The Light That Shined upon Darkness

Michael Higgins

Order this book online at www.trafford.com
or email orders@trafford.com

Most Trafford titles are also available at major online book retailers.

Print information available on the last page.

ISBN: 978-1-4907-7121-2 (sc)
ISBN: 978-1-4907-7120-5 (hc)
ISBN: 978-1-4907-7119-9 (e)

Library of Congress Control Number: 2016903667

Trafford rev. 03/04/2016

 www.trafford.com

North America & international
toll-free: 1 888 232 4444 (USA & Canada)
fax: 812 355 4082

PROLOGUE 1990

It was a clear night in Cleveland, Ohio. The bright white moon lit up the dark-blue sky beautifully. The city's main streets were unusually quiet. Traffic was at a minimum nearly everywhere; most of the cars that normally occupied these exhaust-polluted roads were now part alongside curbs of the treacherous side streets and back alleyways. All the homes on Lil Dave's family's street, which was on East 149th and St. Clair, were dark and quiet—all except his. And every light downstairs of his parents' white-and-red two-and-a-half-story home was on. Dave's mom was having her usual get-together with some friends. Lil Dave, a recipient of all the noise from the party, could literally smell all the smoke and alcohol coming from downstairs. *Man, how they expect me to get some sleep with all of this noise?* Dave asked himself. Dave's mom yelled over the blazing music and drunken slurred voices of her friends, "Boy, I know you hear me calling you!" Lil Dave was engrossed in his game system, and he tried his best to ignore his mother's inebriated voice. "Dave, I'm not playing. If I come up there and catch you on that game, I'ma tear yo lil ass up!" Lil Dave could hear his mother Lisa's voice quickly approaching his bedroom door. Her footsteps grew louder and louder with each step she took on the creaking tan carpeted floor. Then before he knew it, his old wooden door swung open like it was being kicked in by the CPD. Luckily, Lil Dave had already managed to turn off his game system and jumped in bed. With the glare of the hallway light invading his bed area, Dave took it as an opportunity to rise up from the fetal position. "David," his mom called out. "Yes, Ma," he replied while squinting his eyes as if to imply that she had awakened him. "I know you were up here playing that game, and you bet not be late for school in the morning either. Don't think I forgot about that teacher calling here today."

"Ma, did Dad come home from work yet?" Lil Dave asked somberly. "No, your father hasn't come home yet, and if you're wondering whether I'm going to tell him or not, yes, I am." With no further discussion, Dave's mom shut the door. "Maaan," Lil Dave mumbled in discouragement then laid his head back upon his pillow.

Getting in trouble by Big Dave for being assigned detention was the last thing Lil Dave wanted. He was terrified of his father. For what reason, he couldn't explain, especially since his father never laid so much as a finger on him. Big Dave had this extremely authoritative presence that surely demanded obedience. Just the mere thought of his mom ratting him out to his father about detention scared Dave. But after closing his eyes and replaying the whole scenario, Lil Dave knew that what he did to receive detention was well worth it.

"Dave, I bet' choo won't blow the new girl a kiss," one of Lil Dave's elementary friends dared him. Little did they know, Dave had been trying hard to find ways to get this fine-looking girl to notice his existence since the first day he laid eyes on her. "I'll do you one better than that," he whispered back, accepting the challenge. All three of the boys sat in the back of the classroom, looking on at Dave as he began writing what appeared to be a love letter. After completing it, he neatly folded it and handed it to the girl in front of him. "Pass that to Tracie," he whispered. She did just as he asked her to. Tracie grabbed the letter, then tried to ease it inside of her textbook, but it was too late. The teacher noticed it. "So we're passing notes in the middle of class now?" the teacher asked sarcastically. The classroom became so quiet that you could hear a spider crawling. "Tracie, hand me that note, please."

Tracie immediately handed her the note. The teacher opened the note and read it to herself, then read it to the class. "'Tracie, will you marry me? Check yes or no.' Cute!" the teacher said, pacing back and forth in the front of the room. "Whoeva wrote this marriage proposal better stand up now, or the entire class will be put on detention and have extra writing duties." Instantly, the class began pouting. Just before the teacher could silence them, Dave stood up and owned up to the responsibility. "Oh, so it was Mr. Smith who wrote this note, huh? Okay, Mr. Smith, please step out into the hallway, and I'll come get you when I'm ready to talk to you."

Just like that, Dave had earned himself a detention. Dave's failed attempt at a convenient marriage proposal, ironically, intrigued young Tracie's interest, which would lead them to becoming inseparable friends. The two of them, along with Jay, Dave's other best friend, began walking to school together, eating lunch together, and even studying together. Before long, the three Collinwood Area friends had finished grade school and were on their way to senior-high life at Collinwood High School.

Collinwood High School was located off 152nd and St. Clair, just a few blocks from Lil Dave's home and across the street from the neighborhood police station. Its appearance was of an older oversized church house. There was a skywalk leading to the gymnasium, which added a little prestige to it. The hallways were tanned brick, with camel humps about them. The students' lockers were stretched out side by side along the hallways. This three-story schoolhouse was a pillar of the city.

Attending Collinwood, Dave, Jay, and Tracie would quickly learn that life at this high school would be more of a popularity contest than an educational experience. If you weren't in the "in crowd" or a sports star, then you were basically a nobody. Having good grades or just staying out of trouble didn't spell good for most students. Sadly, it only meant that you were probably more susceptible to being picked on or cheated on. Even with the school having a dress code, somehow, those crafty in-crowd trendsetters would find ways of spicing up the boring dress code. Dave and Jay, who had swiftly became an exception to the rules, cared nothing about playing ball or being accepted by anyone; their main concern was making money.

Tracie, on the other hand, had befriended some sassy female cheerleaders. In the process, she had acquired their insatiable desire for designer things and developed an attraction to the type of men who could get those things for her. Her friendship with the young ladies would soon put a strain on her, yet her taste for luxuries and men had become a part of her character—a character that would soon recapture the once-lustful eye of the lil guy who previously proposed to her through a letter in grade school.

As fate would have it, Dave and Tracie's friendship would become one steamy teenage love affair. Everybody in the school knew that they were an item. They walked down the hallways hand in hand in between classes, they took turns escorting each other to class, and they even shared lockers.

Finally, just as everyone had already suspected, fresh out of high school, Dave and Tracie wound up getting hitched. For the first few years, everything was peaches and cream. Unfortunately, for the young couple, it wouldn't take much time to learn that marriage was a very complex union, which would be much more work and significantly different than just being boyfriend and girlfriend.

PART 1

CHAPTER ONE

J ay, whose birth name was Jayson Hill, was born to Jerry and Debra White. His parents, who both migrated to Cleveland separately from different parts of the South, were still children themselves when they unintentionally conceived and birthed Jay into the world. Not really wanting the responsibilities of a child, his parents decided they'd pawn innocent Lil Jay off to Debra's mom. Debra knew that her mother would not object as she's loving and caring. Debra knew her mom couldn't say no.

For the first few years of young Jay's life, his parents would occasionally stop by his Big Ma's (the name he had given his grandmother as a child while pretending to play momma and daddy). They'd buy him little outfits here and there. They'd even give some of their food stamps to Big Ma, hoping that the stamps would recompense for all the food Big Ma needed to buy and feed their son. Occasionally, they'd find time to come and hang out with Lil Jay, at least until either he or they would become exhausted. Never once, though, did they ever attempt to take little Jay with them.

As time progressed, Jerry and Debra's simple efforts to support their child slacked off worse than America's search for Osama bin Laden. Big Ma hadn't heard a word from them. Word on the street was Jerry was mistreating Debra in nearly every way possible. To make matters worse, people were telling Big Ma that her daughter was using drugs and selling herself. Not wanting to believe the gossip, Big Ma just brushed off the negativity and continued to look after Lil Jay.

Eventually, Jerry wound up leaving Debra out in the cold and dangerous streets of Cleveland to fend for herself. Meanwhile, he became a well-known marijuana dealer, with a host of other kids. Debra just fell deeper into the clutches of the drug of her choice: heroin.

Jay's last time seeing his mother or father was around the age of eight. Strangely, he had grown accustomed to their permanent abandonment. Big Ma had done more for him than his parents could ever have. So as far as he was concerned, his Big Ma was his mother and his father. "Well, Big Ma, I'ma gone and get outta here. I gotta go pick up Candace from the house. We're supposed to be goin' out tonight." Candace was Jay's live-in girlfriend. They met while they were both in high school.

Big Ma lived in a canary-yellow two-family house off 140th and Kelso, next to a large building. She owned both the upstairs and downstairs of the home. The house was an older home that looked to be sinking. The front lawn was sloped and only about 10 feet long, the grass was worn and patchy, and the driveway was narrow but lengthy, stretching about thirty feet long. The front door of Big Ma's house led straight to the living room; it was off-limits. From both the side and the back doors, the upstairs and downstairs could be accessed through the hallway. The side door led directly to the old wooden kitchen door, and the back door led to a long flight of stairs, which took you up to a landing where a balcony, a bathroom, and a kitchen door were all located. On a whole, the old house was comprised of five bedrooms, two bathrooms, two living rooms and dining rooms, an attic, and a basement. The upstairs had two bedrooms, and the downstairs had three. "Ya'll plan on goin' somewhere special, huh?" Big Ma asked inquisitively while relaxing comfortably on the doodoo brown couch, which matched the rest of her antiquated furniture that she had since Jay lived there.

Visiting Big Ma was like a ritual for Jay. Ever since he'd moved out of her house and in with Candace, he made it his business to stop by every chance he got to check on her. Big Ma loved every single visit too. "Naw, not really," Jay said as he grabbed hold of his keys from off the wooden-looking kitchen counter. "We're just goin' to get a bite to eat. You need anything, Big Ma?" he inquired before walking over and kissing her on the forehead. "I'm okay, baby," Big Ma retorted. Jay immediately headed for the kitchen toward the door, but before he could exit, Big Ma turned toward him and asked the unthinkable. "Jay," she called out.

"Yes, Big Ma!"

"When are you gonna marry that girl?"

What did she just say? Jay asked himself silently. Was she serious?

"Why you say that, Big Ma?"

"Because I like that girl, Jay. She's a really good girl, and she truly loves you. Trust me, Jay, Big Ma knows. Now if I was you, I wouldn't let her slip away. She's the type of woman that you want to start a family with."

"Okay, okay, Big Ma, you're getting too deep now," Jay cried. After a momentary pause, Jay continued, "I don't know, Big Ma. Maybe you're right."

Jay then pushed open Big Ma's rotted wooden door, jumped his six-foot-something frame inside his banana-yellow '76 Monte Carlo, and headed for his house. "Candace," Jay spoke into his hands-free Bluetooth.

"Yes, Jay."

"I'm on my way. I'll be home in about fifteen minutes."

"All right."

Before disconnecting, Jay whispered, "Candace!"

"Yes, Jay," she replied.

"I love you."

"I love you too, baby," Candace responded before saying bye and hanging up the phone.

CHAPTER TWO

Outside of Dave and Tracie's new three-bedroom ranch-style home on the west side of Cleveland, all was well. Children were outside playing in the open field; they rode their bikes inside the circle of the cul-de-sac and chased around the neighborhood hound. One of the women homeowners on the street was outside, watering her beautifully landscaped garden, while another was mowing her lawn. Everything seemed to be of the norm. Inside, though, things were just the opposite. "You know what, Tracie, you ain't right," Dave hollered disappointingly. "You actin' real selfish right now, and you know it. You know how much this mean to me. You need to quit being childish for once and come support me!"

"Support what, Dave? You make it seem like the club ain't been open for damn near a year already. I don't understand why you making such a big deal out of it. It's just anotha day."

Dave rushed toward the foot of the oak-framed bed, where he had his light-gray-and-white pinstriped suit matching his gray-and-white pants, lying perfectly flat. He slipped into the Sean John suit and then nudged his tie a bit to make sure it was centered perfectly.

"What the fuck you mean it's just anotha day? Tracie, it's my grand reopening," Dave emphasized as he worked his feet into a flawless pair of light-gray gators he'd not too long ago purchased. "I'm gone have a few of my people there that'll be looking forward to meeting you When they ask me, 'Where's my wife?' what am I supposed to say?"

"Say, it ain't none of their damn business where I'm at! Dave, I'm not finna be up there with you while all them skank-ass hoes are strippin'. Now, maybe if you changed it to anotha day, then I might reconsider." Tracie made a few final adjustments to her eyeliner in the bathroom mirror. She then found her way to the guest bedroom, where she had laid out a red bra and panty set. *Bitch, you look gooooood,* Tracie reassured herself as she stood in front of her full-length closet mirror, checking the profile of her curvaceous figure. Her breasts sat up perfectly perky, her ass stuck out like a hill in a plain field, her waistline was almost as small as that of a Victoria's Secret model. As Tracie listened closer, she could hear Dave power walking, back and forth, through the hallway. Dave would've been pissed to see her sporting the hell out of the red thong and translucent bra top she had on. Before he could even think about easing his way into the guestroom, Tracie slipped into her sundress. She again checked her profile before pushing up on her breasts as if they weren't sitting just right already. Next she slid her feet into a pair of mustard-yellow Jimmy Choos, which highlighted the likewise flower pattern inside her dress. She threw her Rafe bag over her shoulder, then glanced at the clock sitting on the dresser. It read six o'clock. "Dave, you betta hurry up. It's already six o'clock," Tracie informed him as if trying to be considerate. "Don't choo gotta be there at seven?" Despite her nonchalant attitude, Tracie knew how much this grand reopening meant to Dave. Why was she acting so stubborn? To add insult to injury, she had the nerve to be going out. When the two of them crossed paths in the hallway, the enticing smell of Tracie's Allure perfume danced around Dave's simply nose. Dave sniffed a few times. "Damn, Tracie, who you smellin' all good fo' if I may ask?"

Unfortunately, for Dave, her sense of smell was pretty keen too. Dave had all but drenched himself in Unforgivable, a new fragrance by Sean John. She wasted little time sarcastically exposing him. "I should be asking you the same question. Hell, I smelt yo' unforgivable ass before I even hit the door. That's a shame," she said, using reverse psychology. "Them heffas even got choo smellin' good fo'em too, huh?"

The Reason, a bar and an exotic strip club that Dave had opened only a year ago to the date, was located on Cleveland's southeast side. The building was a completely red-brick one that sat on the corner of two intersecting streets. Around its perimeters was a ten-foot universal fence to deter thieves. The pavement of the parking lot was rigid and rough and looked to have needed some work. To the left of the club was a street named Matilda, and to its front was 116th. To the right was a two-family house owned by an older couple; the couple lived upstairs, and they ran a mom-and-pop store by day downstairs. On a whole, the building that the Reason sat on was ideal.

Dave unlocked the doors to the Reason at 7:00 p.m., looking like the business executive that he'd worked so hard to become. He stood next to the steel-gray door that read Entrance on it, ready to greet any and every newcomer. Where was Tracie, though? Where was his better half? She was supposed to be alongside him, waiting to greet those folks too! This was supposed to be their night. They were supposed to reopen this place together.

With a somewhat fictitious smile on his face, Dave scanned around the inside of the club and nodded his head in agreement. His club's new look was magnificent. The contractors he'd hired had totally remodeled the place. They lengthened the bar to the left so that it wrapped around the front. They rebuilt the stage in the back with ceramic tiles and two copper poles to double the pleasure. Dave's office, which was next to the girls' dressing room in the back to the right, was also enlarged. An upstairs room that wasn't in use before was remodeled and transformed into a VIP room. The contractors even slapped a couple of fresh coats of glossy gray paint upon the walls. Along with security, the bartenders, and the waitresses, Dave had helped to spit shine the place from top to bottom. Collectively, they had the place spotless. For him and his staff, this was truly an accomplishment beyond measure. That's why that Grand Reopening banner, with the Reason's name upon it, on the brick wall outside the establishment meant so much to him. Now the Reason was already known even before the grand reopening for being one of the nicer, more popular clubs in the city, especially when it comes to just hanging out, having a few drinks, and maybe hitting the dance floor or something. It's true success and notoriety, though, rested solely on the shoulders of the dancers. Dave hated to admit the fact, but he knew that those strippers, both male and female, made his place the hot commodity. He had a group of male dancers called BDS (Big Dick Slangers) that performed on Wednesdays. Every week they'd shut the place down. Then he also had arguably eight of the finest female dancers on this side of the Mississippi River. All the women were extremely thick. They all too wore scantily clad outfits that usually covered next to nothing. Their signature dance moves and lap dances kept men rushing from everywhere to see these professional pole dancers hard at work.

Dave worked the doors for over an hour and then went to hibernate behind the walls of his office. Thoughts of his wife immediately sprang up like a bad leak.

What could she be doing that is so important? he asked himself while lying back in his black leather chair, with his eyes closed. *Maybe she'll surprise me and show up.*

Dave's thoughts were then interrupted by a knock on the door. The knock was so gentle he could barely hear it. "Come in," he cried.

It was his waitress with a strange-looking smirk upon her face. "Dave, there's a lady outside that says she wants to audition tonight." The waitress's voice came off soft like. Her body language reeked of intimidation.

"Tell her I said come up here Monday and I'll see what I can do." "But, Dave, she's standing right behind me."

Before Dave could respond, the lady boldly stuck her beautiful face in between the waitress and Dave's office door. Normally, Dave would've had a fit about someone invading his space like that, but for some reason, tonight was different. Maybe it stemmed from the fact that Tracie's absence had him feeling sort of devalued. Or perhaps that caramel-complexioned medium-sized head on the lady was just too cute to turn away. Whatever the case was, Dave surprisingly said to the waitress, "Go ahead. Let her in." After shutting the door behind her, the woman waltzed right in, stood in front of Dave, and looked directly into his eyes. Dave tried doing the same, but her sensual eyes and her voluptuous body caught his full attention. This woman had a beautiful round face and some piercing ebony eyes. Her heavenly built body was so blessed that it looked like it dropped straight out of the sky—oh, so perfect. The low-cut body shirt she sported was causing a major cleavage spill.

"Hi! What's your name, sweetie?" Dave politely asked after finally making eye contact.

"My name is Chanel, but my stage name is Caramel." By the time she opened her mouth to speak, Dave was already captivated. Those inviting eyes, succulent lips, and pretty white teeth had Dave's mind wandering to places that it shouldn't have been. Her soft and seductive voice came off so subtle and sweet. Before Dave could even articulate exactly what he wanted to say, "You're hired" rushed past out of his mouth. Something was telling him, though, that the words he'd just let fall out his mouth would eventually come back to haunt him.

"Man, Teddy, can you believe Dave tried to get me to go to the grand reopening of his so-called club tonight? This idiot has the nerve to be having a grand reopening for a club that has been open for a year," Tracie mocked, chuckling, as she's lying on the hotel bed, with her head in between Teddy's exposed thighs. Now Teddy was a short stumpy guy with a slight beer gut that clearly protruded over the waistline of his pants when standing. His complexion was of a high-yellow tone, and he had a sea of jet-black waves spinning across his scalp. His eyes were light brown, and he was a very fashion-forward kind of guy.

"What's so wrong with that, Tracie?" Teddy asked as he sat in just his boxers with his back up against the wooden headboard. Teddy gently rubbed Tracie's beautiful face.

"Stop it, Teddy," Tracie pleaded as he slid his hands from her ears down to her breasts. Teddy didn't stop; he kept caressing them until Tracie let out this soft moan, then answered his question, "I don't know. I guess nothing's wrong with it. Maybe I'm just upset about the whole stripper thing."

"And I can totally understand how you feel, baby," Teddy interjected. "Maybe you should just tell him how you feel." Teddy then eased from underneath Tracie and then gently mounted her. He began planting soft kisses upon her lips and continued down until he reached her navel.

"Teddy, STOP IT NOW!" Tracie tried to reject Teddy's sexual advances and finish the conversation, but they were just too much. He began nibbling around paradise, and that was all she wrote.

Teddy and Tracie had met about three months prior to the date at The Mirage on the Water, a club in the flats. Teddy spotted Tracie chatting up a storm at the bar with some of her girlfriends. The minute he'd saw her, he instantly knew that Tracie was the finest thing he had ever laid eyes on. She had this mocha complexion that shone in the light. Her jet-black hair hung loosely down her back. From what he could see, she looked to be about five foot four inches and 140 pounds of pure thickness. Without hesitation, Teddy informed his homies of his next pursuit, then jumped out his chair, and eagerly approached Tracie. Tracie, oblivious to everything, didn't even notice Teddy paying any attention to her. So when Teddy lightly tapped her on the shoulder, it startled her. Even more startling to Teddy was when he looked over Tracie's shoulder, he noticed a massive wedding ring. To his surprise, that didn't stop them from discussing their obvious age difference and natural attraction to each other; Tracie was a ripe twenty-six years old, and Teddy was only nineteen. The two of them laughed and drank the night away before eventually fucking each other's brains out. From that day on, they crept around together every chance they got.

"Fuck me, Teddy," Tracie screamed as Teddy flipped her over and thrust his manhood deep into her from behind. "Oh shit, you fuck this, pussy boy. Aw, don't stop."

"Whose pussy is this, huh?" Teddy yelled back in ecstasy. His face was drenched in sweat and his manhood with juices from the sexual friction.

"It's yours, baby. It's Y-O-U-R-S. Aw, God," she hollered in passionate spurts.

Teddy had Tracie bent over the foot of the bed like a bitch in heat. They had rough yet emotional sex for what seemed like forever. Both of them were buck naked and perspiring profusely. They looked worse than two slaves out picking cotton in 120-degree weather.

"Aw shit. Teddy, I can't take it no more." Tracie's upper body, including her arms and head, collapsed onto the bed. "Please, cum inside me, baby." That was all Teddy needed to hear. It's just something when a woman tells a man to shoot his load inside of her. It seems like those words instantly excite a man, forcing him to do exactly what's been told of him. Teddy quickly shifted his gear into five and pumped everything he had into Tracie. After the sex, the two of them talked for a good while. Teddy mostly spoke about the problems that he was having with his car. He had ordered some rims for his 2002 Chevy Monte Carlo. He came to find out the ones he ordered had the wrong bolt pattern. He explained all this to Tracie as if she didn't understand why he had to send them back.

Tracie, on the other hand, spoke about more heartfelt subjects such as how much she'd fallen in love with Teddy and the little problems she and Dave's marriage was having. Tracie, out of pure lust, told Teddy she wished she had met him before she'd gotten married.

While Tracie continued in her venting, Teddy just put all his problems aside and held her close. He was now doing all the right things; he was saying nothing but doing everything right! Teddy was playing the part of a man she'd only dreamed of: compassionate, emotional, selfless, and loving. Yes, to her, Teddy was all that and more. And for the last few-hours plus, he had captivated her physically, emotionally, and, most of all, mentally.

The two of them left the Radisson on Rockside Road the very next morning and went their separate ways. Teddy hopped on the freeway toward the east side while Tracie bypassed the expressway toward the streets. She then rode Broadview to Pearl Road, coasting right past her home, praying that she didn't run into Dave in the process. Tracie's mission now was to get back to her mother's house, the place she used to lie to her husband, telling him that that's where she would be. Her mom's house was just off 155th and St. Clair. Tracie was determined to take her time getting there. That was the purpose of her even taking the scenic route. She could've easily jumped on the highway and gotten there in no time. She had too much on her mind, though—too many mysteries that just couldn't be solved while sitting next to Dave. So Tracie drove the west-side streets like a consort. She had the top down on her pearl-white Lexus, her Chanel shades, on and her hair blowing in the wind. Her favorite Mary J. Blige song was turned up to capacity, causing her factory speakers to sound more like ten-inch subwoofers. Everyone that she rode past or that drove past her had to observe her. They had to stare in admiration. Her Lexus complemented her nicely. Her beauty, her style, and her way of living could be captured with one glimpse. Just one look said all the things that she couldn't say to every passerby.

From the outside looking in, one would have thought that Tracie was the happiest woman on the planet, which she probably should've been. She had a good husband, a beautiful home, an expensive car, and an access to a nearly endless supply of currency. Her wardrobe was unlike that of any other young woman her age in the whole city. Her family looked up to her, her old friends respected her, and all her enemies envied her lifestyle. What more could a girl her age want? For some reason, though, Tracie's heart just wasn't content. She wanted more—mainly more out of her man. Yeah, she might've been ungrateful, but she felt like she deserved to be.

Regardless of her inappreciative attitude toward him, Tracie couldn't deny the fact that Dave took really good care of her. He was the sole reason for her great fortune. His endless love for her compelled him to purchase nearly everything she asked him for. He took Tracie on exotic trips to places like Jamaica, the Bahamas, and Puerto Rico. He would be spontaneous, buying her roses, candy, and different stuffed teddy bears. He did everything that he could to spice up their marriage and try to keep his wife happy. With all these different luxuries at her disposal, one would've never guessed that Tracie was unemployed. Yes, Tracie was jobless. In fact, she hadn't ever had a job in her entire lifetime. The way she saw it, she didn't need one. Every guy that she'd ever been with, from grade school 'til now, did their best to provide for her. If Tracie wanted it, Tracie got it. And that's just the way it was.

Dave, believe it or not, didn't mind taking care of his wife. He loved her very much and felt that she deserved nice things. His motto was "What I won't do, another man will." Taking care of her the way that he did too made him feel like more of a man. He wasn't a control freak by any stretch of the imagination. He just felt like it was the right thing to do, especially since he saw how his father spoiled his mother.

Now Tracie's mom—who looked like Tracie's twin with her medium height, mocha-colored skin, and banging body—loved her daughter deeply. Despite the unconditional love, Mom was opposed to her daughter's behavior. Mooching off a man, even if it is your husband, was not the way she reared Tracie. Tracie's mom would always tell her, "If you let a man take complete care of you, and you give them too much power, before long, they'll start thinking they own you!" Through her exceptional example of single parenting and working multiple jobs, Mom thought that she'd shown her daughter how to be independent— apparently not, though. The real slap in the face was when Tracie's mom found out that she was unemployed with no intentions of getting a job after she spent her hard-earned money to send her daughter to Cleveland State.

"Tracie, are you going to use that degree that I paid fo', or are you just going to let it go to waste?" her mom would ask. Tracie's inconsideration made her mother feel like sending Tracie to school had been in vain. One other thing that concerned her mother was Tracie's adulterous nature. See, Tracie told her mother about everything including her sexual encounters. Mom would express her opposing opinion but tried not to condemn her daughter or even bash her too hard. For some reason, though, when Tracie told her about Teddy, Mom's attitude was unreserved. "Listen, Tracie, that boy is too young for you. In my opinion, you need to quit seeing him. He don't got a job, and all he does is sell crack all day, and he's immature. Tracie, listen to your mother. That boy ain't nuthin' but trouble. If I were you, I'd leave him alone." But just like a child that knows more than their parents, Tracie brushed off her mother's comments like dandruff.

CHAPTER THREE

Nearly two weeks after the successful grand reopening of the Reason, Dave's club was at it once again. The inside of the Reason was an unreserved fire hazard. The place was smoke filled from wall to wall, with minimal elbow space, except for the seated area of people watching the strippers. The only illuminators were the flat screens and strobe lights decorating the walls and ceilings. You could barely hear yourself thinking let alone talking because the music from the speakers was overpowering everything. Outside, the parking lot on 116th and Matilda was also packed to capacity. The nearby side streets were flooded with fly classic cars likes Regals, Cutlasses, Chevelles, and Monte Carlos. Dave, Jay, and a few others had their big-ass SUVs parked near the front entrance. Ladies barely old enough to drink, at least that's how they looked, were darting across the main street, half-damn naked and full of raging excitement, wanting to be a part of this atmosphere. Everybody who was somebody, from hood to hood and even some suburb dwellers, was in the place to be! St. Clair, down the way to Ninety-Third, E.C. fellas and even Maple Heights ladies and a gang of others were representing in the Reason. There was also a great polarity concerning the men and their attire, but somehow, it all worked. Some men had on mink coats and gators while others wore a pair of fresh Jordans and Jerseys or a pair of Lebrons and crispy black jeans. Occasionally, you'd even see some fellas in white tees and torn blue jeans scattered abroad. That's that good old hood shit, though. Most ladies were adorned with either something short and revealing or something skin tight and tasty. Majority of them were representing their Apple Bottoms in leggings or boy shorts or low-rise jeans, revealing all the goods, plenty of thongs, and ass cracks in sight. Halter tops with miniskirts and pumps were also extremely prevalent. There were even a few beautifully shaped women gracing the scene in full-body catsuits and full-length sexy dresses and a pair of spicy stilettos or wedges, looking oh so lovely.

"Dave, I must say this bar sure has come a long way since the last time I was here," Candace shouted over the loud music after taking a sip of her apple martini.

"Thanks, Candace. It better had cuz I have put a lot of money in this place. I'm just happy to see it prosper and filled, you know."

"I know that's right. Let me say dis too before I forget. The next time ya'll ask me to come up here, I'd appreciate it if it wasn't the same night you got these females up there strippin'!" Candace looked at her boyfriend, Jay, crazily then continued to say, "When are your normal bar hours anyway?"

"My normal bar hours?" Jay repeated over the immense crowd of people. "Mondays and Tuesdays are normal bar days, and we open at seven. Wednesday, Thursday, and Friday nights, the ladies dance. Saturday nights are our party-request nights."

"So ya'll closed on Sundays, huh?"

"Yeah, oh, and we run a happy-hour special from seven till eight too."

"That's all right," she replied at the top of her lungs as she was taking another sip and then said, "I know Tracie sho'll be trippin' 'bout all deez females around her husband every week. Damn near naked too! Shit, I'm 'bout ready to yolk this big-eared nigga up and head toward the exit." Jay and Dave couldn't help but laugh. Candace continued, "Nigga, you laughing, but I'm oh so serious. If Dave wasn't my dude and yo best friend, trust and believe, yo ass would be out of here immediately, and you know what else?" Then she was cut off by Jay.

"Candace, chill out now. You know I'm here strictly for my nigga. These girls in here, all of 'em combined, don't even compare to what I got, so quit trippin'."

"Yeah, aiight nigga, whateva," Candace yelled back vigorously. You could tell by the slur in her speech that she was starting to feel the effects of the few drinks she had consumed already.

As the night went on, Dave, Jay, and Candace all continued just shooting the breeze. They talked a little and drank a whole lot more. Eventually, all of them were good and wasted. Out of nowhere, Dave was approached by the new dancer, Caramel. Caramel's beautiful face and voluptuous body looked good and edible. From head to toe, every inch of her skin looked smooth and milk chocolaty, like a sugar daddy. Her jet-black hair hung literally below her neck. Her seductive cat eyes sized Dave up. She was wearing a money-green bikini top and thong with the matching garter belt. Her breasts looked so succulent underneath her bikini top that if one hadn't known any better, you'd think they were filled with silicone. Plus, she had an ass that could make Beyonce a bit jealous. Her measurements were a healthy 34-24-42, and she was holding up D cups.

"Would you please give me a ride home, please, Dave?" Caramel begged Dave in his ear while she was behind him. Under normal conditions, her tone of voice would've been heard across town but not tonight. To Dave, Caramel was not just any old fine woman—she was a temptation. She had the looks, the attitude, and, from what he could tell, the brains too. The last thing Dave wanted to do was to cheat or even think about cheating on his wife, Tracie. But with Tracie's attitude lately, he couldn't help but to pay attention to Caramel's obvious advances. So without a second thought, Dave turned his head around, paused for a split second, and then replied, "Yeah, I think I can do that."

"Thank you, Dave," Caramel said and then walked away slowly and seductively. As soon as she left from where Dave was, Caramel began working the room. Heads immediately turned and eyeballs got larger as she graced through the aisles that were instantly created. Dave, feeling a bit ambivalent about his earlier decision, just looked on in utter lust.

Before long, two thirty rolled around, and the club was starting to empty. Most started evacuating around 2:00 a.m., and all the pretty cars and trucks that dominated the parking lot and surrounding streets had vanished. Most of the dancers had either left by themselves or left with customers. Jay, Dave, Candace, and two of the bartenders and Caramel were the only ones still there; and Jay and Candace were on their way out. Dave then escorted them both to the door. Before leaving, Jay turned toward Dave and asked him, "You comin' to the creek tomorrow?"

"I'on know. It all depends on what time I get to bed," Dave answered.

"You know we gotta do that one thing tomorrow, or did you forget?"

"Yeah, I know. I ain't forgot."

"Aiight, my nigga, I holla at choo tomorrow then."

"Aiight, ya'll, be careful getting home, and, Candace, take good care of my nigga."

"I got 'em," Candace said.

"I'll see you later. Tell Tracie I said hi, okay?"

"I will, aiight, ya'll."

Jay and Candace then left. The two bartenders, after finishing up inventory along with some minor cleaning duties, left too. That left Dave and Caramel all alone.

"You ready, Dave?" Caramel asked after exiting the dressing room and now looking more like a significant other as opposed to an apparent stripper. Just looking at Caramel was becoming a burden to Dave. As she sashayed toward him, all he could imagine was himself, in the next couple hours, being somewhere that he wasn't supposed to be, doing something that he wasn't supposed to be doing, with somebody that he wasn't supposed to be with. If Tracie found out that he was taking this girl home, she'd kill him and her. But the way Tracie had been acting lately, with her apathy and all, he thought to himself she might not give a damn anyway.

"Yeah, c'mon, I'm ready."

The two of them left, and Dave locked up behind them. Then they jumped in his truck and pulled off. Rolling down 116th to the boulevard, with one hand atop his wood-grain steering wheel, Dave felt like the king of Cleveland; and oddly enough, Caramel felt like his queen.

"Caramel, I hope you're not in a rush to get home 'cause I gotta drop this money off at the night deposit," Dave said as he grabbed his lighter and already-rolled blunt from out of his cup holder and attempted to fire it up.

"Actually, Dave," Caramel began replying while gently grabbing the smoking contents from out of his hand, "I was hoping that we could kick it a lil bit. Maybe get to know each other a lil better." She then lit the blunt and took a heavy pull. The thick cloud of smoke rolled from her mouth to her nose. The alluring and sexy gesture turned him on even more.

"Shit, cool with me," Dave answered back.

And with that said, they were off. The two of them rode around for over an hour, smoking, sipping on a bottle of Patrón, and vibing to the Isley Brothers. Because of the liquor, weed, and smooth ambiance, Caramel started getting really horny. With little inhibition, she reached over and placed her hand on Dave's thigh. By this time, Dave was so high and drunk that he didn't even think or care to stop her. Caramel's hand then quickly slipped into Dave's pants, and she began to massage him slowly. Without hesitating, Dave found the first motel parking lot he saw and pulled right in. That didn't stop Caramel, though. She pulled Dave's manhood out and began stroking right in the parking lot. Then, as she was about to go down, Dave stopped her and moaned out, "Hol' up, baby, let me go pay for this room, okay?"

Both of them breathing heavily, they jumped out of the truck; and as soon as they got the key from the motel manager, Dave and Caramel began going at it. Kissing sloppily, they hurried toward the room. Once inside, they wasted little time. Dave's shirt was off, and his pants were down to his ankles. Caramel quickly stripped butt naked. Then Dave grabbed her from behind and rushed her over the cheap wooden dresser. He aggressively threw Caramel's left leg upon the dresser, then stuck everything he had in her. Caramel screamed in satisfaction before Dave stuck his finger inside her sexy, seductive mouth. Full of passion and her libido steadily rising to the highest degree, she nearly sucked the blood vessels out of Dave's finger. Dave and Caramel's sexual escapade lasted most of the early morning. Every which way they could, they devoured each other. From one position to the next, from one place in the room to another, upside down and sideways, from the window to the wall, they made magic happen. They went so long and hard that Dave wound up falling asleep inside her. They checked out of the room at around seven in the morning. Dave rushed Caramel home, then hopped on I-90 back toward his house on the west side. All he could think about while driving on the highway was how he was going to explain this to Tracie. When he got home, though, to his surprise, his home was empty. Tracie was nowhere to be found.

Chapter Four

Jay and Candace both woke the next morning with slight hangovers, Candace's being the worse of the two. Jay's hangover was a bit more subtle; after all, he was used to it. Waking up early after unaccountable amounts of liquor was almost normal so to speak for Jay, considering the fact that his best friend owned a prominent local club. Jay took a quick look at his alarm clock, which read 9:00 a.m. He yawned a couple times, then got out of bed. Flashbacks of last night's sexcapade between him and Candace immediately hit him. The evidence was literally everywhere. Her panties and bra were dangling from the ceiling fan like Christmas ornaments. Every piece of clothing that he wore last night looked like footprints leading to the bed from the main entrance: first, his all-white Air Forces; then, his ankle socks and his nice watch; followed by the Rocawear blue jean pants and jacket. It was as if a minitornado had swept through their bedroom.

"Baby, where you going this early?" Candace asked as she turned her body over toward Jay, exposing a part of her perfectly perky C-cup breast; the rest of her body was being covered by their blue satin sheets.

"I'm finna meet Dave and them at the creek. I told 'em that I'd be up there by eleven."

"What time is it now?" Candace asked.

"A lil after nine."

Candace paused for a second and then continued, "Well . . . why are you getting up so early then? Can't you get up around ten or ten thirty? I mean, it's right around the corner."

"Baby, you know I gotta get up and get movin' so I can shake this lil hangover. I be damned if I stay in bed too long and get on the court feelin' drunk, so them clowns can take advantage of the situation. I can hear them fools now, talkin' 'bout my game done fell off and shit. Won't be me," Jay responded in a tone of sheer confirmation. Surrendering all hopes of winning this confrontation, she proceeded, "Well, aren't you at least going to let me cook you something real quick? I know you hungry after all that drinkin' you did last night. I know I sure am!" Jay didn't even respond this time; his facial expression spoke volumes. It told Candace that she was pushing it again. Candace was known for overdoing it, especially when it came to her man. It wasn't bad to Jay; it just got a little annoying sometimes.

The two of them stared each other down lightly before Jay finally broke and said, "Go ahead, Candy. I'll be down after I get out the shower."

"Jay, don't have me cook this food and you let it get cold." You could clearly see hangover all over her face as she sat straight up on the bed. Her golden-brown hair was as wild as a deuce of spades. She lifted her left arm, cupped her forehead, and then began to massage her temple with her fingers.

"I'on know how you do it, but I feel like shit, like I'm being hit upside the head wit a hamma! It'll be a cold day in hell before I get drunk like this again, I promise." That was really just the pain talking as the thumping inside of her head continued. It sounded to her like an old grandfather clock. "I'm so serious," she cried. But she really wasn't. As soon as the pain abandoned her, she would be sipping another martini or two or three and talking shit again at the bar, forgetting her previous head pain and promise. While Candace hobbled down the stairs to make breakfast, Jay rummaged through his things in search of something suitable to play a few games of B-ball in. Cleveland's weather, however, had a funny way of changing on its dwellers in a moment's notice. You could put on a waist-length leather jacket and a pair of Timberlands on to face the cold and then look up and the sun would be eyeing one harder than a high school teach during a pop quiz and burning a hole in the back of your neck. On the contrary, come outside dressed pretty light because it's warm and sunny and temperatures will drop like hotcakes and the snow will fall quickly. Jay stumbled across a navy-blue Windbreaker jumpsuit in his closet, and he threw it on the end of the bed, along with the matching head- and wristbands. He then grabbed his hygienics—underclothes, facecloth, and towel—and then hopped into the shower. Jay stood underneath the water for at least twenty minutes. The water was so hot; it fogged the bathroom mirrors and the glass shower door in record time. You could even see the rose-pink toilet sweating condensation. It resembled a big old steam room. Dave loved the feel of that perfectly hot shower in the early morning, especially since he had been drinking all night. To him, it was rejuvenating and refreshing, almost like he'd prayed to God, asking him to wash his sins away, and he accepted. It felt like heaven to Jay! After his twenty-minute long trip in the throne of grace, Jay jumped out of the shower feeling like new money—so fresh and so clean. He was ready to face all fourteen and a half hours that were left of this particular Saturday. Fourteen hours doesn't seem like much to many others, but to Jay, that was a whole lot of time. He was from a different world, though. In his world, he had seen the rich lose it all and the broke, busted, and disgusted get paid overnight and gain it all—all in a matter of fourteen hours. Jay dried himself off and began getting dressed. He put on his Windbreaker outfit and slid on his navy-blue head- and wristbands with the jump emblem on them. Next, he slipped his feet into his custom-made navy-blue-and-white Jumpman basketball sneakers. Underneath his outfit, he even had on some navy-blue-and-silver balling shorts just in case the weather decided to switch up and get warmer.

"Jay, c'mon now, you know this food is getting cold!" Candace hollered from the bottom of the stairs, hoping Jay could hear her voice over the music he was blaring upstairs.

"And you betta not leave those towels and stuff in the middle of the bathroom floor! I'on know how many times I gotta tell you, you ain't got no maids around here!" Before he could reach the bottom step, Jay's olfaction was aroused by what Candace had put together: scrambled eggs, turkey bacon, butter toast with a side of strawberry jelly, sausage biscuits and a bowl of grits, and a glass of Minute Maid orange juice. The aroma was alluring and enticing to him. You could damn near smell each unique individual delicatessen separately.

"I love you, baby" was all he could manage to say after seeing the meal that she'd put together for him in no time at all. Candace really had a way of showing Jay just how much he meant to her. She even had special ways of making him remember and recognize just how much she meant to him. Candace loved Jay beyond belief, and she tried to show it every chance she got. In fact, she didn't even want to get out of bed that morning, but she felt obliged to feed her man and send off the right way.

"I love you too, baby," Candace replied after they passionately kissed on the lips while heading in opposite directions; Jay was going toward his plate on the kitchen table, and Candace was headed back upstairs. By the time Jay sat down, Candace was standing at the bottom of the steps with her food and drink in hand. As she started up the wooden stairs, one could see the imprint of her petite backside showing through her red silk slip. She turned toward Jay and demanded, "I know you betta eat all that food or we gon have a problem!" Candace relayed.

"I don't think you want no mo' problems, babe, not after what I put down last night, cuz I know you gotta be runnin' on fumes right about now!"

"Boy, shut up." She giggled, then continued, saying, "I'm serious now. Don't waste that food, Jay."

"I won't, baby. I won't. Now gone back upstairs before I give you something to be serious about!"

Jay tore through his meal quickly before hurrying to grab a few things so that he could jump into his Cadillac truck and ride out. Next, he eased a box of Swisher Sweets cigars out of his pocket; there were only three left. He clutched one, licked it up and down, split it down the wet seam, then dumped the contents of the cigar inside and old Macdonald bag that was occupying a little space in his truck. Replacing the tobacco with a hairy fluorescent-colored bag of marijuana, Jay then rolled up the Swisher Sweets ever so lovely. He repeated the same process with the other two cigars remaining. After rolling up all three blunts, he lit one, puffed it just enough for it to burn, and then keyed his ignition. Jay's burnt-orange Escalade then took off out of their driveway and onto the street, off their street and onto the main street, out of Richmond Heights, and into the city of Euclid. Before hitting the blunt three good times, Jay was in the parking lot of Euclid Creek.

The historic creek was somewhat of a large open area surrounded by plenty of full trees and many broken trees leaning, rusty-colored flowing water streams, falling rocks from the adjacent hills, and dark-rustic-brown-colored gazebos strategically placed about with picnic tables underneath some. There were grassy areas and a small jungle gym with kids at play and patchy areas from big boy trucks and old-school whips riding up on the grass in an effort to been seen and get the ladies' attention. Plenty of women loitering around, young and old, some dressed in casual cute outfits and others in the skimpiest outfit possible, even on a cold day, also in an effort to be seen and get attention. The ladies usually hung around the court and pranced around the gazebos and even lollygagged in the parking lots, hoping to take a ride with any cute guy that asked. The creek had one main basketball court located at the front entrance of the long private two-lane road that stretched a few miles long, taking you from Euclid City and into the city of South Euclid once at the top of the hill. It was the place to be in the spring, summer, and even fall. Sometimes one could catch a gaze of sunshine, but usually, the shade was overpowering because of the many tall trees and the fact that the creek sat so low, almost seemed nestled down in the earth, with all the tall mountains and hills surrounding the creek.

Everybody that usually played ball at the creek was already there, all except Dave. Jay didn't have to look around long to notice Dave's invisibility either because he didn't see his truck there. Jay got out of the truck and hollered at everybody as he began to shoot around the ball. He started out with some finger-roll lay-ups, and then he moved to the arc. It didn't take long for that pretty jumper of his to warm-up. Before they finished the session, Jay was hitting from near half-court.

"Yo, Jay, was sup wit Dave? Is he comin' or what?" one of the players asked.

"'Cause, if not, we might as well get started."

"I'on think he comin', Tay. Just go ahead without 'em. If he comes, he'll just have winners."

The game started just a little after 11:00 a.m. At first, everyone's game looked a bit rusty; passes were being over- and underthrown, everyone's dribbling looked pretty bad, and nearly every other shot across the court was an air ball. Eventually, things finally started to pick up. The game was on. Midway through the game, things got quite hot. The temperature rose up, and so did tempers. It was only about seventy, but the whole court was filled with sweat and bad attitudes. Jay immediately came up out of his sweat suit. Other players yelled as he took the ball out at half-court. The ball was passed in to Tay, who dribbled through the lane and shot a lay-up over Jay's whole team. The ball bounced off the backboard, and then it hit the front of the rim. Before the ball could get off the rim good, nearly everyone on the court jumped for the rebound. Elbows flailing around in midair, bodies grouped up against one another, one bouncing off the other, then Jay came down with the rebound. He tried dribbling the ball out of the ferocious pack but was brutally elbowed in the mouth by Tay.

"Damn, Tay! What da fuck wrong wit choo, nigga?" Jay said angrily as he was running toward Tay.

"Nigga, what?" Tay yelled back as he threw his dukes up, ready to fight. "Nigga, you betta watch who the fuck you talkin' to like dat, fo' you get what you lookin' fo!"

"Nigga, what I'm lookin fo' yo bitch ass don't possess!" Jay spoke aggressively as he put his thumb to his mouth, incidentally smearing the blood that seeped from the corner of his mouth.

Nell, Tay's teammate, swiftly stepped in between the two of them before any punches were thrown.

"Chill out, yawl. Yawl betta than dat. This shit ain't nuthin' but a game. Play ball, yawl. Play ball!"

Jay walked away with the ball in his hands; he was pissed, and there wasn't denying it. You could see the vein next to his temple bulging out and his face was beet red. After wiping the corner of his mouth with the inside of his shirt, Jay took the ball out at half-court, and the two teams went back at it. Both sides scored buckets, grabbed rebounds, and played some great defense. They played as physical of a ball game as one could play without someone taking it to the next level or too personally.

"Eleven, nine, our way," Jay informed everyone as he took the ball out at half-court again. And this game point!" After passing the ball in bounds, his team began distributing it around, pass after pass. Everyone on his team touched it at least once, and then the rock was kicked back to Jay at the top of the key. He took a couple of dribbles then pump faked. The man on him jumped to anticipate the shot, and as soon as he came down, Jay shot a three-pointer. Good! Game over! As of lately, hitting the game winner was becoming a ritual for Jay. He had done it the last three games in a row. After the magnificent shot, Jay stood around and trash-talked for a while.

"This, my court! What! What! I tol' ya'll this is my court!" He bragged for a couple of minutes before walking off the court. His boasting was all in fun, though, and the other players knew it. So the fellas didn't mind his gums flapping because he was the best player at the creek, hands down, and they all knew it.

"You still runnin', Jay?" Nell asked as he began picking up his new team.

"Nawl, I'm cool. I got something I gotta take care of." Jay raised his arm and chunked up the deuces. "I'm out, ya'll," he yelled and then left.

Jay may have had something to take care of, but that wasn't the only reason he was leaving. He left because he was hotter than a hundred suns in the desert. His lip had a small cut, and his ego was bruised a tad bit. Jay was still a bit angry and feeling some type of way because Tay didn't have the balls to apologize for his actions earlier. And he had the nerve to flare up on Jay like an STD. That in itself was a sign of trouble and enough to give Jay a change of heart. So he thought to himself, *Staying and playing another game might not be too wise. Things may go even further, so I'll do the smart thing and eliminate myself from the equation before I have to eliminate someone else from the equation.* So that's exactly what he did with the win under his belt yet again.

As soon as Jay jumped in his truck, though, it was as if he forgot about everything: the game, the foul, the confrontation, the flare-up—everything. After all that, all he could instantly envision in that moment was those two succulent unlit blunts and the one already in the ashtray he was working on before arriving at the creek, and he clearly could see himself enjoying the sweet taste and feeling real good smoking them. He used his thumb to strike the lighter, put the flame to that half blunt that he had left, and took a nice long pull. He then inhaled the smoke through his nose and then exhaled it through his mouth. It immediately left a thick white cloud of smoke lingering inside. Jay keyed his ignition, and as soon as the engine started, you could hear the speakers in the back rumbling like a roaring avalanche. He cranked his sounds a little and cracked the tinted windows two inches. Smoke from the inside began to leak out, creating a winglike effect over the top of his truck. It was time to hit the road again. He tapped the horn a couple times to let the homies know he was leaving the scene as he pulled off smoothly.

Was it intentional, or was it just a mistake? Did Tay have something against him, or was he just so into the game that he lost control? Maybe Jay was just overreacting or overanalyzing the circumstances. Of course, the more he hit the blunt, the more he continued to analyze the situation that occurred on the court.

I mean, what the fuck was that shit? We ain't never had a problem any other time, and that nigga know not to try me. He know I ain't havin' dat shit, Jay unconsciously vocalized.

It wasn't till Jay left the semi-suburb and hit the inner city streets of Cleveland that his attitude to begin to change. The Cleveland City atmosphere can do that to a person's demeanor, especially when it's too hot or nice out. The ambiance can captivate the best of them: streets filled with underdressed ladies; cars still dripping wet from the jet-off, big rims, deafening sound systems blaring; paint jobs so clear they look like mirrors when it's hot out them Cleveland boys and girls do it like the best of them. As soon as Jay passed the Welcome to Cleveland sign, near the green-light shopping plaza, he instantly became the focal point. The bass from his music made heads turn, the burnt-orange paint on the Cadillac Escalade nearly blinded other drivers, and the chrome-and-burnt-orange-colored spinning rims had onlookers dizzy. Even women who were riding in the cars with their own men, were staring at Jay recklessly. This was the feeling Jay lived for: the spotlight. Top of the world!

Jay traced the Cleveland streets for over an hour, hitting every corner he could possibly hit. He drove down almost every back street that existed on the east side. Smoking on his purple chronic and setting off every parked car alarm that he rode past. Jay's little city street creeping escapade came to an abrupt halt, though, when he noticed the red LED light on his phone blinking. It had been ringing for the last ten minutes or so, but of course, Jay didn't hear it or feel it vibrating because the music was so loud. It was Dave. Jay turned the music down and answered the phone.

"Hello?"

"Wut'up, Jay?"

"Wut'up, my nigga," Jay replied back.

"Ain't shit shaken but the leaves on the trees. I been tryna' get in touch wit you fo' da last ten minutes. I just got off the phone wit Sleeze, right? He probably gone be callin' you soon as we hang up if he ain't already been callin'," Dave explained.

"Wus da word?"

"He want us to meet him at his restaurant in twenty to thirty minutes. Can you make it?" Dave asked.

"Yeah, I'll be up there in a minute."

"Aiight, bet, I'll see you up there," Dave replied.

"Aye, Dave, wut happen to you comin' up to the creek?"

"Man, I got a room wit ol' girl from the club. Shit, by the time I got home, you was probably on yo' way up to the creek."

"Oh shit, fo' real. Nigga, you betta watch it fo' yo' ass fall in love."

"Nawl, it ain't even like dat. That's just my new lil homie." Dave laughed back.

"Yeah, homie, lover, friend—all dat," Jay said, joking around.

"Cum'on, man!"

"You know I'm fuckin' wit choo. You my nigga regardless."

"Aiight, my nig, ill see yo' ass at the spot in 'bout twenty!"

"Aiight!"

Still a bright and sunny day and temperatures were somewhat high to where you could see a bit of steam off the metal signage of Sleeze's restaurant. The two-story restaurant was a rather large historic brick building with a modern twist containing an abundance of huge mirrored glass windows. The restaurant was on a side street in the flats of downtown Cleveland, strategically placed in the heart of the most activity, surely where a more-than-generous profit could be made. The building sat on the corner attached to a high-rise building full of eloquent condos occupied by a few wealthy business owners, a few college students with trust funds, many classy high-paid strippers with money to blow, and even some prestigious lawyers with attitudes and business cards. Sleeze made sure his restaurant was near the money—the action—and the atmosphere was just right.

Upon entering the restaurant, guests would notice the decorative art sculptures highlighting the walls that were the most striking and simply exotic. There was a wine and sushi bar situated to the left with marble siding and glass inset along with glass barstools with burgundy velvet-like cushioning. Plenty of fine ladies at the bar, sipping wine and holding amusing conversations with the attractive gentleman sitting nearby, and fellas sending drinks and smiles across the bar to women of interest. Another bar was on the right that was decorated with a plethora of liquor options. This bar had lighted mirrors on rotating glass shelves that reached all the way up to the ceiling, and the shelves would be lowered and put in rotation at the touch of a button. The first-floor floors were black marble, and the ceiling of the first floor was all glass containing Cleveland's largest restaurant fish tank with only the finest and most exotic selections swimming around above the patrons' heads. Of course, if you were to fine dine on the second-floor level, you would experience the sight of the foreign fish and sea creatures underneath your feet. The fish tank ceiling was now your floor.

As patrons enter the exclusive restaurant, they can't help but admire the many visual attractions, have a seat, stay for a while, and spend plenty, which is what happened daily for this restaurant. Customers dining would notice the beautifully painted royal-blue walls, gold and a money green with a couple large art sculptures protruding out of them to superbly complement the walls, the bar setting, the colossal fish tank, and the seats in the perfect way. Ironic as it was, the fish ranged from many different colors, shapes, and sizes; and many of them were the same vibrant colors of the walls of the restaurant. The perimeter of the restaurant was lined with VIP booth-like seats that were moon shaped and seemed more like fancy couches; they were surrounding beautiful steel oval-shaped tables. The rest of the tables in the restaurant were steel as well, only triangular shaped, and the chairs were steel with the same soft burgundy velvety cushioned seating. When the restaurant catered to bigger groups of eight or more, they could dine at one of three master tables that were large oval-shaped tables nestled in the very center of the room. There were also private party rooms just as decadent and lively, that could seat a private party of two or a party of one hundred guests at a time.

Sleeze's restaurant was definitely one of a kind and drew customers from all over the place, especially people who were in town visiting and heard about the restaurant's sheer beauty and excellent food choices. The restaurant sold a bit of everything under the sun, from Italian style to Brazilian meals, American delicatessens to Japanese style, and even a bit of Southern home cooking and Puerto Rican cuisine too. It was a great place to dine or even just stop in for a drink and admire the ambiance and exotic fish exhibition.

When Jay pulled up to the restaurant, he was graced by the presence of Dave's baby-blue Navigator truck and Sleeze's burgundy 600 Benz parked out front. He parallel parked in between the two, shut off the engine, and made his way toward the door. He gazed inside the restaurant's vast front window and saw that the two of them were already engrossed in conversation. Then, he proceeded through the door and heard Sleeze's strong Jamaican accent, saying to Dave, "Dos are da tings you cont worry about, you hear me! Women are hard ta undastand, ya know."

Their conversation was then interrupted by Jay's entrance. Dave, facing the front door, had seen Jay as soon as he stepped in the restaurant. Sleeze, with his back to him, turned around as soon as he and Dave lost eye contact. Jay walked over to the table. Both Dave and Sleeze stood up and greeted him with a one-armed hug after which they all sat in unison, then got down to business.

"Listen, da best I can do is eight hundred a pound. Take it or leave it," Sleeze exclaimed.

"But, we buying fifty apiece!"

"I know what'cha buyin'. Ya dun tol me a hundred times now! And I con't go no lower dis time, but I promise I gotcha da nex time, ya hear me!"

"Aiight, Big Sleeze," Dave replied.

Jay made it home around eleven o'clock, half drunk and as high as a seven-fifty seven going straight to heaven; and he was about forty grand poorer than yesterday. That's the life of a hustler, though. It's sort of like a see-saw: one day you're down forty; the next day you're up fifty.

With an appetite as big as a lion, Jay headed straight to the kitchen. Candace had prepared a plate for him already and left it on the table: fried chicken, mashed potatoes and gravy, collard greens and cornbread, and a big-ass cup of Kool-Aid. The plate was wrapped in foil. He took off the foil, put the plate inside the microwave, and set it on warm for five minutes and thirty seconds. It came out steaming and ready to be demolished. Jay added a little hot sauce to the chicken and greens and devoured the entire meal after which he headed for the sack. Once upstairs, he could see the glare from the fifty-two-inch plasma screen percolating through the doorway. This shocked him because Candace usually came downstairs when she would hear him come in and she hardly ever went to sleep with the TV still on. Jay eased toward the door slowly in a tiptoe-like fashion. Then he opened it and looked in. Candace was lying in a fetal position—knocked out. He took off his clothes and then tried to ease in the bed. Candace woke up immediately.

"Baby, it's past eleven, and I been callin' you all day. Why you ain't call me back?"

"I'm sorry, baby, me and Dave been kickin' it all day. By the time I checked my phone and realized you called, I was on my way home. So I said, forget it. I'll talk to you when I get in."

"Did you see your plate on the table?"

"Yeah, and I smashed dat already, baby. Thanks. It was real good too."

"You welcome, but the next time you gone stay out without telling me, Jay, please just call home. You know I get worried."

"I know, baby, and I apologize. Now gone back bed, aiight?"

"Good night."

"Good night."

CHAPTER FIVE

The crowd at the Reason the next week was kind of diminutive. Saturday nights sometimes were like that too. If there wasn't reservation for a big party being thrown by one of the dope boys or some prominent person in the city, then things pretty much would be humdrum. After more than a year in the business, this was something Dave had gotten used to. Tonight was no different either. Including Dave, the waitresses, and the bartenders, there might've been about thirty people inside the Reason this night. So for that reason, Dave had every intention on closing up early to save himself some money. The sound from the television and the music coming from the speakers were about at equal volume. Various conversations could be heard fluxing among the room. The lights were only partly dimmed. One side of the Reason was shut down completely, and it was time to close up shop. Dave counted down and added up all three registers, then had the waitress and bartenders clean up, while he kindly dismissed the small throng of people. After they left, he turned off the music, the televisions, and the lights and then proceeded out the door behind his employees. He then locked up and hopped inside his blue '69 Cutlass. After watching his employees drive off, Dave pulled his car just outside the gate, locked it, and then drove off too.

Not even two minutes into the ride, Dave's cell phone rang. It was Caramel. The call shocked him because he'd normally still be working, and she was well aware of that. So what was she calling for? Was there something wrong?

"Hey, Dave, how are you?"

"I'm good, Caramel. Why? Wuz'up?" Dave replied in an apprehensive tone.

"Nothing's up. Can't I miss you?"

It doesn't seem that any good can possibly come out of Caramel missing her boss, who happens to be a married man. Caramel's growing attachment to Dave is not quite what Dave had in mind.

"Yea, I guess, but you never call me at this time. You know I'd still be working right now," Dave answered as he turned off Ninety-Third and onto Harvard Road.

"I know. I was kinda hopin' I caught you before you left."

"Why? Wuz'up, Caramel?"

"So I could see you," Caramel responded defensively. "Geez, wuz'up with all the interrogating and aggravation in your voice?"

"I'm not interrogating you. I just wanted to know why."

Caramel waited a couple of seconds, then said, "Well, anyways, I just wanted to see you tonight, but I see that you're not in the mood so—"

"Caramel, I'm sorry, boo," Dave said, cutting her sentence short. "Today just wasn't a good day, that's all."

"Why? What happened?"

"I had to shut the spot down early."

"Really! Why?" Caramel's concern was genuine, and Dave could hear it even underneath that naturally sensual and sexy voice of hers.

"It was pretty much dead. The person who reserved it for the night didn't even show up, and neither did their guests. I'd be lucky if we broke even tonight. Then, I made a move earlier, so I'm kinda down right now. Shit just ain't lookin' dat good."

"Baby, if you need sumthin', all you gotta do is ask. If I'm able to do it then, consider it done."

"Thanks, but I'm okay. I'm really just venting a little."

"I understand. So you gone let me see you today, baby, or what?"

Having sex with Caramel that week prior was the first time Dave had ever cheated on Tracie, and he totally regretted that night, and he resented himself for his infidelity. He also knew that he was extremely attracted to Caramel, and if he didn't keep things professional, he could easily fall into the same trap again. So how could he turn her down without hurting her feelings? he thought.

"Baby, I don't feel like the hotel thing tonight" was what Dave mustered up saying before he dropped his phone beside him. He then took his eyes off the road for a split second to retrieve it. All he could hear was endless tooting of car horns.

Honk! Honk! Honk!

Dave's Cutlass had drifted over into the other lane. After grabbing the phone and regaining control of the wheel, he began talking to Caramel again.

"Damn . . . I'm t-r-i-p-p-i-n'. I almost crashed my fuckin' car."

"What choo do?"

"Dropped the phone. I dunno what the hell I'm thinkin' about." He took a long deep breath, then continued, "Naw, but, Caramel, I don't feel like doing the hotel thing tonight. I just wanna lay in the bed—a comfortable bed."

"Who said anything about a hotel? I wanted you to come over my house tonight. Well, you know, my house, my apartment, whatever."

"Are you serious? I never thought you'd let me spend the night at your house." Caramel's invitation unconsciously compelled Dave to toss his inhibitions away.

"Well, I'm quite sure it's nothing like where you lay yo head at, but at least, it's clean."

"Girl, quit trippin'. I don't get down like dat, I ain't into judging you by what choo got." Instead of continuing down Harvard, Dave made a right onto the highway.

"So you cumin' or what?" Caramel asked.

"I'm on my way, but I gotta be home by four."

"I'll leave the front door unlocked, okay?"

"Aiight."

Dave got to Caramel's apartment at around one o'clock in the morning. She stayed across town off East 185th Street. Dave had been there before but only to drop Caramel off. He had never stayed or came in to see the inside of Caramel's apartment. He had never even parked. He had only stopped in front to make sure she had made it in safe. Caramel stayed on the first floor of the two-story building, the first door on the left. Tenants had to buzz everybody in because the steel hallway door had an automatic lock to it.

Dave parked his car in the back parking lot then walked around to the front of the building. He then opened the door, looked toward the names on the mailboxes, and realized he'd forgotten Caramel's real name. This was an embarrassment to him because Caramel was his employee. Since he was used to paying the girls "under the table," though, he didn't ever write out any checks to them. Therefore, he really had no reason to remember their legal names anyways. Standing in front of the mailboxes, looking at the names, Dave was trying to see which one seemed the most familiar. Dave had looked down at the door and noticed it was held ajar by a small piece of wood. He pulled the door open, then kicked the piece of wood aside, and let the door close and lock behind him. He was just about ready to hop on his cell phone and call Caramel to ask her the apartment number. Staring at all the wooden doors made him feel confused and uncomfortable. Something inside of him wished he could've just started ringing bells until someone sounding like her answered their intercom. Dave walked toward the bottom of the steps, passing up the first and second doors on his left. The he turned right as he was about to head up the stairs when he noticed the first wooden door was cracked open just a little. He walked back toward the door and was startled by Caramel's voice.

"Dave, come in."

Dave walked into the candlelit apartment. He could barely see Caramel's body as she was lying there on the couch. Dave reached back to shut the door and locked it.

Caramel stayed in a nice and comfy one-bedroom apartment. Her place was very spacious. Upon entering, he noticed her kitchen was a small space immediately to the left. It was just big enough to hold a fridge, stove, and a mini kitchen table with two chairs. Next was the living room. All she had in it was her forty-two-inch flat-screen TV and brown leather sofa and a glass table with black legs trimmed in gold. As he left the living room, down the narrow hallway was her small bathroom to the right and her semi-spacious bedroom in the back. Caramel's apartment wasn't very big, but she loved it.

Walking toward her couch, he whispered, "It's dangerous out here. Leaving ya doors open in the middle of the night is real dangerous."

"About as dangerous as peeping into an open door," Carmel replied back.

Dave sat down next to Caramel on her black leather couch. Caramel raised her legs up then put them over the top of Dave's thighs. Her beautiful feet were pointing straight up toward his face. He rubbed the shin of her legs with his left hand and massaged both feet with his right hand. Without saying a word, he continued the process for a minute or two; then out of nowhere, he asked Caramel, "Why did you leave the door open anyways?"

She responded with a question, "Why do you think?"

"You knew that I didn't know which apartment you lived in and that I didn't remember your name, didn't you?"

"Yes, Dave, I knew."

"Why come you just didn't tell me on the phone, so I could buzz the bell?"

"Because you didn't ask," Caramel replied.

"So what if someone else woulda came in the building and locked me out?"

"Woulda heard'um and then put the wood back."

"Dressed like this?" Dave asked.

"Not the first time I'd be caught half naked and probably won't be the last."

"Truthfully, though, why didn't you just tell me your name again? It ain't that big a deal, is it?"

"Because, David, I didn't think I would need to. I never thought this relationship would even get this far, and I really truly didn't think that I would let choo see the inside of my apartment!" Caramel replied earnestly.

"So why did you then?" Dave asked curiously while still rubbing her shins and feet gently.

"Because, David, somehow I've developed strong feelings for you. Feelings that I didn't even know I had, that's why!" She paused for a few seconds then continued, "Hell when I told you to come over, I didn't realize what I said till I had hung up the phone."

Caramel raised her body up so that she was sitting aside from him. The light from the candles highlighted her partly covered body. Shadows of her goodies were enlarged on the wall. They began kissing, deep throat kissing, and swapping spit heavily. The kisses were so passionate, sloppy, and wet.

Caramel pulled away slowly, leaving Dave stuck in midair, looking thirsty. Dave's eyes were still closed, and his lips poked out, wanting more.

"Nina," Caramel said softly.

"What?" Dave retorted back after opening his eyes and regaining consciousness.

"Nina. Shanina Tucker. That's my name."

"Shanina Tucker, huh? I probably should've remembered that!"

"You can't remember something you never knew," Caramel said softly.

"What! What choo mean?" Dave asked while giving her his puzzled look.

"David, I gave you the wrong name when you hired me. That was just in case things didn't work out. But now that you know my real name, you better not forget it."

"D-A-M-N. I wonder just how many of the girls gave me the wrong name."

"Trust me, Dave, you'd be real surprised," Nina said, nodding her head back and forth.

Dave sat there for a second then came back with "So am I supposed to call you Caramel or Shanina now?"

"Dave, call me Nina. It sounds much more personal, considering it's real."

"I agree. I agree. Well, what about at work? What then?"

"Caramel's good," she replied.

"And so . . ." Were the only words Dave managed to mutter before Nina placed her pointer finger over his juicy lips.

"Shhh . . . Don't say another word and kiss me."

Their spit swapping began again as both tongues explored places that the naked eye can't see without a telescope. They bumped gums and teeth and sucked on bottom lips, top lips, and bottom again. After tongue wrestling for over five minutes, the two of them were hotter than Hell's Kitchen. Dave lay Nina down on her back on the sofa, positioned himself in between her thighs, then leaned toward her, and pecked her on the chin. He kissed her neck, in between her breasts, then licked down to her navel. Nina's temperature rose quickly. Dave had her open like a twenty-four-hour convenient mart. Her body was sweaty and moist just from pure anticipation. The more Dave licked and kissed, the more her body convulsed. Enjoying every minute, she just closed her eyes and moaned softly to her own tone. Dave slowly pulled down the purple thong that separated his face from Nina's paradise. He slid them over her feet, tossed them to the floor, then made his way toward heaven.

Nina helped guide him to that sacred place by grabbing his head and forcing it down paradise lane. Dave didn't fight her, though. He wanted to do it as much as she wanted it done. Dave's tongue met Nina and was delighted. Her love below was soaking wet. Juices ran all down her inner thigh as his tongue dove as far into her inner walls as it could. He used his fingers to spread her open further. Then he began maneuvering side to side, up and down, slowly with his tongue, as if he were in search of something. Nina couldn't withstand much more of it. Her moans became heavy and got even more intense as he started sucking on her clitoris.

"Ooooh S-H-I-T, David. I c-a-n-t t-a-k-e a-n-y-m-o-r-e!" Nina came all over her couch and his face. Dave loved it. He watched as she jolted crazily, squirming like a fish out of water. She shook and moaned unconsciously like Dave wasn't even present.

Finally, her body settled down as she took a couple of minutes to catch her breath. After her short breather, Nina sat upright then unstrapped the front of her matching purple bra. He 34D-cupped breast spilled out, exposing her dark areolas and fully erect nipples. With haste, she stood straight up then grabbed Dave underneath his shoulders, standing him up as well. She reached down, unbuttoned his pants' button, then unzipped his zipper. His hard dick fell out from between the slit in his boxers. Nina hungrily dropped to her knees in pursuit of Dave's manhood. Before she could get him in her mouth, though, Dave's phone rang. Nina, relishing in the moment, told him, "Answer it, baby."

"Hell naw, girl. You ain't finna get me killed."

"Answer the phone, David. I'm not go get choo in trouble. So wait a minute. You don't trust me now?"

Dave conceded. "Aiight, but choo betta not say nuthin'. I'm serious, Cara—damn . . . I mean Nina."

"I'm not. I'm not."

Dave answered the phone, and it was his wife, Tracie. Her belligerent tone shook him up.

"Dave!" she yelled with authority.

"Yes, baby."

"Where are you at right now?"

"Uuhh?"

"Nigga, don't uh me! Where are you at?"

"Why you ask me that?"

"'Cause I just called the club and nobody answered the phone."

"Oh yeah. I closed the club early. We weren't doin' too good, so I shut it down for the night. I was gon call 'n' tell you. I guess I just forgot." Nina grabbed his thang and carefully caressed it. She began licking the head and massaging it with her thumb. Pre-cum oozed out slowly, causing her thumb to rotate quicker. Dave tried to stop her but to no avail. She wasn't stopping.

"I like how you just avoided the question, David."

"What question?"

"WHERE ARE YOU!" Tracie screamed.

"What you mean where am I at? Where you at?"

"I'm at home, David. Now answer the fuckin' question!"

"I'm waiting on our food."

"Waiting on OUR food? Where, David Daryl Smith?"

Dave was as hard as steel, still standing straight up. Nina took it all in her mouth with no hands and deep throated as far as she could without gagging.

"At S-l-e-e-z-e's r-e-s-t-a-u-r-a-n-t," Dave replied.

"If you at Sleeze's restaurant, then let me speak to him."

"Fa' what?" Dave asked uneasily.

"'Cause I don't believe you."

"Oh, but choo a believe him?" he asked in an awkward tone of voice. You could just about tell Nina's head doctoring was starting to become a hindrance on his speech. By now, Nina's lips were slipping on and off the shaft off Dave's dick religiously. Quitting hadn't even crossed Nina's mind. Not with all the work she'd put in. not to mention his wife being on the other line. She wanted this volcano to erupt NOW!

After Dave's response to her wanting to speak to Sleeze, Tracie sat quietly on the other end of the phone for a bit. Then she insisted, "You know what, Dave, if yo' ass ain't in this house in the next 20 minutes—I'm . . . I'm not even gonna go there. Be here in twenty minutes. Bye!" Then she hung up the phone. As soon as he saw the words *call ended* on his cell phone, Dave instantly began moaning. "Aww shit. Nina, what-the-fuuuck? I'm finna cum. You betta watch it."

Nina just kept sucking. Spit was everywhere: all over her mouth, her face, her chin and her chest, and even some on her hands from when she grabbed his dick and took control. She kept going faster and faster and hoping Dave was ready. And that he was. He shot cum all in her mouth rhythmically, and she swallowed every bit of it.

Dave got in his truck and did eighty-five miles per hour down Interstate 90 from Nina's apartment all the way to Bratenahl, only slowing down when he saw cops ahead.

Leaving the scene of the adulterated crime wasn't easy for Dave, but he knew it was only for the best. Dave still loved his wife more than life itself, and if rushing home to be with her after an ardent encounter with someone that he only had strong feelings for was what he had to do to prove it, then so be it. As he raced passed Fifty-Fifth, then around a dead man's curve, Dave was in deep though—no music was on, no weed smoking, no drinking, just driving fast and deep thinking. He tried everything in his power to figure out what he was going to say to his wife when he got home. For some reason, though, he couldn't keep his mind off Shanina and all the events that transpired: the spontaneous phone call, the invitation to her home, Shanina telling her real name, the brain surgery. Everything that felt so foreign about her was now being revealed. All the things Dave used as excuses to say this is not an affair were now being dislodged. Not that he didn't want them to be, but the question was, why were they?

What puzzled Dave the most, though, was Nina's head. It was sort of kinky and freaky, downright nasty even. But he liked it, and he realized, from the way she participated, she liked it too. Besides that, it was an act his wife rarely performed. She did it, but the way it was done was so traditional. Oh, and doing it while he talked on the phone—Tracie probably didn't know that existed.

Why did I like that so much? he asked himself. Was he just thinking with the wrong head, or was he beginning to fall for his subordinate?

The clock on Dave's dashboard read two o'clock in the morning. Time was moving faster than usual. That wasn't unusual, though, especially when you had somewhere to be. He'd just left Nina's apartment at one forty, and here it is, already two o'clock. So much for making it to the house in twenty minutes. Dave put the pedal to the floor, flying past the downtown scenery: Jacob's Field, the Q Arena, Tower City, and all the rest of those beautiful monumental buildings. They quickly became distant memories in his rearview. He drove in the fast lane until he got to the Jennings Road exit. He got off there, beat the light, and darted over the train tracks, running the next two lights. He made a right on Crestline and another right onto Crest Drive, which was his street. He pulled into the driveway, put the truck in park, shut off the engine, got out, and walked to the door. After chirping his alarm, he put his key inside the door, unlocked it, and right before he went inside, he said to himself, *Goddamn, I forgot to bring home some food!*

"Hello, Nina. How you doing?"

"Hey, baby! Did everything go all right last night?" Shanina asked about Dave's frantic dash home when his wife called him to come home the night before. It really disturbed Nina because she truly wanted Dave all to herself. That was the whole reason for Nina's spontaneous call. But after a few hours of contemplating, then a good night's rest, Nina woke with a completely different attitude than she had the night before.

"Yeah, everything went cool," Dave responded in a whispering tone of voice. It was only nine thirty in the morning, and to his knowledge, Tracie was still in the bed. The last thing he was trying to do was get caught sneaking on the phone talking to Nina or any other female. While Dave was sitting on the toilet, he kept his eyes on the door, making sure it stayed locked. The door was kind of tricky, and he didn't want Tracie bursting in on him in the middle of the conversation with Nina. After he explained how things went, Dave continued with "Nina, listen, I need to tell you something."

"Go ahead, David. I'm all ears!" True enough, she was listening to David, eager as she was. Her heart was beating a mile a minute. She was nervously anticipating his news. Dave's tone of voice wasn't exactly receptive, so she knew his news might not be what she would like it to be. She could almost sniff the bad news through the phone before he even put the words together.

Dave flushed the toilet and flipped the switch on the bathroom vent and turned the hot water on to begin washing his hands. With his cell phone wedged close to his ear, resting on his shoulder, Dave unenthusiastically said, "Listen, Nina, this isn't going to be the easiest thing to say, but it's necessary."

"Go ahead, boo. I'm okay with whatever it is you have to say to me."

"Okay, I'm glad you said that, baby, 'cause I need you to hear me and hear me good.

"First, you should know that I love you!" Dave couldn't believe what he was saying, but he meant each word. Last night was the icing on the cake that they'd been baking for weeks. Those feelings he was having were the exact reasons why he had to end this affair quick, fast, and in a hurry before it had gotten out of hand.

"And I mean that, Nina! That's why we have to stop seeing each other."

Nina's heart fell to the floor. She thought she might have been prepared for any and everything Dave had to tell her but apparently not. She was hurt. She remained quiet on the phone. To Dave's surprise, she didn't reply immediately. She just remained patiently and painfully silent, recovering from a state of shock and disappointment. Dave said a few more words, but she didn't hear a thing after. "We have to stop seeing each other." Caramel was devastated, and it showed. Dave had just stated something that he felt Nina should have answered to, even though he wasn't asking her a question. He realized she had gone completely hush.

"Nina, you still on the line?" he asked and then waited for her to respond.

"I'm still here, baby." A part of her was still there, and a part of her was somewhere else, trying to figure out what she had done to deserve this. Last she remembered, she'd just told him her real name, let him come in her home—something she never did—and to top that, she'd even given him an incomparable blowjob that was worth top dollar. *Now this,* she thought to herself.

"Nina, I want choo ta know you have not done anything wrong, okay? This has nothing to do with you," Dave whispered to her.

Just then Dave heard something go boom. It sounded like a door slamming. "Nina, hol' on for a second, okay?"

"Okay," Nina replied with a worried yet delicate voice.

Dave put his cell phone on the bathroom sink, then opened the door, and ran straight up the stairs to his and Tracie's bedroom. Tracie wasn't in bed. The bed was made up, though, and the room was clean too. So where the hell was Tracie? He checked all the rooms upstairs and then ran downstairs to check the basement—still no Tracie. He checked the bathroom to see if it had been used, and sure enough, his intuition served him correct. Dave looked out the window to see if Tracie's car was still outside, and it was gone. Tracie had gotten up, gotten dressed, and left. Her leaving was clearly all he heard because he sure missed the sounds of her grooming herself and water running in the other bathroom. Dave was now asking himself, *Did she hear me whispering on the phone in the bathroom?*

Dave rushed back to the bathroom, picked up his cell phone, said hello, and to his surprise, Nina was still there, waiting for his return to the line.

"Yes, I'm here!" Nina replied.

"Baby, I'm sorry for leaving you on hold like dat. I had to check something out."

"That's okay. Is everything all right?"

"Yea, I thought I heard someone at the door that's all."

"Hey, David, before you continue, let me say this one thing, okay?"

"Go ahead, baby," Dave urged, walking through his house shirtless, with a pair of Carolina blue ball shorts on.

"David, I hear what you're saying, and I think I understand where you're coming from, but I want choo ta know dat I love you too . . . regardless. I know I've never said I love you before, but trust me on this one. I do. I'm not saying this for you to change your mind or take back anything you said. I'm saying this for you to know that no matter what, I'll be here for you, and I mean it." Nina was speaking strictly from the heart. The things that she was saying, she couldn't make up or form sensibly unless she meant them, and she did.

She had truly fallen for this man. The only problem was she might've waited too late to tell him how she felt. Dave took in everything Nina said. It was even kind of soothing for him just to know that she felt this way.

"Nina, baby, you just don't know how good that makes me feel to hear you say dat. Now listen, I'm ain't crazy, and I don't expect you to put yo' life on hold for lil ol' me, but I want choo ta know dat if anything was to happen with my marriage, you'd be the first and only one I'd call."

"And I hope that if and when you do call, I'm not spoken for."

Dave was really surprised at the way things ended. Nina had taken the news a lot better than he'd expected: no crying, no whining, no threats, no violent rants about plans of sabotaging his marriage or any of that childishness. This affair thing, for him at least, was okay considering. It would even be much better if he hadn't had such strong feelings for her.

Now, where did my wife go? Dave asked himself next. Last he checked, she was knocked out cold, lying beside him. All he did was get up for a few minutes, actually thirty minutes, to talk to Nina and Tracie woke up and left. Just as he was about to call Tracie, his house phone rang.

"Hello," Dave answered.

"Hello, may I speak to Tracie?"

"She's not in. May I take a message?" Dave asked.

"This is her cousin Nikki. Is this her husband, Dave?"

"Yes, it's me!"

Nikki and Dave conversed for a good ten minutes. The conversation was very interesting, and as far as Dave was concerned, Tracie had a lot of explaining to do.

Chapter Six

"**S**o where you want to meet at?" Tracie asked, talking into her cell phone while steering her Lexus up Harvard Avenue. Tracie had gotten dressed and headed over to Sleeze's restaurant. She had plans on finding out the truth about where her husband was last night. After he came in without something to eat, suspicion arose immediately. Tracie told herself not to bring it up to him—just go ask Sleeze in person. She wasn't very familiar with Sleeze, though. She had only met him twice: once when Dave took her with him to pick up a package and another time when they ate at his restaurant. Both times Sleeze seemed to be cool to her, so she convinced herself that he wouldn't mind her questioning him a bit. "I guess we can meet at the Radisson again," Teddy replied.

"What time you talkin' 'bout, Tracie? You know it's kinda early."

"I know. I'm on a mission right now, anyways. I'm talkin' 'bout more like two o'clock," Tracie said in a defensive tone. To her, Teddy's voice was a little overconfident. She didn't want him thinking she'd gotten too thirsty for him.

"Okay. Well, yeah, we can do that. By then, I'll be ready for whateva. Ya know."

"I hear ya talkin'." They both laughed devilishly.

"What choo gone wear over there?" Teddy asked in a Barry White–like tone of voice. He already had a deep voice, but the way it deepened accentuated his attempt at being sexy.

"If I tell you now, then it won't be worth waiting for now, will it?"

Tracie hung up the phone with Teddy around Ninety-Third and Harvard. As she channeled her emotions back to Dave and where he was last night, her thoughts began wrestling with one another. *If he was there last night, then he ain't got nothing to worry about* was what she continued to recite aloud like a crazy woman in her car. Tracie then rode past 120th and was stopped by the red light at on 131st. Sitting alongside a black-on-black H2 Hummer, with sparkling chrome rims, Tracie stared inside the tinted windows thirstily. After cracking the windows just enough for the two of them to make eye contact, the bald-headed black brother stared back intensely. *He is fine as hell! And bald-headed too,* she mumbled under her breath. The light then turned green. *All his chocolate ass got to do is say the word,* Tracie continued as the two of them began coasting through the traffic signal.

Tracie continued to weave in and out of traffic, unconsciously keeping up with the H2 Hummer. Again the two of them get caught at a red light, this time on Lee and Harvard. With Tracie now in the left lane and the guy in the H2 on her right, the two of them began staring. Inside the drop-top Lexus, Tracie's thighs looked thick and enticing. Her tropical-colored tennis skirt was hiked up so far he could practically see her panty line. She watched as he quickly undressed her with his eyes. Then, after what looked to be a lust connection, the guy turned right onto Lee Road. *If I wasn't so close to Sleeze's restaurant, I'd follow his ass,* Tracie whispered to herself.

The light then turned green, and Tracie proceeded. After driving past the Lee and Harvard Plaza, she remembered Sleeze's restaurant was just after it. The distinctive sign popped up like a billboard. CAROLINA'S was what it read. Tracie got over in the right lane, then stopped in front one of Sleeze's many restaurants. There was a parking space at the curbside right in front of the door. She let the oncoming traffic pass by, then parallel parked in between a Navy Chevy Lumina and a powdered-white-colored Olds Alero. She then put her car in park and shut the engine off.

Carolina's was a three-thousand-square-feet building with lots of curb appeal. The rest of the surrounding buildings either didn't quite have its mass or couldn't match its outer decor. The beautifully constructed brick building looked newly renovated. It was definitely an eye-catcher.

Before exiting her vehicle, Tracie took a moment to check her makeup. Inside her rearview mirror, she examined the mascara that highlighted her eyelashes. It looked proper. Her eyebrows were arched just the way she liked them. The lip gloss that smothered her full lips had them looking juicer than a medium steak fresh off the grill. Everything was on point.

Tracie finally exited her car and headed toward the bar. After opening the expensive glass entrance doors and walking inside, she glanced around at its interior. At quick glance, Tracie was impressed. Carolina's was wonderfully decorated. Standing atop some softly carpeted stairs, she looked to the left and admired the large bar. The bottles of liquor and glasses along the wall where brightly lit. Straight ahead was the dining room floor, where some contemporary black table and chair sets that were perfectly positioned for space and convenience. To her right was an elevated semi-private VIP section. She shook her head in approval.

As Tracie began to walk down the stairs, all eyes were glued to her. With each step, her multicolored tennis skirt revealed her thick and well-toned chocolate thighs. Her breast jumped loosely in the matching halter top. Her mustard opened-toe heels with the corked soles enlightened her sexy feet. Her healthy jet-black hair hung just below her neck. The light that set just above Tracie had her milk-chocolate-colored skin glowing gracefully. Tracie looked stunning.

As she strutted toward an open table, reality set in. She began asking herself questions like *What am I doing here? What if he doesn't even remember me?* Tracie didn't even know Sleeze's name for crying out loud. She just knew *Sleeze. How am I going to get his attention?* she then asked herself. *What if he ain't here?* All the necessary questions that she should've asked herself before leaving home were now surfacing.

Tracie reached down to grab a chair and sit, and to her surprise, Sleeze's dark five-feet-ten-inch somewhat-muscular frame came from behind the bar. His timing was impeccable. It was almost as if he knew Tracie was coming. With an air of confidence, Sleeze walked gracefully over to Tracie's table. "Ello," he spoke in his strong Jamaican accent. "You're Dave's wife, Tracie, right?"

"Correct. And you're—" Tracie dragged, hoping he'd says his name before she made a fool of herself by asking.

"Cedric," Sleeze answered, cutting her short. He had this feeling that Tracie barely knew his alias, much less his real name.

"Yes, Cedric," Tracie retorted, going with the flow of the conversation. "How have you been?"

"I've been jus' fine, tank you." With every few words, Sleeze's accent would rear its ugly head. "Do ya want me ta send you me best waitress?"

"Actually, that won't be necessary. At least not at the moment anyways."

"Well, what can I do for ya, Tracie?" Sleeze asked, looking very puzzled.

"Well, I was kinda hoping you could help me solve a few unanswered questions about my husband's whereabouts last night. But if you're unwilling, I could respect your confidentiality," Tracie spoke in a low tone and very eloquently. This was due to Sleeze's oozing confidence and the intimidation his sheer aura gave her.

"No, no, me be glad to help. Follow me to me office. I'll have da cook make us sumting small. Anyting you want in particular?"

"Maybe a penne pasta with a glass of white zinfandel, if you don't mind," Tracie said while following Sleeze's lead. Her walk was so alluring it captivated the room. The size of her rea end, and the way that it shook loosely with each stride had both the ladies and men stuck in a trance.

Sleeze left Tracie waiting for him in his office for over ten minutes before he reentered the room with food and drinks. The two of them ate, drink, and conversed about Dave, his whereabouts, and everything else that came to mind.

Tracie left Carolina's feeling much happier than when she first walked in. Sleeze had eased her mind. She could not believe how friendly he was or how willingly he gave up information. He even managed to slip her his business card with his cell number written on the back. Tracie left the restaurant saying to herself, *I don't know if Sleeze is telling me the truth or not, but I do know that with this card on file, David sure won't be using Sleeze as an alibi no mo!*

Feeling relieved, Tracie hopped in her pretty white Lexus and set her sights on her next mission: Teddy!

Tracie and Teddy's rendezvous ended somewhere around seven o'clock that Sunday evening. A few last-minute hugs and kisses, then the two of them abandoned the hotel room and went their separate ways. Teddy went back toward his side of town while Tracie headed home. To her surprise, when she pulled in the driveway, her husband's truck was in the same place that it was when she first left. Usually, by this time in the day, Dave would be out and about. Although Sunday was his only night off at the club, and one would think he'd need his rest, Dave did his best to take full advantage of his free day!

Tracie entered her home through the back door and was greeted by a sarcastic "Hey, baby!" Dave's voice didn't seem pleasant to her at all.

"Well, hello, David," Tracie responded back defensively.

"Guess who called today?"

Guess who called today? Tracie repeated to herself. *Why would he ask me that? I was just with Teddy, so I know it ain't him. I don't mess with anybody else, sooo . . . it must be Sleeze,* she figured. After seconds of contemplation, she finally just went ahead and blurted, "I don't know. Who?"

"Nikki," David replied in a dry tone.

"Nikki? What did she want?" Tracie asked inquisitively.

"She said something about you picking her up from the Greyhound station."

"Oh shit! I was supposed to pick her up. I completely forgot." By this time, Tracie was just realizing she never even asked her husband if Nikki could stay with them. "By the way, baby, I meant to ask you if it would be okay if my cousin Nikki stayed with us for a little while. Not long, though, just until she gets on her feet. Don't worry, I already got a job lined up for her and everything," Tracie uttered convincingly. After a stern look from her husband, she continued, "Baby, I'm sorry for not coming to you earlier. I-I," she stuttered, "just have a lot of things on my mind. Honestly, though, I had every intention of telling you."

"Yeah, okay. Tell me anything!"

"No, seriously, I did mean to tell you. She had asked my mom if she could stay with her first."

"So why ain't she staying with your mother then?" Dave inquired.

"Baby, you know my mother ain't really the company type. Plus Nikki—well, Nikki's used to be kinda fast. Anyways, baby, we got two extra rooms that we don't even use. So I just figured it wouldn't hurt to let her use one 'til she got herself together."

"But that's just it. Y-O-U ain't the one paying bills in this house. So how are Y-O-U gonna tell anybody that they can stay here without asking me?"

"Baby, I said I'm sorry. Now can she stay pleeeeaaase?"

"Well, it's a bit late to be asking that now. She's been at the Greyhound station since four thirty or so," Dave said walking toward the refrigerator. Tracie hustled her way toward the door, but before she could open it and leave out, Dave yelled, "Next time you decide to do some shit like this, you make sure the one who pays this $1,000 house note is informed first." Dave's demands fell on deaf ears.

Tracie leaped into the driver's seat of her car and hit the streets like a bat out of hell. *I wonder if she left me any voice messages or texts,* Tracie questioned. Then she checked her voicemail. To her surprise, Nikki's voice was on the other end of two voice messages. "Hey cuz. I'm at the Greyhound. It's about 4:45 p.m. right now. I'll be on the inside waiting on you. See ya." The Greyhound station was on Fourteenth and Chester. "Tracie, it's almost six," Nikki said with trepidation. "I'm going to go outside and wait for you. Please come as quick as you can. Okay. Bye."

Racing down West Twenty-Fifth on her way to the Greyhound station, Tracie, for some odd reason, began to have mixed emotions about these planned living arrangements she made with her cousin. *I hope this is the right thing to do,* she thought to herself. Tracie thought herself to be a pretty secure woman, but Nikki was fine. She was young too! Nikki had just turned nineteen this year, but her voluptuous curves begged to differ. Tracie hadn't seen her in a while, though. *Everything will work out,* she convinced herself, quickly dismissing all negative thought.

Tracie then made a right onto Superior Avenue and headed up the bridge. She got up to a speed of nearly seventy as she weaved in and out of traffic like a NASCAR driver. As she almost hit a car, a white man yelled, "Hey, watch where the hell you're going!" Slowing down at the light, she looked in her rearview and saw him flicking her off. She just smiled and proceeded to stop.

As Tracie got closer to the bus station, her anticipation to see Nikki grew. *How does she look now? How is she gonna act? Is she the same cousin that looked up to me like a big sister, or has she become some fat ass?* The last time they saw each other was when Tracie graduated high school. She then went to spend the summer with Nikki and her mom in Cincinnati before coming back up to Cleveland for the start of her first semester at CSU.

Tracie made it to the station a little after 8:00 p.m. She pulled into the entrance and saw Nikki, with a large suitcase and a couple bags, sitting on the wooden benches. "Hey, Nik," she blurted out of her open window after realizing Nikki wasn't familiar with her Lexus.

Nikki left her luggage and rushed toward the car. "Hey, Tracie," she yelled eagerly, dislodging the fact that she was supposed to be angry with her cousin for being over three and a half hours late. The two of them hugged tightly. "Girl, you don't know how much I appreciate this. You are truly a lifesaver."

"Girl, don't mention it," Tracie retorted. Tracie then stepped back, looked her little cousin up and down in amazement, then said, "Girl, what diet plan are you on? You lookin' real good. You weren't hardly this slim last time I saw you."

"Thanks, girl" was Nikki's only reply. Tracie was right about one thing: Nikki looked good. She was ten pounds thinner than the last time Tracie saw her. Her body was now well proportioned. Nikki was five feet six inches and 130 pounds. Her skin was high yellow, and she had some deep hazel eyes. Her hair was light brown and hung just below her neck. Her embellished shirt revealed her small but firm breasts. The gauchos she wore accentuated her curvaceous hips and plump behind. In totality, she could pass for Halle Berry's stunt double.

Tracie and Nikki both took turns stuffing the backseat and the trunk with Nikki's things. "Damn, girl, you sure you ain't got a body in this suitcase," Tracie joked as she stuffed Nikki's last bit of luggage in the backseat.

"Ha-ha, girl, you silly." Nikki laughed, then hopped in the passenger side of the Lexus. Tracie then drove them to get something to eat at a well-renowned place in Cleveland called Zanzibar in Shaker Square. The two of them ate, drank, and caught up. Then, after over an hour, the girls made their way to the Westside.

"David, come here so I can introduce you to my cousin," Tracie insisted after walking through the door.

"Tracie, girl, ya'll got a lovely house," Nikki commented while glancing around in awe.

"Thank you, girl." Before they could continue conversing, Dave entered the room in a white T-shirt and his favorite Carolina blue shorts. "Baby, this is my younger cousin Nikki. Nikki, this is my husband, Dave."

"It's nice to meet you, Dave." The two of them shook hands.

"It's nice to meet you too, Nikki," Dave replied.

"You and my cousin have been together for so long. It feels like we already know each other."

"I know, right?" Dave giggled.

"Well, I want to thank you for letting me stay here 'til I get on my feet. I really appreciate it."

"Don't mention it. Any family of T's is family of mines." Dave, Tracie, and Nikki all small talked for a few; and then everyone went their separate ways. Dave went back to his bedroom, Nikki to the guestroom that Tracie pointed her to, and Tracie to the showers.

PART 2

CHAPTER SEVEN

"**D**id you call yo job and tell 'em that you weren't comin' in tomorrow?" Jay questioned Candace as she rushed her way toward the porcelain god. Candace had been hurling off and on for the past few days. But like every person in denial, she refused to go to the doctor. Jay's concerns were heightened, though. He had done all he could do for her. Chicken noodle soup, tea, and Tylenol could only do so much. Jay pressed the mute button on the television's remote control and heard his girlfriend nearly puking her brains out. "Candace," he yelled. "Tomorrow, you're going to the doctor. I don't care what you talkin' 'bout. Now you can go on your own, or I'm taking you myself. Pick your poison."

By the tone in Jay's voice, Candace knew that he was serious, especially since he said that he'd take her. Jay wasn't the take-off-work type, even though he owned the construction company and did very little manual labor. "I called earlier and made an appointment for tomorrow morning," Candace managed to convey over the sound of the flushing toilet. Holding her face over the toilet bowl to rid her mouth of the excess puke, Candace straightened up and began to brush her teeth. "I promise I'ma go tomorrow, babe. You ain't gotta take off," she assured him.

"Aight, Candace, I trust you. Don't let me down."

"Have I ever?" she retorted. His comment disgusted her, and Jay could hear it.

"Well, I'm not counting, but this is the third time I've asked you to go. So in the case, naw, you haven't let me down."

"Jay, come on now, I said that I'm going," Candace exclaimed after shutting of the water, then putting away her toothbrush. Candace then entered their room and walked over to her side of the bed.

"Baby, I ain't tryna be funny, but I hope you washed your hands." Jay chuckled, then continued, "I'm just saying. You tryna get into the bed and all."

"Boy, shut up," Candace replied, then hopped onto the mattress. "You know I did."

"Naw, I don't know nothing. I know you shut that water off mighty quickly," Jay teased, laughing even harder. Candace, laughing playfully too, just nudged his arm. The two of them then kissed and said their good nights. Jay then shut the TV off, and they both went to bed.

Candace got up early the next morning and found her way to the doctor's office, like her man had requested. Her appointment was for ten o'clock. She barely made it on time. Candace hated going to the doctor. Ever since she was a kid, she feared doctor's appointments. No matter how sick she would get, she'd still find ways out of going. It got to the point that Candace would rather go to school sick than go to the doctor.

Candace's doctor's office was a multilevel, brown-bricked building located on Euclid Avenue. It neighbored a very small car lot and a run-down vacant hotel. Inside the building where her doctor was were over fifty rooms, all individually occupied. Candace's doctor's office was on the first floor, first room on the right.

Once inside, the nurse checked Candace's vitals, took her temperature, and checked her weight. Then she sent Candace back into the lobby to wait on the doctor.

"Long time no see, Candace," the doc uttered after receiving the message that Candace had arrived, then meeting her in the lobby. "How have you been?"

"I've been okay, Doc," she replied as she followed him into the room.

Candace was getting more nervous by the second. "So I see you're allergic to Aleve," the doc said as he perused her chart. Candace didn't respond. "You seem to be a bit nervous, Candace," the doc said, still looking down at her chart. Before she could respond, he continued, "Don't worry. You're in good hands. Everything will be fine."

The doctor then got up and left the room. He returned with a clear plastic cup that had a blue lid. "Candace, I'm going to need a urine sample, okay? I'm also going to take a blood sample if it's okay with you."

"What's wrong, Doc?" Candace asked frantically.

"Nothing's wrong, Candace," Doc said then chuckled slightly. "We just wanna run some tests to make certain everything is okay. Sound good to ya?" Doc asked in a calming tone.

"I guess," Candace responded in relief.

"Great then."

Candace then gave him the urine sample, and Doc stuck her with a needle to obtain her blood. Afterward, he concealed them both. Next, he wrote a few things down inside of his notebook. "Okay, Candace, we're just about set here. In about three days, we will get in contact with you to let you know the results, okay?"

That's it? Candace thought to herself. *Wow, that was quick!* "Okay, Doc!" was her only reply.

"As far as meds go, I don't want to give you too much until I get the test results back. So I've prescribed you some Tylenol with codeine plus some cold tablets. You take these to your local pharmacy, and they will take care of you. If things manage to get worse before we contact you, call me."

"I sure will," Candace said while giggling.

"If there's nothing else, you're free to go."

"Okay, Doc. Thanks," Candace said with gratitude.

"No problem. Take it easy."

And just like that, Candace was out of the doctor's office. Candace eagerly shut the main office door and then walked hesitantly toward the stairs at end of the hallway. Still feeling ill, though, she was still happy to be out of that office. Holding on to the rail, she slowly and cautiously strolled down the steps, walked out the front door, and headed toward Jay's Escalade. Candace was only driving it because he took her Ford Explorer early that morning.

Candace got into the truck and was getting ready to back out when she noticed someone on her passenger side. It was a tall dark-skinned brother with a deep-waved haircut. He had begun tapping on the window. She was about to pull off because he scared her half to death. Something told her to roll down the window. "Excuse me, may I help you?" Candace asked the guy after letting the window down halfway.

"Oh, I'm sorry. I thought choo was this dude named Jay. My nigga got a truck just like this one."

"This is Jay's truck! I'm his girlfriend," Candace replied.

"Oh, okay. Hi you doing? My name is Nell."

"Hi, Nell," Candace said. "Do you want me to tell Jay sumthin'?"

"Naw, not really. You know what, yeah. Just tellum I was looking for him. He'll know what for." Nell and Tay wanted some weed, and Jay and Dave had the best in the city. Tay, though, remembering the altercation that he and Jay had previously, thought that it would be a perfect time for some payback.

"I can do that," Candace assured Nell. Just as Nell was about to walk away from the truck, Tay stuck his head out of the '85 Grey Buick Regal they were in and yelled, "Aey, sweetie, you should let a nigga get a number or sumthin. You need a nigga that's gone take care of you."

"Gone wit all that bullshit, Tay," Nell insisted as he opened up the driver-side door. Candace just gave them and their too-old two-door Regal that look of disgust. Then she backed up and drove off. Jay left his work site later that evening around six thirty. Instead of going home, though, he went over to the Reason." He hadn't seen his homie

Dave in a few weeks. So Jay decided to drop in, have a few drinks, and release some stress.

When Jay got there, he drove into the open gate and parked the Explorer next to Dave's Navigator and the bartender's blue Chevy Malibu. Then he got out and walked over to the door. After firmly pressing the doorbell twice, Jay noticed someone peeping out of the peephole. "Who is it?" they then asked.

Who doesn't know me here? Jay asked himself before yelling his name to the unidentified person.

Then, Jay heard Dave's voice render from the background. "Let him in," Dave demanded.

The eye behind the peephole quickly disappeared. Next, there were the unbolting of a few locks. Then the door opened. Jay entered. "Hi, how are you doing?" Jay asked the new waitress that he had never seen before. She was gorgeous. Her skin was high yellow, and her body was flawless. Dave looked her up and down then kept walking over to the bar, where Dave happened to be standing.

"I'm okay," she retorted while trying to get a good look at him.

Dave came from alongside the bar to greet his ace. The two of them tightly gripped hands, then embraced each other. Then Dave walked back behind the bar and stood next to his bartender. Jay went over to the barstool and took a seat.

"Dayum, homie! It looks like somebody forgot to go home after work." Jay had sawdust and dirt all over himself from the sanding of some wood floors he was doing. "Everything's cool, ain't it?" Dave asked, then put two glasses on top of some coasters he'd set out.

"Yeah, everything's cool I guess. Candace has been sick for the last couple of days, though. She's been keeping me up all night!"

While Jay continued venting, Dave walked over to the freezer and grabbed a couple of ice-cold Heinekens. He popped the top on then with a can opener, then stuffed them both with a couple of freshly sliced lemons.

Then he partly filled the empty glasses that sat on top the coaster with a few cubes of ice and a significant amount of Hennessey. After surrendering both of Jay's drink to him, Dave took a sip from his own Heineken and inquired, "So has she thought about going to the doctor, or is Candace playing the I'm-too-proud role?"

"I told her last night to make sure she went. Plus, she said that she made an appointment yesterday for this morning. Now, when I get home, if she ain't been to the doctor already, I'ma take off tomorrow and drive her myself," Jay said, holding his beer close to his mouth as if ready to take a sip.

Hearing the locks on the door click, Dave looked and saw the new server unlocking it. *It must be seven o'clock,* he thought to himself as he glanced up at the clock on the wall. Sure enough, it was seven. "Showtime," he eagerly announced, then focused back in on his homie Jay.

"Enough about me, man. What's been goin on wit'choo? We ain't kicked it in forever. Tell me something new." Jay then took another nice gulp of his Heineken.

"Man, I ain't even gone lie to ya. My household is a hot mess," Dave said in a soft-spoken tone so that the two customers who'd just walked in and sat at the bar wouldn't hear him.

He continued, "Me and my wife, man, we was beefin' heavily. Do you know she had the nerve to tell one of her cousins that she could move in with us till she gets herself together?"

"Did she?" Jay asked, then paused, and proceeded, "And what did you have to say about that?"

"Hell, I couldn't say shit. By the time I found out, the girl was already at the Greyhound station, waiting for Tracie to pick her up."

Dave's voice was starting to rise a little. You could tell that he was getting somewhat upset. "Man, was I heated!"

"How old is her cousin?" Jay asked inquisitively.

"Nineteen," Dave answered with a strong emphasis. "And truthfully Jay, gurlee look niiiccee."

"Man, don't cross that bridge. I'm tellin' you, it'll kill you."

"I know, man. I ain't even on all that, but for real, shorty nice, though, and she seems kinda cool too."

"So what you so mad about it for?"

"I'm mad cuz Tracie's ass is inconsiderate. She didn't even think to ask me about it. Hell, knowing me, I probably would've said yes anyways." Jay just stared harmlessly at his friend all the while nodding his head in agreement. "Jay, man, I give this woman everything, and you know it. All I ask for is some respect. You feel me?"

"Ain't no mystery. I feel you," Jay said, nodding his head in agreement again. Jay's buzz started kicking in. One could tell by his somewhat lazy posture and his slurred voice. Jay had even spilled some of the Hennessey that he nursed in the glass onto the counter.

The two of them went back and forth, sob story after sob story, with Dave dominating the conversation. You could tell that his problems far outweighed Jay's minor mishaps. Jay, being the unconditional friend that he was, just sat and listened while polishing off more than three brews and two glasses of cognac in the process.

When Dave finally snapped out of his zone, it was somewhere close to nine o'clock. Time had crept up on him so quickly that he didn't even realize it. The bar was starting to fill up. The DJ was set up and ready.

"Dave, I'm gonna get up outta here, my nigga," Jay said after downing the backwash of his last Heineken. "You gone be aiight, ain't you?"

"Yeah, I'll be cool," Dave responded back. "The question is, are you gon be cool?"

"I'm aiight," Jay assured him as he got up and headed toward the door.

Dave followed close behind. After a gripped-tight hug and a firm handshake, Dave watched Jay walk to his Explorer, jump in and pull out the gate, and ride off. To his surprise, as soon as Jay pulled out the gate, Dave watched as some dude in a red Dodge Magnum pulled in with his ex-fling Shanina on the passenger side.

Ain't this a bitch? Dave spoke angrily to himself as he watched the red Dodge Magnum work its way through the gate of the parking lot. *She couldn't wait for us to break up so she could get to acting like a hoe.*

When Dave saw Shanina pull in that gate with another guy, it bruised him internally. He felt like his heart had been sliced open by a freshly sharpened knife. The sheer hurt, pain, and sadness was written all over his face. The feeling he felt, during that moment, immediately let Dave know that he was lovesick; and somehow, some way, he'd have to straighten this out before his feelings got the best of him.

Things didn't get much better for Dave when Shanina and her new guy friend stepped out of the car to make their way into the club. Shanina's attire could've made a blind man see. She had on a light-gray skin-tight body dress that accentuated her curves wonderfully. Every inch of her well-proportioned body was being lustfully defined. Her silver-grayish high-heeled sandals matched her dress, and hooped earrings helped create a star-like mental image. Her beautician had her healthy jet-black hair covering part of her face. Shanina looked like a model on her way to a cover shoot for Smooth magazine.

Shanina's male companion wasn't slacking either. He wore a form-fitted tan-colored shirt that hugged his chiseled chest, arms, and stomach like a glove. His backside was covered by a pair of hand-cut polo jeans, and he was stomping on the crust of the earth with a fresh pair of tan

Timberlands. Around six feet two inches, dark skinned, and bald-headed, this was one handsome brother.

When Shanina and her guy friend got close to the door, where Dave was standing, one could see the tension between Shanina and Dave lingering. Their fierce eye contact spoke volumes.

They stared each other down like two rams, facing off and about to engage in battle.

"Caramel, I need to see you in my office before you go onstage," Dave demanded in an upset tone while watching Nina strut past him.

"Yeah, okay," she retorted sarcastically. Nina's tone wasn't exactly inviting either. In fact, the harshness of it compelled her friend to look at her skeptically. "I'll be in there as soon as I get dressed, BOSS!"

Boss, Dave said to himself, after letting Nina's words replay in the back of his mind. *Where did that bullshit come from? Hell, if anyone should be mad, it should damn sho be me.*

Shanina left her guy friend sitting near the end of the bar while she went and got dressed for work. Her anger and disgust was apparent. She remained completely silent as she walked past her co-workers. They spoke to her, but the rebellious attitude she held toward Dave wouldn't allow her to speak back. "Damn, what's gotten into her?"

"You mean what didn't?" the girls whispered, then giggled collectively.

Nina put on her sleaziest outfit, drenched her caramel body in baby oil, then prepared her mind to go out and tease the shit out of every man in the audience, including Dave.

Nina's friend—who sat at the bar, drinking by himself—was still somewhat oblivious to the situation. He had no idea that Dave and Shanina had previously been intimate. In fact, he had just met Shanina last week. Everything about her to him was still novel. Just escorting this siren to work was enough for him to be proud.

"Give it up for skittles ya'll. Give it up," the dude Jay spoke into the microphone. Skittles waltzed her high-yellow self with those thick thighs and itty-bitty titties down the stairs and off the stage while picking up the excess twos and fews that weren't attached to her hot-pink garter belt or matching thong. "Up next to the stage, ya'll, we got Caramel. Give it up for Caramel!"

Before the DJ said Caramel's name in the mike, Dave had been oblivious to the fact that Shanina had just disregarded his bid for her to meet him in the office. Even when her name was announced, it still didn't register to him. But as soon as Caramel stepped out of that dressing room, she instantly caught his attention.

When the crowd heard Caramel's name over the loudspeaker, everyone got excited. Caramel was a crowd favorite. She had somewhat of a spell on the place. Men would literally sit in their chairs or at a barstool until they heard Caramel's name. Once heard, they'd flood the front of the stage with money in hand just to get a glimpse of this pole practitioner working her magic.

Dave met up with Caramel in the middle of the aisle on her way toward the stage. "I thought I asked you to meet me in my office before you go onstage, Caramel." Caramel was speechless. She just stood there, looking dumbfounded. "Can I please see you in my office before you go onstage, Caramel?" Dave said aggressively. Then he looked toward the DJ, shook his head from side to side, and muttered, "Call Sunshine to the stage. Caramel will be back in a minute."

"What the hell is your problem, huh?" Caramel screamed immediately after Dave shut the door behind the two of them.

"You, that's my problem," "so I guess you just gone waltz up in here in my place of business, I might add, with some other nigga and I'm just supposed to be cool with it. I mean damn, Shanina, we just broke up."

"Dave, you're married, remember? Why should I have to answer to you?" Caramel asked with her arms crossed, crutching her healthy breasts.

"So all that—"

"So all that what, David?" she yelled, cutting Dave's words short.

"Listen, damn, so all that stuff you said the other day didn't account for nothing, huh?"

"I never said that! Listen, Dave," she said after calming her tone. "I just met this guy. All I did was call him and asked him to take me to work, and the guy said he would. That's it."

After a faint exhale, Caramel continued, "David, I still love you, and you know it. And nothing's gonna change that. But I must say that our little separation hurt me a little more than I thought it would. No, I'm not having sex with anyone, and no, I'm not about to get into a relationship. But, baby, I can't stay single forever." Nina was lying about the sex part.

"I know, I know." David said as he grabbed ahold of Shanina ever so tightly, trying to hug the life out of her. "Baby, I promise, I'm going to straighten this out, okay? I promise."

"I love you, you lil ole baby." Nina conveyed after kissing Dave's lips.

"I love you too. Now get back onstage and get daddy's money." They both laughed as she pinched Dave's arm playfully.

After a hectic and emotional night at the Reason, Dave wrapped things up, then headed straight home. When he got there, to his surprise, things were quiet and tranquil. All the pieces of electronic equipment were turned off, and Tracie and Nikki were sound asleep.

Dave took a nice long and hot shower, quickly dried off, then put on a blue wifebeater and his favorite ball shorts. Next, he plopped himself down on his red leather sofa in the living room directly in front of their forty-two-inch flat screen. *What a night,* he thought as he began surfing the channels. Concerning the club, Dave had every reason to be ecstatic. He had made a ton of money from cover charging, to the bar drinks, dancing fees, etc. Dave had made a killing. On the contrary, him seeing Nina with another guy, then their imminent argument continued to puzzle him.

"Why thank you, David. You look pretty damn good yourself, I must say."

Dave sported a long-sleeved striped blue button-down shirt designed by Ralph Lauren with matching blue jeans and a pair of construction blue Timberlands. His blue Indians pro-model was cocked to the side. What was even more puzzling, and quite periling, was their reconciliation. Even though their reconciliation consisted of nothing more physical than a kiss on the lips, those three words—*I love you*—touched his heart much more than sex could've ever done.

What am I gonna do now? he asked himself silently while his ears were being unconsciously entertained by the voice of a sportscaster on ESPN Sports Network. Dave knew that he had put himself back into the same awkward position as before. Pulling the stunt last night with Nina was the last thing that he wanted to do, but he couldn't contain himself. When Nina arrived with the guy driving the red Magnum, it nearly crushed Dave's spirit. Why did he care so much? Why couldn't he just let Nina live her life? Had he truly fallen for her? The only true question that needed to be answered was, how was Dave going to straighten everything out with Nina like he told her he would?

Dave lounged on the couch for at least thirty minutes, just letting the TV watch him, before realizing that he'd been thinking about Nina since he'd first sat down. Sounds of the toilet flushing snapped him out of his late-night daydream. Dave then sat up and turned back toward the bathroom and found Nikki dressed in a midnight-blue silk slip, easing her way back to her bedroom. Before making it to the door, she turned to her right, looked down the semi-dark hallway, and saw Dave looking back at her. She just waved and then went back to bed.

Seeing Nikki walk past in such a sexy outfit immediately aroused Dave's sexual appetite. At that moment, he knew that he had to have his wife. He needed to touch her, hold her, and feel her; he needed to become one with her again.

Dave shut off the television, then immediately headed toward his bedroom. When he walked in, he found Tracie lying on her stomach, knocked out cold.

Without hesitation, Dave slid in between their midnight-blue satin sheets and gently grabbed hold of his wife's shoulders. Then, he leaned in and began planting soft kisses about her neck. Only, she, after waking up, wasn't very receptive. "David, stop now," she requested in a groggy voice. Dave didn't comply, though. Instead, he just started unstrapping her purple bra. Once unsnapped, he began licking in the vacant spot where the strap once was. Tracie, now fully awake, quickly showed her displeasure by rising up off the bed, her juicy breasts now fully exposed, and hanging just below her bra. "David, I'm not in the mood, okay?" Tracie yelled with an attitude. She restrapped her bra, turned opposite him, and got back into the bed.

"Damn, it's nice to see you too!" Dave's pride was crushed. He felt as if he'd been stabbed in his heart with a dagger. *I wonder if Nina would act the same way,* Dave thought to himself before getting underneath the covers and reluctantly falling asleep.

CHAPTER EIGHT

About three hours after relieving herself and seeing Dave's head pop up from behind the couch, Nikki had begun rubbing the crust from the corner of her eyes, trying to wake up and prepare herself for her first day of work. As soon as her mind fully grasped the thought of the task at hand, Nikki was inundated with jitterbugs.

Nikki's cousin Tracie had somehow managed to use one of her connections to hook her up with a job at Progressive Insurance Company. She was very appreciative of her new gig and grateful to her cousin for providing her with it, but what she wasn't too fond of was all the adjustments she had to make. Working a job, dealing with people, and being accountable were usually not Nikki's style; she was more of the carefree, I-do-as-I-please type. Waking up and traveling during the wee hours of the morning were now also her dreaded realities. The traveling part she could get used to since she had already been familiar with the bus routes since a kid. The early-morning wakeup, though, was another story.

After wrestling with her spirit for a few minutes of sleep, Nikki's flesh finally consented and slowly made its way toward the upstairs shower. It only took a touch of the steaming hot water, discharging itself from the showerhead; and Nikki was completely up, alert, and, for the moment, jitterbug free.

Her petite frame stood directly in front of the gushing hot water, letting it pound against her soft yellow skin. She leaned her head forward, causing the water to pounce loudly upon her shower cap.

Nikki completely covered herself in a thick foam of soapy suds from face to foot. Then she got up under the water, thoroughly rinsed herself, shut the water off, and then stepped out. Grabbing a towel to dry off, she then wrapped it around her. Next she gently opened the bathroom door and made a dash toward her bedroom, clutching both ends of the towel with her right hand across the trunk of her body and holding a bottle of cocoa butter lotion in her left hand. Nikki strolled through the hallway toward the room. Then out of nowhere, Dave opened his bedroom door. It startled Nikki so much that she dropped everything, including her towel. She just stood there, completely naked and embarrassed.

"I am soooo sorry, Nikki! I did not mean to scare you like that," Dave apologized as he reached down to help her retrieve the things that she'd dropped. Nikki bent down simultaneously, causing their bodies to brush up against each other.

"That's okay," Nikki assured him, and then she grabbed her towel to rewrap herself in it. Dave reached out and handed her the lotion. After gaining complete composure, Nikki then mustered up the strength to say thank you.

Then, without hesitation, they both went their separate ways. Somehow or another, Tracie never heard a thing.

Nikki's first day on the job was monotonous and very repetitious. Accounts receivable at Progressive Insurance wasn't exactly a fun day at the beach for her. As if any job was for that matter. Nikki had been conversing through headsets and punching keys on the computer in front of her since almost eight o'clock in the morning. Her lips and throat were exhausted. Her fingers were aching, and her spirits, for answering another ten minutes worth of calls, were all but broken. Thank goodness, there were only two minutes left in this eight-hour abyss.

Nikki logged off her monitor right around 4:00 p.m. She was so relieved when she saw the clock change that she didn't know what to do. She had met her quota for the day as far as successful calls went, so coming back next week was all but a shoe in the door.

After grabbing her pink Baby Phat jacket that hovered the back of her chair, Nikki got up and made her way toward the door. Her new boss said to her before she exited the room, "Good-bye and see ya Monday." That was all the job assurance she needed.

Nikki politely turned around and said, "Good-bye. See you Monday, Ms. Taylor" as she pushed open the glass door that stood between her and freedom. A few of her co-workers were in front and behind her, walking with determination toward the cars that sat out front, waiting to pick them up. She kindly spoke to the ones she knew and then headed toward the bus stop.

At the back of the parking lot, near the bus stop, there was someone in a pearl-white drop-top Lexus that looked very similar to Tracie's playing music extremely loud. At first, Nikki paid very little attention to it. But as she got closer, the music got louder, and Nikki was all but forced to look at the car. Plus it was parked near the bus stop she was heading toward. Ignoring the music coming from the car for as long as she could, Nikki finally looked at the car and recognized that it was her cousin Tracie. Nikki walked hastily toward the Lexus. All she could hear coming from Tracie's stereo was "Down here we riding slooooow."

Nikki leaped into the passenger seat and softly shut the door. Then Tracie turned down the volume of the music slightly so she and Nikki could acknowledge each other's presence. "Hey, gurl! Didn't think that that was cuz over there beat'n up the block like a gee did ja," Tracie said with laughter.

"Hell naw, gurl. I didn't know who you was," Nikki replied as they embraced each other. Tracie said, "Gurl, you know we gone have to celebrate ya first week back in the land. So what you wanna do, go out or get a bottle and kick it at the house?"

"It's whateva, gurl. You know I ain't trippin," Nikki said submissively.

"But if we do go out, you know, I gotta change."

"Gurl, fo what? You look fine. Plus, that outfit makes you look older. With that on, you won't have to worry about getting carded."

"Well, you know I'm game," Nikki said softly to Tracie as the song that had been blasting finally faded out.

"I think I'm gonna have to show you how we get down in the land then," Tracie expressed exuberantly while the next song on the CD began playing.

"Let's do it then, gurl."

"Let's do it."

CHAPTER NINE

Déjà vu, for Dave, arrived much quicker than he could've ever imagined. While walking outside his club at around 7:30 p.m. to get a bit of fresh air, he spotted Shanina again being dropped off by her so-called friend with the red Dodge Magnum. Dave was again livid. It had only been a week since the last encounter that he had with the two of them, so to him, Nina was now picking at a fresh scab. Nina had assured him, though, that the guy that had been dropping her off was merely a friend, but Dave begged to differ. "What choo doin here so early, Nina?" Dave asked while watching her make her way toward the front door, where he was standing. "You know it's only 7:30 p.m."

Dave really wanted to ask Nina why Sport Coat was dropping her off again, but he figured that it wasn't the right time.

"I know what time it is, David," she responded while holding the door open as if to say, "You first." "I have something that I need to discuss with you."

Nina followed behind Dave to his office. The heels from her pumps could be heard clanking against the floor as she strutted through the club. The two of them made it inside Dave's office, and he gently shut the door behind them.

He then walked over to his desk and leaned on its surface. Nina stood against the wall, facing him. "Before we proceed, Nina, baby, I must say you look gorgeous!"

Nina had on a tannish-colored evening gown that matched her blocked heels and her Louis Vuitton handbag. A perfectly pinned hairstyle displayed the tan earrings that she was wearing. Her face shined like the sun along with her silky smooth skin. There was an aura of sexuality hovering her.

right just a tad. A hefty two and a half-carat diamond earring weighed down his left earlobe.

"Well, thank you Shanina. I truly appreciate the compliment. Now, tell me," Dave said, before

Pausing to look at Shanina again, "What brings the lovely Ms. Tucker to my establishment an hour and a half before time to work? This must be something important."

"This time, David, I must say that it is. I don't even know where to begin, though. Do you mind if I sit down?"

"No, no, not at all. Here, come sit in my chair." Coincidentally, Dave's chair was the only one in his office.

Nina made her way over to Dave's chair and sat while he continued to rest his rear end on the edge of his desk. Silence then governed the room for what seemed to be an eternity before Nina attempted to express herself. After a slight hesitation, she finally blurted out, "David, as of today, I will no longer be working here."

The expression on Dave's face was blank. His eyes were squinted, and his mouth was wide open. Her announcement had caught him completely off guard.

"What! What choo mean you can no longer work here? Why not? I know that nigga outside ain't done turned you against me?"

"No, no, Dave."

"Well, what is it then?" he asked, eagerly anticipating the answer.

"Well, let's just say I found another job."

"You found another job?"

"Yes, David. I found another job."

In a sarcastic tone he asked, "Doing what?"

"Well, right now, I'm in training, but hopefully within the next year, I'll be a full-time writer for the *Plain Dealer*."

"Are you serious?" Dave looked more stunned than ever before.

"Yes, I'm serious. What, you thought I planned on stripping all my life or something?"

"Naw, I just figured—"

"Figured what?" she cut him off, "That I wasn't going to do anything else with myself? I shoulda known you were no different than the rest of deez niggas. Ya'll think just 'cause a girl strips to make a few ends meet that she don't have any plans or goals. Well, guess what, buddy, I do."

"Nina, come on now, It ain't like that."

"Then what is it like?"

"It's just that you and I—we never talked about anything like that."

"Hell, I just told you my name a month ago. What do you expect?"

"You also told me that you loved me a month ago! Remember that?"

"Yeah, I remember. I also remember you breaking up with me too. Look David, I'm not here to argue with you or go back and forth about this. The reality is I will no longer be working here. So if that's it—"

"Wait, Nina. Wait, wait, wait," Dave pleaded with her as she was rising up out of his chair. "I didn't mean to turn this into an argument. How about you sit back down and we start this all over, okay?" After a deep exhale, Nina consented. Dave then congratulated her on her soon-to-be new career. Then, he asked her a bunch of questions, proudly showing his interest. Nina answered every question elatedly. Dave could feel her passion for both writing and her new job.

The two of them conversed blissfully for the next ten minutes before Dave asked a mood-evolving question. "Nina, I don't mean to change the nature of the conversation, but I'm sort of curious to know why you just didn't tell me this sooner."

"Because I just found out today. I didn't want to inform you until I got the job."

"Understandable. Well, answer me this then. Why didn't choo just work your last day, then quit? You know that I wouldn't have had a problem with it. And you can still do that if you want to, by the way."

When Dave asked Nina the last question, he had no clue that the answer he was about to receive would be a life-altering one.

"Dave," she said hesitantly, "I'm P-R-E-G-N-A-N-T. I found out today."

Dave's heart nearly skipped a beat. "You're what?" he asked with skepticism.

"I said I'm pregnant." Nina sensed his skepticism, so she told him, "But don't worry you don't have to tell your wife."

"You mean it's mine?"

"What the fuck do you mean it's yours? You know what, David, I'm gone!"

"No, no, no, Shanina, wait. I didn't mean it like that," Dave pleaded with her as he grabbed hold of her arm, pulled her back to him, and squeezed her tight.

"Let go of me, Dave," she urged, trying her best to yank away from him.

Dave just wouldn't let go, though. "Then what did you mean, David? You can't clean this one up."

She explained to Dave that she found out when she took the piss test for the job. They had just called back earlier today. She told him how many months.

Nina's voice was filled with devastation. Tears began streaming down the right side of her face as she soaked the side of Dave's shirt up in the process.

Dave was in dismay. His mind began running a million miles a second. With Shanina's feminine feeble frame leaning on him for complete support, Dave just stood there in disarray.

Nina and Dave have a life-changing talk about him and her and his lifestyle like how she never slept with a married man. She told Dave that in order to be forgiven for his wrongs, he had to confess like she did.

What am I going to tell my wife? he asked himself. But it didn't stop there. Questions just continued to gyrate through his mind, questions like if this was her baby or if did dude with the Magnum slip in between the sheets. Had Nina been trying to trap him all along, or was he just being careless with their sexual endeavors? His inquiries was longer than the Mississippi River.

Dave's thoughts: his first child and it's not even with his wife. How was he going to explain that?

After what would seem to be an endless mutual consolation, Dave and Shanina finally let go of each other. And that's when it hit him. "Shanina," Dave said in a strong tone. Shanina had somehow found her way back into Dave's comfortable office chair by this time. "If you knew you were already pregnant when you first came here, why were you about to walk out the door when I started that argument? So what, you weren't gonna tell me that you were pregnant? You were just gone walk outta here like you didn't have a care in the world, huh?" Dave's tone was very convicting. With each syllable, Nina could feel the vibrations of his voice penetrating her eardrums ever so harshly.

Nina was now at a loss for words. David was right! She was going to walk out of that door without telling him that she was a month pregnant. But in her mind, she had a good reason.

For one, David was a married man. Second, getting pregnant right now was not a part of Nina's plans. And believe it or not, for Nina, those were just the tip of the iceberg. Nina's biggest concern was having a child out of wedlock. That was something she just didn't believe in.

Something else she didn't believe in was birth control and apparently condoms too! What a conflict of interest.

Nina searched high and low for the right words to say to David, but she just couldn't find any. "Answer me, Nina! Were you gone ever tell me that I was gonna be a father?" Dave yelled.

"I . . . don't . . . know. I . . . don't . . . know," Nina somehow managed to holler out before a range of emotions overtook her. Nina commenced to crying like a milk-thirsty infant. "David, I'm scared. I . . . don't . . . know . . . what . . . to . . . do."

David, like any good man, should've deleted his selfish thoughts and immediately became a solicitous partner. "Nina, baby, don't worry about nothing," he said. "Somehow or another, we're going to make it through this, okay?" Dave said while hugging her and the chair collectively.

CHAPTER TEN

"**B**aby, are you going to answer the phone or not?" Jay asked Candace before completely covering his head with the pillow to avoid hearing the obnoxious ringing coming from her side of the bed.

Candace stretched her arm out toward the night table in an attempt to grab the receiver off the base. The phone had rung at least eight times prior, and it didn't seem like the person on the other end had any intentions on hanging up. Candace wrestled with the receiver for a couple of seconds; then, she finally gained control of it, put it up to her ear, and said hello in a deep-toned, scratchy, I-was-asleep type of voice.

"Hello, may I please speak with Ms. Candace Johnson?"

Candace immediately sat up in the bed to gain her composure.

"This is she. May I ask who's calling?" Candace's reply instantly got Jay's attention.

Who could that be? Jay thought to himself. Jay knew for Candace to sit up straight in the bed and begin to speak properly, it had to be someone important. Hell, it was eight o'clock in the morning on a Saturday; and for Candace to even say anything more than hello, call me back, and good-bye on the phone would've been a miracle.

Jay, being nosy, surreptitiously twisted his neck toward Candace and began to eavesdrop in on her conversation.

"Yes, I am aware that I was supposed to receive a call," Candace said. "No, I have no problem with you discussing the situation over the phone."

Jay's antennas were up and all ready for reception now. Once he figured out that it was the doctor's office on the other end, his curiosity level shot up to the sky.

He rotated his body up under the king-sized quilt that covered him, sat up straight, and turned toward Candace. Jay then looked her directly in her face as she continued to talk, "Yes, ma'am. Yes! Yes! Well, if you don't mind my asking, do you know how far long I am?"

When Jay heard Candace ask the doc how far along she was, he was extremely happy and relieved. For the last few days, Candace had been vomiting; and at one point, she was damn near bedridden. It took a huge load off Jay's shoulders when he learned that Candace's sickness stemmed from a little him growing inside of her.

"Well, when should I come in?" Candace asked. "Okay, I'll see you then. Thank you and you have a wonderful day."

As soon as she hung up the phone, Candace's face lit up like a bunch of Christmas lights. "Jay, baby, I'm pregnant. You're going to be a father," Candace said as her eyes began to redden.

Jay and Candace's minicelebration lasted for a while: they hugged, they kissed, they caressed, and they consoled. They even began to comfort each other, assuring each other that they'd make good parents.

Believing it was a good morning what had turned out to be a very good morning, Candace made her way to the kitchen and prepared the two of them a hearty breakfast: flapjacks, scrambled cheese eggs, links, buttered biscuits with grape jelly on the side, and two cups of Minute Maid orange juice. Jay grabbed his cell phone off the dresser and made a straightway call to Dave.

"Wuz up, my nigga?" Dave said after picking up the phone on the fourth ring. "I don't think I'ma be able to make it up to the creek this morning, man."

"Who said I was calling 'bout the creek? Hell, I ain't going either. I do got some good news I wanna holla at choo about, though," Jay expressed as he found his way into the kitchen.

"Plus, I don't feel like fuckin' with them knuckleheads, Nell and Tay, no ways."

Dave then subdued the conversation and said, "Man, I got some shit to tell you too, my nigga! You still tryna get together and holla at Sleeze today or you need a minute?"

"I'm ready."

"Okay, then, this what we gone do. After we finish eatin' at the spot," Dave said, "you take care of yo business, I'll take care of mine, and then we meet up at the club later on tonight, aight?"

When Jay ended his call with Dave, he heard Candace just getting off the house phone with her mother. Apparently, Candace had told her the good news.

"Hey, baby, what's with the long face?" Jay asked Candace with a concerned tone. Jay could see that the look on Candace's face was contrary to that of the one about fifteen minutes prior.

"It's my mom. I had a feeling she wouldn't be happy for us."

"What makes you think she ain't happy for us?"

"She didn't sound enthused at all! I started not to tell her till later."

"Baby, don't let nothing and nobody spoil yo' day, you hear me?"

"Yeah, I hear you. You know what then, Jay, I probably shouldn't tell you what I had to tell you, huh?"

Jay instantly gave Candace a look as if to say, "Gurl, if you don't say what it is you have to say, there's going to be a misunderstanding." "Candace, I don't appreciate you hiding shit. Now gone and tell me what it is you got ta tell me."

"Jay, you know I ain't hiding nothing. It just slipped my mind till I heard you say them names while you were on the phone."

"What slipped yo mind? And what names?"

"Listen, baby," Candace said after being rudely interrupted by a now-eager Jay. "You remember when I went to the doctor the other day?"

"Yeah. Why?"

"Well, when I came out the building, two of your friends were parked right next to your truck."

"And?" Jay said, looking somewhat demented now.

"If you quit interrupting and let me finish, I'm gone tell you. Their names were Nell and Tay." Jay immediately exhaled.

"The guy Nell was cool. He had thought it was you driving your truck, but when he seen that it was me, he told me to tell you that he was lookin' for you. Then when Nell started walking away from the truck, the dude name Tay said something like, 'Let me get yo number or something.' I just rolled up the window, backed up, and pulled off."

"How you know that the other dude was Tay, Candace?"

"'Cause Nell said it. As soon as Tay said that ignorant shit, Nell said Tay man gone with that or something like that."

Jay flared up like a disturbed lion. "See, baby, this chump gone make me fuck'um up."

Jay's six-something, 250-pound frame looked far more intimidating than ever before to Candace.

"Now, baby, you just told me not to let nobody spoil my day, and here it is you finna let this nuthin'-ass nigga spoil yours. Baby, don't even waste your energy on him or anybody else for that matter. You know I'm all yours."

Jay embraced his companion and began kissing his sexy yellow beauty queen over her entire face. "I love you more than life itself. You know that, right?"

"Yes, I do. And you know that you are my life. Now come on, let's eat before this food gets cold."

* * *

Dave and Jay's phone conversation ended somewhere close to nine o'clock in the morning. By that time, the sun had snuck its rays through Dave's venetian blinds. Several voices could now be heard creeping through Tracie and Dave's open bedroom window. Dave, worn out from a late night at the Reason, was still lying in the bed; his sheets covered all but his chest, neck, and head. He didn't find his way home until near four o'clock in the morning. Nina unexpectedly needing a ride home was one of the causes.

While on their way to her apartment, Nina said some things to Dave about himself that had stuck in his mind. After gently placing his cell phone on top of the night table, Dave laid his head back onto his soft down pillow and began to recollect. "Dave, you need to start taking control of your life" was what he heard Nina strongly insisting in the back of his mind.

"You've got a good business that brings in some good money. You own a house and a nice truck. Dave, you really don't have reason to continue selling drugs except greed!"

The real shocker to Dave came when Nina asked him to inform his wife about the child and the affair that they were having. *Come clean to my wife?* he thought to himself. *She must be crazy!* Then reality set in, and he was quickly reminded that Nina could possibly be his new baby's mother.

Although some of the things that Shanina mentioned to him sounded ridiculous to him, Dave understood her reasoning; and because of it, his respect for her was beginning to increase by the second. See, as far back as Dave could remember, no one ever really cared enough about his well-being to tell him the cold-blooded truth—no one except Jay—and the two of them were one in the same. That's not to say that his family didn't love him. They just had their own issues. –Mike- explained that his mother and father loved him, but he raised himself.

Dave's mom had a slight drinking problem; so she barely ever took the time to tell him about the goods, the bads, and the uglies. His father was a workaholic, so he didn't have the time.

As he got older, money began to grow on trees, in a figurative sense, so his extended family constantly had their hands out. His wife, Tracie, basically just went with the flow.

As long as she had money to do what Tracie wanted to do, she couldn't care less how Dave earned it. For some strange reason, though, Nina was different. Nina truly cared; well, at least that's the image that she was starting to portray. But then again, it could've just been the pregnancy speaking for her too.

Dave's recollection was stopped by a few light taps on his bedroom door. "Come in," he said.

Nikki twisted the doorknob, then lightly pushed the door open. "Good morning, Dave," she said as she along with the silky blue nightgown that draped her body eased in the doorway.

"Hey, Nikki, where's Tracie?" Dave inquired.

"I thought she was in bed. That's why I came in here. I guess she didn't get back home yet."

"Wasn't ya'll together last night?"

"Yeah. She picked me up from work."

"Yeah, I know. She told me that cha'll was goin' out. So what happened with that?"

"Oh yeah, we went out last night," Nikki confirmed while switching her stance, causing her nightgown to work its way open. Nikki's black see-through bra and panty set, along with her flat smooth bare stomach, was now very visible to Dave's naked eye. "She had dropped me off around two o'clock then left. She told me that she'd be back, though. I thought she'd be here by now."

Dave's eyes were glued to Nikki's petite frame. He couldn't stop staring at her erect nipple as they protruded the fabric of her bra. Blood immediately began rushing to the calling of Dave's manhood. Nikki took a glance at the sheets and noticed the imprint that Dave's hard and extremely jumpy wood was making. That's when she said, "Oooowweee, I'm sorry, I didn't even know my nightgown was open like that. You'll have to excuse me." Then she made an attempt to close it.

Dave, now straining to control himself, replied, "Awh, Nikki, don't worry about that. Shoot, you act like I ain't neva seen that lil stuff before."

"Little stuff. Hold up. What choo tryna say, David?" Nikki asked with a smirk. Then she dropped her nightgown to the floor, teasing him seriously. Dave's eyes grew to the size of golf balls. "I bet choo like this little stuff." She pranced seductively while turning around and giving Dave an eyeful of her luscious behind.

"Oh, I neva once said I didn't like that little stuff. All I said was I've seen it before. Am I right?"

Nikki grabbed her nightgown off the floor and covered her gorgeous youthful-looking body back up then asked, "That was some crazy stuff that happened yesterday, wasn't it?"

"Hell yeah, it was! I probably was just as scared if not more scared than you was. You know what, though, truthfully, I was just praying that Tracie wasn't behind me. If Tracie would've seen that—oooh my goodness," Dave implied as he began to shake his head.

"I thought you was gone tell her about it!"

"What?" Dave interrupted Nikki in midsentence.

"Yeah, I thought you was gone tell." You could see from the expression on his face that he wanted to interrupt her again, but Nikki, feeling the need to continue her sentence, strengthened her voice and continued expressing her concerns.

"So you could just imagine how I felt when I seen her car parked outside my job." They both immediately began chuckling.

Outside the open window in Dave's bedroom was the sound of an approaching car that was blasting its music noticeably loud.

You could tell by the music's continuous escalation that the car was getting closer to Dave's house. This could have only meant one thing: Tracie's home!

It didn't take long for both Nikki and Dave to put two and two together.

"Let me gone and get back in this room before Tracie come in here and have a fit," Nikki insisted as she began to make her way out the door. I'll see you later, Dave, okay?"

"Aight then, Nikki. I'll see you later, "Dave uttered. Then, Nikki shut the door. Just as she made her way inside her room, Tracie was inserting her keys in the door.

Dave and Jay both made it to Carolina's around two o'clock that afternoon. Dave parallel parked his Navigator in front of Sleeze's forest-green Range Rover. Jay eased the Escalade into a parking space two cars behind them. The two of them hopped out of their trucks and immediately walked over and acknowledged each other. Then, they made their way toward the restaurant.

When they entered, they couldn't help but notice Sleeze relentlessly gawking at the doorway. Sleeze had impatiently been waiting on Dave and Jay ever since the two of them called his cell phone and set up the meeting.

"Wuz up, fellas?" Sleeze asked and then firmly shook both their hands.

"What up, Sleeze?" they replied together.

"Why are you standing at the doorway like you were spying on someone?" Dave inquired out of curiosity.

"Awh, no reason," he answered. "Just observing dah Cleveland Streets—feel me."

"Boy must be getting homesick," Jay interjected with laughter.

"Jamaica Queens, babe, Jamaica Queens!" Sleeze began walking toward his office with Dave and Jay following closely behind. "Fellas, before we get down to biz, I thought I'd ask ya'll if yah'd like tah go see Mike Epps and Sommore at the Improv. On me."

The two of them glanced at each other then muttered in unison, "Awh, naw, man."

Sleeze, knowing what was on their minds, interrupted them both. "Wait a minute. Wait a minute. Before yah decline, just tink 'bout it. Da tickets are a gift. I go dem from a friend. You can take yah women too! I got two tickets, apiece, fa both of you."

After a few seconds of deliberating, Dave said he wouldn't mind going. Jay again turned down the offer, though. "I'm sorry you're not gone be able ta make it, Jay. Dave and I are going ta have a lovely time."

The three of them small talked about the comedy show for a minute then got down to business. As usual, prices were once again the topic of discussion. It took them fifteen minutes or so, but the three of them finally negotiated a reasonable offer for the drugs.

Dave and Jay followed Sleeze to his storage place where he kept the bulk of his marijuana in East Cleveland to pick up the weed. As soon as they all got there, they made the transaction. Dave and Jay impatiently stuffed the back of their trucks with fifty pounds apiece of pure potent hydrated marijuana. Then, with the same impatience, he dumped $35,000 apiece on Sleeze.

"Sleeze, I appreciate you droppin' the price baby—fo real," Jay happily expressed as he walked nervously over to the driver-side door of his truck. "You just don't know how much of a difference $5 makes."

After the transaction, all three of them went their separate ways: Jay went straight down Euclid Avenue to his home in Richmond Heights, Dave took I-90 to his home on the Westside, Sleeze jumped on 271 and did eighty-five miles per hour all the way to the Harvard exit. Then he took Harvard all the way down until he got back to Carolina's.

Dave drove a cool sixty miles per hour on the highway all the way to the Jennings Freeway exit. He then played with the speed limit until he got to his driveway. When he pulled up, he saw Tracie's Lexus parked right in front of the garage.

Needing to switch places with her to put his truck in the garage, Dave used his spare key to do so.

"Hey, Nikki," he said as he walked through the front door. Nikki had her feet on one arm of the couch while she rested her head on the other. Out of his peripheral, he could see that she was munching on some popcorn and watching the television. The popcorn was set on the table, and the remote control to the television was gripped in her left hand.

"Wuz up, Dave?" Nikki replied unenthusiastically. Nikki's full attention was on the music video that she was watching on BET.

Dave strolled right past her, through the hallway, and into his bedroom. Tracie was sitting peacefully on the bed, reading a book written by her favorite author Zane entitled *Addicted*.

"Hey, sweetie," Dave said as he walked over to his wife and stole a kiss from her luscious lips. "How would you like to go see Mike Epps and Sommore live?"

Jay wound up arriving at the Reason, like he and Dave had planned on earlier, near the end of happy hour. Dave was already inside, helping the servers prepare for what was supposed to be a pretty large crowd; an associate of his had made reservation for a birthday party that he planned on having today.

When Jay walked inside the club, he could see Dave and the girls were working steadfast. The girls were meticulously wiping off tables, cleaning stools, and sweeping and mopping the floor. Dave and the bartender were rotating bottles of liquor and filling coolers up with fresh beer and slicing up lemons and limes. All the action going on made it somewhat easy for Jay to just slip right in and sit down at the bar unnoticed.

One of the patrons sitting a few seats down from Jay made a call for the bartender. That's when Dave turned his head around and saw his partner Jay sitting on a stool, with his forearms resting on the ends of the bar table.

"Wuz up Jay, man? How long you been sittin' right there?" Dave asked as he began to rip open another case of Budweiser.

"I just got up here a couple seconds ago. I seen you in bump-'n'-grind mode, so I didn't wanna break ya flow."

"Awh, come on now, you know I do this type of stuff in my sleep."

"I know. I just haven't seen you work this hard in a minute. I figured I'd just enjoy the sights," Jay said with a smirk.

"What choo want to drink?" Dave then asked him.

"Uhh, just give me a double of Remy, straight, and a Corona with a lemon."

"Okay, my nigga."

Dave prepared Jay's drinks. Then he fixed himself a double of Belvedere mixed with orange juice and a Heineken with a lemon. After passing Jay his drinks, Dave looked over at his bartender and asked, "Can you handle the rest of this, or do I need to stick around?"

The bartender looked back at Dave and answered, "I'm fine. Go right ahead."

"Are you sure?"

"Yes, I'm sure. Now shoo!"

"Okay, but if you need me, don't hesitate to bang on my office door."

"You know I won't."

Jay and Dave grabbed their drinks and strolled over toward Dave's office. Along the way, Dave occasionally overlooked a table or two just to make sure the girls were doing a good job. Jay grabbed one of the wooden chairs from underneath the dining table and took it into the office with him.

"Man, do I got some news to tell you," Jay said with a slight grin on his face after they both sat down.

"Trust me, Jay, you ain't the only one wit news," Dave replied while taking a sip from his half-filled glass of brown liquor.

Jay turned his Corona up one time. "You know Candace had been throwing up and all that, right?"

"Yeah," Dave responded.

"Well, she got a call from the doctor this morning, and they told her that she's pregnant."

"Fo' real?" Dave said, enthused.

The two of them immediately stood up and clasped each other. Then, Dave patted Jay's back.

"Congratulations, family! Congratulations!"

"Thanks, my man. Now what was it you had to tell me?"

Jay's intuition came forth with, causing him to answer his own question.

"Don't tell me Tracie's pregnant too. Man, that'll be some shit."

Dave began stroking the top of his head all the while trying to figure out a way to explain this uncanny situation to his best friend.

"Actually, Jay, somebody is pregnant. It just ain't Tracie."

"Wait a minute. Run that by me again."

"Shanina! That's the one who's pregnant, man."

"Who the hell is Shanina? And since when did she come into the picture? Man, don't tell me you keepin' secrets on me now."

"Come on now, don't even play me like that. Shanina is old girl who used to work here," Dave said with emphasis.

"You mean the one stripper?" Jay said with his head cocked to the side.

"Yup. That'd be her."

The look on Jay's face was priceless. He sat in complete silence for a good ten seconds before asking, "Have you told Tracie yet?"

"Man, hell naw. Tracie woulda been trying to kill me!"

"You think I don't know? Hell, she done tried ta kill you for less, so I know this woulda been a fo-sho catastrophe. Anyways, man, what choo mean by used to work here? You mean to tell me gurlee quit too, huh?"

"Hell yeah, she quit on me yesterday. But check this, though. Last week I called myself breaking off our little affair or whatever, right? Tell me why when she showed up to work wit some lame in a Dodge Magnum last Thursday. I flipped the fuck out on her like I'm her man or something."

"You did what?" Jay looked hypnotized.

"Hell yeah, I did. But listen, listen. We wind up getting back cool before the end of the night, right? Not even a week later, she comes to work early. Mind you, dude drops her off again, okay? Well, to make a long story short, we go to my office and talk. She tells me that she's quitting because she got a job working for the *Plain Dealer.* So I asked her, why come? She just didn't tell me after she finished working. She had the nerve to tell me that she can't work tonight 'cause she found out she was pregnant today."

"Man, that's some deep shit. So you think it's yours or what?"

"I asked her the same question, and she damn near had a heart attack."

"That was probably just a front, though," Jay said. Both Jay's and Dave's glasses plus bottles were damn near empty now. Dave stood up and was about to go to the bar to get some more drinks when they both heard a knock at the door.

"Come in," Dave said. It was the waitress with a fresh set of drinks. Dave's bartender had read his mind and sent the drinks in by the waitress.

"Thank you, Tonya," Dave said. "Tell Darlene she read my mind."

Tonya left the office and shut the door behind her. Jay got right back on the subject, saying, "Yeah, man, that probably was just a front."

Dave took a nice-sized gulp from his ice-cold Heineken and said, "Man, I don't think she was frontin'. Gurlee told me I ain't even gotta tell my wife. But the way she said, it was like, 'Nigga I'll take care of this baby myself.' So just with that attitude alone, I believe it's mine. Plus, man, we weren't using no protection."

"You weren't using what? Dave, man, I know you ain't go out like that."

"Hell yeah, I went out like that. Thank goodness, Nina told me that I'm like one of the few people she's ever slept with."

Jay polished off a nice portion of his Remy. Then, he chased it with a sip of Corona. Then, after a few seconds of silence, Jay looked directly into Dave's eyes and spoke, "You know what, man, this may sound funny to you, but you might be in love with her, man."

"You know what, Jay, you might be right. I gotta do something, though. Somehow, someway, I got to do something."

Another knock at the door brought Dave and Jay's conversation to a sudden pause. "Come in," Dave said.

The new waitress, Tonya, came in and said, "Excuse me, David. Um, Ms. Darlene said that she needs you out here 'cause the place is starting to get packed."

"Okay, tell her I'll be right there."

CHAPTER ELEVEN

Six weeks—that's how far along Nina found out she was at her doctor's appointment. It had been almost three weeks to the day when she first found out through a home pregnancy test that she was pregnant with Dave's baby. When she first looked on that pregnancy stick and saw that positive sign, Nina was in complete denial. *These things must don't work 'cause I know I ain't pregnant. I feel just fine.* Not wanting to take the stick's reading as gospel, she decided to go to the doctor. It didn't take long for them to reveal to her the news that she would soon become a giver of life.

Although Nina's baby daddy was a married man and there was still a great possibility that she'd be a single parent, Nina was somehow still cool with everything. The only problem though, was, she was afraid that her mom wouldn't be.

"Hey, Mommy," Nina responded after hearing her mother pick up the phone and say hello in her customary screechy-like tone of voice.

"Heeey, baaaaaby, how is my only child doing?"

"I'm fine, Momma. How have you been?"

"Chile, Momma been doin' just fine. I've been thankin' Jesus every chance I get. Praise the Lord! Amen."

Like most black mothers, Nina's mom was very religious. This meant that Jesus's name was usually mentioned in every conversation she had. "Oh, and don't think I don't know about you getting that new job over there at that *Plain Dealer*. I don't know why you think your father can keep a secret. Hell, just 'cause we ain't together no moo' don't mean he ain't gone tell me what's goin' on with my chile." Once Nina's mom began talking, she had a way of taking over the conversation. "Chile, I know more about you than you do," her mother said with laughter.

"When did he tell you?"

"That man told me about that the minute choo told him. I started to call you and cuss you out, but I said, 'Naw, I'm a wait and see how long it takes for her to call and tell me.'"

"I'm sorry, Mommy. I've been meaning to call and tell you. I've just had so much on my mind lately. You know that I'd never intentionally keep something like that from you."

Not only was she keeping something from her mother, it was much more important and like altering than a job.

"I know you wouldn't, baby. Momma was just jiving with you. I just gotta get used to my baby being so independent. You just growin' up so fast."

Nina's mom continued her babbling while Nina lay horizontally on her couch in deep thought. *How am I going to tell my mother that I'm pregnant by a married man?* was the question Nina kept asking herself. My mother will never understand this situation.

"Nina, baby?"

"Yes, Ma?" Nina answered.

"Do you hear me talkin' to you?"

"No, I didn't even hear you, Ma. I'm sorry. I started thinking about something, and my mind just drifted off. What were you saying?"

Ignoring her mother was probably one of the worst things Nina could do in this situation. All that did was piquing her mom's curiosity. Now whatever was on Nina's mind was definitely coming off. "Neva mind what I was saying. Apparently, that wasn't important. I wanna know what it is that got choo ignoring yo' momma."

When Nina's mother asked her what was on her mind, Nina's heart nearly skipped a beat. There was something inside her that made her wanna just pour out her soul to her mother. Something was telling her to just blurt it out.

For some reason, though, it seemed like she couldn't gather up enough strength to say what was on her heart and mind.

"It ain't nothing, Ma," Nina said.

"Okay, but you can't say I didn't ask you. Now don't come running to me later when everything done blew up in yo' face." Her mom's statements were so powerful to her. It was almost like she had a sixth sense, like she could see through Nina's heart or something.

"But choo not gonna understand, Ma."

"And just how do you know that, baby girl? You don't know what choe momma been through. I'll tell you one thing, though. You sho'll would be surprised."

"But, Momma, I don't want you to look down on me. I feel like I might lose your respect." Nina nervously began gnawing at her fingernails.

"Lose my respect? Nina, don't be foolish. I'm a always respect choo. And more importantly, I'll always love you. You're my daughter. My only child. Girl, everybody makes mistakes, Nina. That's a part of life. That's why you have people who love and care for you that will help you get through those situations."

Nina's mom had buttered her up like a freshly baked biscuit. Now, Nina was just about ready to tell her mom every mistake she'd ever made in like. "Mommy, I'm pregnant!" The words that left Nina's mouth were trenchant. When she said them, they immediately crept through the phone and pierced her mom's eardrums.

"Baby, did I hear you say what I thought you said?"

"Yes, Mama. I'm pregnant!"

Nina's mom sat up on her bed and turned sideways so that her legs and feet hung from the side.

"Congratulations, baby! Congratulations," she said in a slightly enthusiastic tone. "See, that wasn't so bad at all now, was it?"

Nina began to pace the tan-colored carpeting in her two-bedroom apartment, thinking of how she could break the ill-fated news to one of the two most important people in her life. "Momma, that's not all I have to tell you," Nina mumbled softly.

"Well, what else do you have to tell me, sugar?" she asked, now puzzled. Then, she stood up to initiate her own bit of pacing the floor.

Nina took an acute pause. "Momma, the man that I'm pregnant by is married."

Nina's mom almost stopped breathing. The news hit her like a ton of bricks. When she asked Nina to tell her what the problem was, Nina's mom had no clue that her daughter would tell her that she was pregnant by someone else's better half. But if Nina's mom was one thing, it was definitely understanding. That's why when she heard her daughter sniffling into the phone, she immediately began consoling her, "Baby, everything is going to be all right. Don't choo worry about a thing. We're going to get through this together."

Nina's conversation with her mom put her back in a blissful mood. Mentioning the situation to her, though, was one of the most difficult things that she had ever had to do. Just the intensity of telling her mother that she was pregnant by a married man was unfathomable to her, but somehow, Nina managed to muster up the courage to pull it off.

Nina and her mother's bonding couldn't have come at a more opportune time, considering her and Dave's relationship—or the lack thereof. As of recently, Dave hadn't been communicating with Nina. She was oblivious to the fact, though. That was until she opened up her mail in the mailbox. "Hello, David," she shouted aggressively after hearing Dave's voice consume the other end of the phone line.

"Yes, Nina. What do you want?" he asked with almost no concern.

"David, do not fuckin' play stupid with me. You know why I called you! What the fuck is this check for? I hope you didn't think I had any plans on getting an abortion 'cause if so, buddy, you're shit outta luck." Nina was angry!

"If this helps out any, no, I didn't think for one minute that choo would use the money to get an abortion. That money was strictly for you and your well-being. And since when did a thousand dollars become the going rate for abortions anyways?" Perplexed, Dave patiently waited on her inexplicable response.

"Fuck you, David," She barked harshly while making her way toward the refrigerator to grab a much-needed snack. When she opened it, to her surprise, the only snacks that occupied her food box were apples and oranges. She reached in and snatched the apple like her life depended on it, bit it, then continued to cuss Dave out.

"I'm not a fuckin charity case!"

"Nina, what are you talkin' about?" Dave was so confused he didn't know how to answer.

"You heard me. I'm not a charity case. And don't choo think for one second that choo can buy me off. I'm not havin' it, David!"

"Whoever implied such a thing, Nina?" Dave asked.

"You are the future mother of my child. That's my only concern—period!"

"David, last time I checked, it took more than money to raise a child." Dave was instantly overcome by silence. Nina's statement was hurtful and downright disrespectful, and she knew it too.

"Well, if you would have answered the phone just once in the last week, then maybe I could've done more." Dave was all but fed up with explaining himself to Nina about a good deed he'd done.

"You know what, Nina, fuck it. Do what the fuck you wanna do with the money. Flush the shit down the toilet for all I care. I'm outta here," he said, then angrily pressed the end button on the phone.

"Dave, wait a—" Nina tried pleading with him, but it was too late. *What the hell have you done now?* she asked herself as she held the phone in the clutches of her fingers, hoping that Dave would overlook her ignorance and call back. Unfortunately, for her, he didn't, though. She quickly slumped into a state of depression. Nina went and lay facedown with arms and legs spread out from end to end on her bed; with her face buried in her pillow, she soaked her pillowcase. Boy, had she done it this time. She had no legitimate reason for cussing Dave out, but she did it anyways. Like making him feel bad would help the situation any. All she did was further push the man that she so-called loved and wanted to be with but was too scared to admit it away. It wasn't enough just taunting his ego by being dropped off at his establishment by her male friend turned companion a few weeks prior.

Now, she had to belittle his character too. If Nina was going to have any chance in reconciling their relationship, and anything else for that matter, she was gonna have to change her attitude and fast.

What a day, Dave thought to himself after hanging up the phone with a deranged Nina. He couldn't believe that Nina had actually took his kindness as an insult. *Was she serious?* he asked himself. Was it just her hormones, or was Nina about to transform into the baby momma that every black man in America dreaded so dearly?

Dave, like the strong black man that he'd become, toughened up, shook off Nina's backlash, then continued on with his day. Nina's unpredictable behavior was still hurting him, though. The week's worth of unanswered phone calls, the degradation of his parental abilities, and just her attitude toward him were beginning to become damaging. All this and Dave still had his wife, Tracie, who wasn't even aware of the situation, to deal with.

After briefly thinking over the argument that he and Nina had, Dave went and flopped down on the couch, then turned on the television. He began breezing through the channels, looking for something—anything—to watch. Then, while surfing, his cell phone began ringing. "Hello," Dave answered in an indignant tone, thinking that it was Shanina occupying the other end. Fortunately, for him, though, it wasn't.

"What up, family? Why you answer the phone like that?" Jay inquired with genuine concern.

"Is everything cool?"

"Yeah, everything's straight. I just got off the phone with Nina a few minutes ago, that's all. Man, I swear that broad is crazy. My blood pressure is probably high den a mug. How you gone trip about something I gave you? Most sane people trip about having to give money, not receiving it. Man, I'm just glad you weren't her 'cause I had some things to get off my chest."

"I see. I see. It must be getting rough on a playa, huh?"

"Somewhat, it is. But choo know me. I ain't trippin. Where you at now anyways?"

Dave's curiosity stemmed from a need for socializing and companionship. He needed the camaraderie. Kicking it with his best friends somehow always changed his mood.

"I just walked out my door, on my way to Beachwood."

"Beachwood Mall?"

"Yea, why you tryna meet me up there or somethin'?"

"I'm finna get dressed right now," Dave assured. Jay knew Dave wasn't about to get dressed immediately. At that very moment, Dave was probably lying around in his boxers or ball shorts doing absolutely nothing, but Jay didn't mind. He need the camaraderie too.

"I'm waitin' on you."

Beachwood's Place looked overcrowded as usual. The only open parking spaces were far and few between. Cars were literally sitting behind other cars, waiting on them to back out, so they could attain a parking space.

Dave methodically maneuvered his mint-conditioned '69 Cutlass up and down the narrow aisles of the parking lot looking for a place to park. In hopes of getting a parking space as close to the door as possible, he continued riding up and down for a few extra minutes. While driving, every man, woman, and child was forced to turn their heads in his direction because the bass coming from his car could easily be mistaken for the rumbling of a train going down a track.

"I really lived it, man, counted soo much money it a hurt cha hands," Young Jeezy's voice could be heard blaring from Dave's myriad of door speakers.

Dave finally convinced himself to park near the back of the parking lot. As he shut off the engine, intuition told him to look to his left. In doing so, he notices Jay's truck resting just a few parking spaces down. Dave pulled into the space, parked, and shut off the engine. Then, he got out of the car. Jay, in an attempt to scare Dave, was waiting right beside his door; he had snuck over to Dave's driver side right after Dave got out and turned to shut his door. "Give it up, nigga," Jay demanded in a strong tone as he pointed his hand formed into a gun into Dave's back.

"Boy, you betta be lucky I wasn't a jack boy 'cause that was yo' ass, Mr. Postman." Jay's smirk turned into a slight laughter when he saw his honey jump nervously. "Boy, you shakin' like a stripper. Tighten up."

Dave's facial expression was nonexistent. His mental preoccupation had him in a serious state of mind. As they began walking toward Nordstrom's front door, the two of them gently clashed their knuckles together. Jay could almost feel Dave's tension pulsating through the clashing of knuckles. "You aight, family?"

Dave took a nice long inhale of the polluted suburban Cleveland air and continued walking. "Yeah, I'm good. I think everything's just now starting to sink in, you know." Dave turned toward Jay and gave him this look as if to say, "You know all about what I'm talkin' about." But for Jay, it was the exact opposite. Jay knew nothing about having a child with someone other than Candace. He couldn't even see himself being with anyone other than Candace. In fact, had it not been for him getting caught cheating a few years back, Jay would not have known any of the females he met during their breakup.

After Dave's comments, the two of them continued walking toward the door in silence. Jay was subconsciously wondering when his best friend could come back around. He pulled the door open and walked through it. Dave followed close behind. They cleared a second set of doors, and at once, beauty hit them both in the face like a ray of sunshine.

"Damn, you see the ass on light skinned." Dave's face lit up.

"Man, she look gooood den a muthafucca." The light-skinned bombshell turned around just enough to see Jay and Dave gawking at her healthy rear end, shaking vibrantly. Then she strutted out the double doors and got lost among the numerous people overcrowding the parking lot. That little bit of communication was all it took for Jay to know that his ace was back.

CHAPTER TWELVE

What a boring night, Nikki thought while lying in the bed on her back with her head propped up on a pillow. Both Dave and Tracie were missing in action. From her observation, there was nothing on television, not even on HBO or Cinemax. Sunday nights were usually like that. She didn't even have a friend to call—not one—and to make matters worse, it was just about time for her to get some shut-eye so she could wake up in time for work in the morning. But for some strange reason, tonight she wasn't tired at all. This new slumberous activity she had been indulging in lately had her spirits feeling like foreign entities of her body. Back home, in Cinci, the way she slept, you would've thought that she was a sufferer of insomnia. There wasn't a day that went past that she wasn't out until the wee hours of the morning. Even when she found her way home early, she'd immediately jump on the phone and chat until she and the voice on the other end both fell asleep on the line—literally.

Now here it was twelve thirty in the morning—fairly early for her—and she was in the house, all alone with nothing but idle time on her hands. With no intentions on going to sleep anytime soon, Nikki figured it was time for a little refrigerator raiding. She really wasn't too hungry, but for this or that reason, her stomach was sending her mixed messages, and her mind's eye kept envisioning her consuming multiple spoonfuls of the vanilla ice cream that she stumbled across earlier. Tracie and Dave's fridge was stuffed to maximum capacity—as always. Whatever one could name, nine chances out of ten, you could find it or a close relative inside: fruits, vegetables, all types of beverages, any type of meat, multiple kinds of fish, and snacks—you name it, they had it. With her eyes wide awake, Nikki meticulously scanned through the fridge. Then, deciding to do the same to the freezer, she pulled the double doors open, and the subzero air rushed her 130-pound frame, causing her already-erect nipples to perforate her black silk gown. She let out a loud moan before stepping back. She was really awake now. Then, it hit her: the gallon of ice cream overshadowing the various bags of frozen goods, directly in front of the rack, stood out like a sore thumb. The wind-chill factor from the freezer had the ice cream stiff as a block of ice. She tried using the ice cream scooper fresh out of the drawer but to no avail. So she pranced over to the kitchen sink and began to run scolding hot water over the scooper. While downing it, her hazel eyes gazed wondrously outside the window over the sink. The sky was pitch black and desolate; not a single star was in sight. Even the moon seemed to be hidden from the naked eye. *What a gloomy night,* she thought to herself. She shut off the faucet then headed back toward the ice cream, scooper in hand, in search of a rematch. This time, though, the heated scooper cut through the top of the ice cream effortlessly. She took three gargantuan scoops, sealed it back, and then put it back in the icebox.

On her way back to her room, her bowl cuffed tightly. She was suddenly stopped in her tracks by the sound of keys jiggling inside the lock. Filled with utter curiosity, she stood in anticipation and watched to see who would emerge from behind the door. The knob twisted slowly. Then the door finally swung open. "Oh! Hey, Dave," she said, concealing the happiness she felt to see him as his presence broke the monotony of the threshold.

He had four nice-sized bags with him, a pair in each grip. "You need some help with those?"

When Dave opened the door to his place of residency, he almost had a heart attack seeing Nikki standing there. He had no idea that she'd be up, walking around leisurely and looking so sexy. He expected her to be halfway through with counting a million sheep by now. What he hadn't expected was for his better half, Tracie, to still be out and about on the town. Although Tracie was known for staying out, partying it was becoming too frequent a thing, and Dave was starting to get a bit suspicious. "Girl, what choo still doin' up? I thought you had to go to work in the morning?" he asked as he stepped completely in the doorway. He dropped the bags by the red leather loveseat before pushing the living room door shut.

"I do have to work in the morning," Nikki responded. "I just can't sleep for some reason." She eased her way closer to Dave, curious about the contents held inside of those bags. Her inquisitiveness was too much for her to control.

"Where is Tracie?" Dave inquired.

"I don't know. I haven't seen her since sometime early yesterday."

Before he could pry any further, Nikki quickly changed the subject.

"What choo got in those bags if you don't mind me bein' nosy?"

Using her spoon, she dug deep into the bowl of ice cream she held captive like an inmate in a mess hall and retrieved a healthy serving. After flipping the spoon upside down, she seductively used her tongue to lick the ice cream off its head. Then, she sucked the spoon dry of its excess.

Watching Nikki suck the contents of the spoon off had Dave's little head rising uncontrollably.

His brown eyes, filled with lust, began exploring her enchanting figure. She started to inch closer to him. His mind wanted to move away, but his body wanted them to be closer. From the lack of a bra, her breasts stood erect slightly underneath the silk of her gown. The splendor of her smooth yellow thighs shined brilliantly with each and every movement. Her aura was a bit overwhelming—to say the least—with her small beautiful feet without a trace of

toenail polish gracing the fur-like carpet. Dave gathered
himself to respond.

"Nothin' big" was all he could muster. Nikki ended
up directly in front of his face, then their eyes met with a
knowing glance. Nikki looked down toward the inside of
the bags and jokingly uttered, "So I guess you didn't buy me
anything, huh?"

"Actually, I did," he replied after a brief moment as he
reached into one of the bags and retrieved a gorgeous pair
of Lady Timberlands, along with a matching Apple Bottoms
shirt and jean outfit.

He then laid them out on the leather of the loveseat.
Nikki's eyes widened with surprise and astonishment.
She was genuinely stunned. Her initial reaction reeked of
bewilderment. "Oh my goodness, Dave. You bought that
for me?"

She still couldn't believe it. Then without any
deliberation whatsoever, she leaned toward him. With
her eyes full of excitement, her mouth half open, her lips
entirely wet, and her bowl of ice cream still in hand, she
tried locking lips with Dave. He could feel the intense
heat generated from their body's magnetic connection.
His willpower was minimal. Before he knew it, his sexual
emotions began taking hold of his being, causing his
extremely moistened tongue to follow suit.

"Teddy, wake up! Babe, get up now! Quit playin'!" Tracie
yelled as she shoved his arm redundantly to no avail. Teddy
was passed out from all the drinking and smoking he'd
done earlier on the bed in the Marriott Hotel room they
reserved many hours prior. *Talk about cutting it close,*
Tracie thought. It was the better half of three o'clock in the
morning and she hadn't been home or seen or heard from
since earlier the day before.

After completely coming to, Tracie sat up in her spot
on the bed right next to her secret lover. Her head was

consistently ringing from the hangover that she'd recently acquired. She palmed her face; then, using her three middle fingers and her thumb, she began massaging her sore temples repetitively. Oh, how she wished she could just relax and sleep! she thought to herself. She pulled the covers back to reveal her nakedness. "Damn it! Where's my clothes!" she hissed. She had on nothing: no panties, no bra, no stockings, not even the toe ring she wore. She immediately discovered that underneath the sheet, at the foot of the bed, all their clothes were in one big pile on his side of the bed. Tracie stood to gather her things. She first needed to take a speedy shower. Her entire body reeked of sex, especially between her thighs. It took her just seven and a half minutes to wash up and dry off. When she emerged from the bathroom, she found Teddy in the same state in the same position he was in before she left him.

Damn! she whispered. She grabbed her clothes and immediately started dressing. She slipped her meaty thighs into her red thong and pulled them tight up in the crack of her voluptuous backside. She then moved to put her strapless bra, matching her thong, over her "milkshakes."

"Shit, Teddy, you gotta get the hell up now!" she wailed. Just as she began to put the rest of her clothes on, Teddy started to regain his consciousness. His eyes began to rise slowly, similar to an automatic garage door. He reached his arm over to where Tracie should've still been lying. When he realized she was no longer there, he called out her name in a low raspy voice. She didn't respond, though, because she was too wrapped up in the task of putting on her red thigh-high Baby Phat shorts that coexisted with a waist-length spaghetti- strapped top.

"Baby, what time is it?" Teddy asked, not really caring. He just wanted to go back to sleep.

"It's almost four o'clock in the morning. Now, get the fuck up so you can drop me off back at my mother's house."

Her voice seemed harsh, but again, Teddy didn't care. He did feel inclined to respond back to her latest words.

"Shut the fuck up and stop rushing me. I'm not finna mutate into Flash Gordon just because *you* gotta get home to your husband. Yo' ass shouldn't be out cheating, anyway!"

Tracie's temperature rose two hundred degrees. You could almost see the steam coming out of her ears. She cut her deep-set eyes like a ginsu knife toward the direction where those words had escaped from. Before saying anything, she nearly sucked all the enamel off her perfectly placed teeth.

"Nigga! Don't ever talk to me like that! Not once have I ever disrespected you, so pleeeaase don't ever, in this lifetime, disrespect me again!" Tracie chided Teddy.

Immediately, thoughts of the first day they met began to rage through her mind. What was once so right and so beloved—or at least that's how it felt—now felt so wretched, so grimy. For a brief moment, she felt low. She felt . . . regret. But she was not the kind of person to cry over spilled milk or dwell on what she couldn't change. But still, Teddy—Teddy hadn't ever, ever talked to her in such a manner. She had never imagined him treating her with such utter contempt and disrespect. It was almost unbelievable to her. Unfortunately, though, she made her bed, so now she had to lie in it. The irony of the thought made her chuckle a bit. Teddy started scooting his chocolate-brown partly-woke body over toward the other side of the bed. With his feet flat on the carpet, he positioned both of his elbows on his knees while leaning to rest his face in the palms of his hands; they still smelled of Tracie's sex. He used the tip of his index fingers to clean the sleep out of the corner of his still-tired eyes. Regretting what he had not so long ago said, he spoke again, this time his voice clear and his words calm. "Babe, why can't we just stay here until later on in the morning? I'm still tired, I'm still drunk, and I know you probably feel the same way too. Come on, babe, I promise I'll take you to your mom's house the first thing in the morning." He then grabbed his white T-shirt from the foot of the bed where Tracie put that and the rest of his clothes in her haste to get ready for them to leave.

"It's already first thing in the morning for your info," she said with disdain. Teddy could tell that she was now getting irritable as she began pacing from the window to their door.

"Anyways, I haven't been home since yesterday morning. Unlike you, some of us have significant others we have to go home to," she added as an afterthought.

Teddy finally slid into his baggy Akademiks jeans, then stood up to put on his long-sleeve shirt that complemented the jeans. Then, he eased his feet into a fresh pair of white-on-white Nike Air Force 1s. Eyeing Tracie the whole time, he said, "I wonder how significant he was to you when I had you bent over, facedown, with your teeth clenching that pillow. I was bangin' that back out!" His words hurt once again not because of what he said or how he said it but because she had wondered and asked herself that same exact question. The reality of the situation was that while she was enjoying the ecstasy of Teddy penetrating her from the rear, with such superb stroking technique, she never even blinked at the thought of her husband or her marriage. So at that moment, he must have not been too significant a person in her life. The only thought that she could muster now was how much she regretted her relationship with Teddy.

"You know what, Teddy," she said in a serious tone of voice, "don't even worry about it 'cause I'll just call a cab." She was dead serious too as she picked up her Louis Vuitton handbag off the hotel room dresser and retrieved her cell phone. When she looked at it, she had five missed messages.

Teddy now knew that she was clearly irritated because as she dialed the numbers to the cab company, he saw a stream of tears run down her beautiful face. Feeling sorry, he walked around to the side of the bed where Tracie was now standing, gazing out the window at the realities of the world. While she waited, with one hand on her hip, for a representative from the cab company to pick up on the other line, Tracie mumbled under her breath. Teddy gently seized the hand that held the phone, took it from her ear, and then closed it just as they heard someone pick up on the other end. Then, he fully embraced her from behind, like he'd done many times before, and squeezed her the way a man in love might squeeze his woman.

"Babe, you know I'ma take you to your mother's house. So please stop trippin'," he pleaded in a low mild-mannered voice. Tracie turned her feminine frame around to meet Teddy head-on. She then leaned her whole being up against him as if she were trying to become one with him. Without a thought, she buried her head in between Teddy's shoulder and neck. It finally seemed as though they had come to a compromise. Now, it was time for her to think about how she'd answer to her significant other. How angry would he actually be? was all she could think of from that point forward.

Teddy hastily rounded the on ramp to Interstate 71, doing well over forty miles per hour. Tracie sat in the passenger seat in utter silence. Teddy started to speak, but he went with his better judgment because he knew exactly what was going through her mind at that moment.

What the hell have I done? Tracie thought to herself for the umpteenth time. Her frequent nights out till all hours of the morning were now starting to push it to the limit. Walking in well after 4:00 a.m. constantly was way over the edge. She knew that this was beginning to be too much. Had she finally lost control of her situation and let her passion for infidelity that she once governed like a true dictator ruin what she had at home? Had she finally sacrificed what was her for sure, for someone else's maybe? In a way, she dreaded what she thought would come out of this, but for some strange reason, a very small part of her was delighted to feel that her reign may be coming to a halt.

CHAPTER THIRTEEN

They met at the pump on her way to work—at her new job. He was a brown-skinned brother, not too light and not too dark. His first name was Tony—not Anthony, just Tony. His last name: Banks. He stood about five feet ten inches from what she could see, with light-brown eyes. His hair was cut short with a crispy Steve Harvey lineup. He had very little facial hair, maybe a shadow of a mustache and a beard at best. The smirk that he gave when they exchanged numbers revealed the slight dimples he had hidden. His build, slim but muscular. At least that's the impression Nina got from the definition of his brawny arms.

When Tony's black Chevy Trailblazer first pulled up beside Nina and her new Chevy Cavalier, she immediately said to herself, *If this brotha tries to talk to me, I am pulling off!* But when he stepped out of his vehicle, looking as fresh as a brand-new pair of gators, her psyche rapidly changed.

Damn, he don't look half bad, Nina said while sitting in the cockpit of her car, poking the lid of her latte with a straw. He was sporting some black slacks with a blue-and-black sleeveless sweatshirt. The black Steve Maddens that covered his feet were trimmed in blue and were dressy but sporty.

Nina sat behind the wheel of her car, sipping her drink through the straw, from the time he left until the time he came back. The two of them made slight eye contact through Nina's windshield as he walked past. Then, he walked to his car and began unscrewing his gas cap to pump his gas. In the back of her mind, Nina was now kind of hoping that he'd come over to the driver side of her vehicle and do what it seemed like almost every other male in the Cleveland area that she had no problem turning down did. But instead, he did the opposite.

Feeling somewhat rejected, Nina put the key into the ignition and was about to start the car when she looked to her left and saw the guy's body frame screening her driver-side window. Part of her wanted to jump from nervousness, the other part wanting to jump for joy. She did neither. She just rolled her window down and asked him, "May I help you?"

"I don't mean to inconvenience you, ma'am, but I happened to have been observing you somewhat, and I noticed that you were about to turn the key in the ignition. Well, seeing as how the gas pump happens to still be inside of your gas tank, it might not be such a good idea."

Nina felt like such an asshole. She had been contemplating about him so much that she'd forgotten to put the pump back on the gasometer. Talk about embarrassing. This was hardly what Nina had in mind when she anticipated his arrival at her window. But you know what they say: "Be careful what choo ask for because you just might receive it!"

"Oh my goodness," Nina said, totally embarrassed. "I was just about to turn the key, put my foot on the gas, and go." Nina had the most innocent simper upon her face. A blind man could see that she was wearing chagrin all over her.

"How could I ever thank you?"

"Awh, ma'am, don't worry about it," he said as he walked over to her gas tank to place the pump back on the gasometer and screw in her gas cap. "I'm just glad I caught choo before you started the car."

Suddenly the guy's voice began to fade. Nina felt his presence departing from the car as he said his last few words. Without hesitation, she took it upon herself to say, "Hey, excuse me, sir." He made his way back to Nina's driver-side window. "You didn't tell me your name."

"My name? Oh, it's Tony," he sputtered before softly shaking Nina's right hand, then sliding her one of his prominent business cards.

"Hold on! Wait a minute," Nina insisted as Tony began walking back toward his car again. She handed him a piece of paper with her name and number on it. "If I don't call you, call me."

"I think I will," he said with a smile. "You have a nice day, sweetheart."

Tony jumped into his Chevy and got lost in between traffic. Nina just sat there for seconds, holding Tony's card between her fingertips.

What a nice guy, she thought to herself while unconsciously gazing into the morning sky. Then, she took a second look at Tony's business card and mouthed, *Oh my god, and he's a real estate agent too!*

CHAPTER FOURTEEN

"So how did everything go baby?" Jay asked, concerned, as he sat up straight on the edge of their white leather sofa. Candace had just come back from her first doctor's appointment; actually, it was her second, but she'd shown up so late for the first one that the doctor made her reschedule.

The eager look upon Jay's face let Candace know that his concerns were sincere. Obviously, she was pretty aware of that already. Sometimes, though, when a woman has to do certain things by herself, like going to a doctor's appointment to check the well-being of her and the child that the two of them created together, she occasionally begins to question her man's sincerity.

"Everything went fine." Candace went into the kitchen and got out her favorite tray of soft-batch chocolate chip cookies and bottled vitamin water. Then, she walked over and sat down next to Jay. "I thought choo had to work today?" she asked and then bit a nice chunk out of her cookie.

Jay looked directly into Candace's eyes. "I did have to work. I left Chuck in charge and took off early."

Swallowing the rest of her cookie, she muttered, "I wish you woulda told me that this morning. I woulda asked you to go with me to my appointment."

"My intentions were to meet choo up there, but I didn't know whether you were going to the office on Euclid Avenue or to Hillcrest. Then when I came home and got dressed, I called your phone about twenty times, but choo never answered. So I said *I'ma just stay here till she gets home.*"

Candace was skeptical about Jay's story. It sounded, to her, like he was making an excuse to be at home and not at work. That was her man, though, and she loved him, so she figured she at least give him the benefit of the doubt until she investigates. "I went to Hillcrest," she said, reaching for her purse sitting on the table in front of them. Her cell phone was buried at the bottom of it.

"Jay, you know I barely ever answer this phone," Candace said as she unfolded it, then checked the screen to see if Jay's claims were accurate. They were close. Candace had over twelve unanswered calls. "I don't even know why I still have a cell phone. I don't use it. Not unless you call, and Dave when he's looking for you. Other than that, nobody else really call me on this phone."

"Baby, you should at least look at the phone when you hear it ring. You never know who it is or what they want." Their little miniquarrel didn't last another second. Instead, Jay cautiously whisked his wife-to-be and their unborn child off their feet and carried the both of them up the stairs to their bedroom. He then lay her down on the bed ever so gently.

"Baby, how about I give you a nice massage?"

Candace couldn't get undressed fast enough. She jumped outta everything that she had on, all except her panties, then lay facedown on the bed.

Jay drizzled a small amount of baby oil on Candace's back then gently commenced to massaging her shoulders. "So tell me what they said, baby," Jay insisted as he began applying slight pressure.

Candace's body wriggled slowly from the sensation of Jay's magical hands. His fingers were exploring all the right spots.

"Who's they? Oh, you mean the doctor?" she asked before letting out a few small moans.

"Well, first off, he told me that I should do my best to get to all our appointments on time." Jay eased his hands to the small of Candace's back and continued massaging.

"Oh, and he checked my blood pressure and my pulse."

"So he didn't tell you how far along you are?" Jay began to ease his hands up off her back as his curiosity heightened.

"Of course, he did, Jayson. But if you don't get back to massaging, you sure won't find out from me." Jay's already-moistened hands quickly traced the back of Candace's thighs all the way down to the bottom of her feet.

He began caressing them with delicateness. First the shaft, then in between her toes. "That's better," Candace stuttered from the pleasure.

"Baby, I'm nine weeks pregnant."

"R-e-a-l-l-y!" Jay made his way toward the top of the bed and then started planting soft kisses upon the back of Candace's neck.

"Baby, I can't wait to become a father," he said with exuberance.

"And I got the perfect baby momma too!"

"Baby momma," Candace said. "Boy, you betta quit playing with me."

"I'm only kidding, baby. You know you're my wife," Jay said as the two of them giggled together lightly.

Candace rotated her oily body around to face her man. "Baby, I love you," she said while tugging on the neck of Jay's white T-shirt, pulling him closer to her.

Jay leaned in toward his woman and retorted, "I love you too, beautiful."

CHAPTER FIFTEEN

Lately, for some odd reason, Tracie's attitude toward Dave and Nikki had begun shifting a bit. Ever since that Monday morning, when Tracie failed to make it home until well after four o'clock, things seemed to had taken a turn for the worse. If she caught the two of them anywhere close to each other alone, she'd quickly let her displeasure be known.

That morning, when she'd finally crept in from her little escapade, Tracie was expecting to come home to her husband, Dave, whom she'd already anticipated would be furious. Instead, she came home to an empty house. That did not sit well with her at all. She had used the whole ride home, in Teddy's and her own vehicle, trying to get her lies in order. So when she discovered Dave's absence, Tracie immediately became suspicious. She called Dave's cell phone at once.

"Hello, Dave. Where in the hell are you at?" Tracie screamed maniacally.

Tracie's anger had Dave flabbergasted. Where was all this hostility stemming from?

He thought why was she yelling at him? Had she somehow figured out what had happened earlier with Nikki? Did someone tell her about Nina and the baby? Dave answered Tracie in the lowliest of tones.

"Hey, baby. I'm on the freeway about to drop Nikki off at work. Why? What's wrong?"

Dave's answer, unbeknownst to him, rubbed Tracie the wrong way. Instantly, her mind began working overtime, trying to come to grips with why he would just up and take Nikki to work.

He hadn't ever done it before. *Why now?* she asked herself. *Why this morning? Had they done something, like have sex, beforehand? Was that the reason for Dave's sudden generosity?* All these things raced through Tracie's mind before she yelled, "What's wrong? Nigga, what choo mean what's wrong? You taking Nikki to work—that's what's wrong!"

"What choo mean by that?" he asked, nervously perplexed. As Dave asked the question, he was heading off the freeway ramp. Nikki's job was off the 90 West 305 exit.

"Well, for starters, I've been tryna get in touch with you since about nine o'clock last night." Tracie was obviously lying.

"My car ran outta gas, and I didn't have any money in my pocket. And anyways, since when did you start waking up at four in the morning?" Tracie's voice was loud and boisterous. Nikki could just about hear every lying word that Tracie said.

"Give me the phone, Dave," Nikki whispered, so Tracie couldn't hear her. Dave hesitantly handed her the phone.

"Hello, Tracie," she spoke. "Yeah, I just wanted to let you know that it wasn't Dave's fault. It was mine."

"What wasn't Dave's fault?" Dave almost caught whiplash. He turned his neck toward Nikki so fast. He had the funniest feeling that Nikki would squeal, and if she were going to, now would've been the perfect time.

"Him taking me to work—that was all my fault. I woke him up and asked him to take me to work 'cause I was too tired to walk to the bus stop. I'd been up all night. For some reason or anotha, I just couldn't sleep. So I said to myself, *If Dave or Tracie don't take me to work, then, I'm not going today.*

"Well, it just so happened that you weren't in the room when I knocked on the door, so I asked Dave. At first, he declined, but when I told him the situation, he finally said yeah. So that's why I said it was all my fault."

Nikki's word fell on deaf ears. Tracie didn't believe a syllable. Instead of expressing her sentiments outwardly, though, Tracie kindly said, "Thanks for telling me, Nikki. Put Dave back on the phone for me please."

"Hello," David muttered after Nikki nervously passed him the phone.

"David Daryl Smith, I'm only going to say this once. After you drop my 'lil' cousin off, do not—and I mean do not—go anywhere else! Bring yo' ass home." Tracie took a deep breath, and before Dave could utter another word, she had hung up the phone on him.

Saturday morning inside the Smiths' home was a little awkward for each resident to say the least. Everyone seemed to be walking on eggshells. Both Nikki and Dave could barely look at each other while in the presence of Tracie. Tracie, on the other hand, couldn't keep her eyes off Nikki; she kept a vigilant watch on Nikki's behavior around her husband, the attire she pranced around the house in, and any little thing Nikki did that triggered a sign of lustful thinking.

Noon came around. Surprisingly, both Dave and Tracie were still cooped up in the house. Dave would've usually been at the creek balling or possibly with his best friend. Tracie would've either been on her way out the door or would've left hours earlier. Today was different, though.

Tracie lay in bed with the bedroom door ajar. Out of her peripheral, she could see Dave coming toward the bedroom. Nikki, wearing a baby-blue bathrobe, was also coming out of her bedroom. Unconsciously, Dave's and Nikki's bodies nearly brushed at the intersection of the hallway. Tracie didn't miss a thing.

"Put some clothes on," Tracie yelled mildly before Nikki could close the bathroom door.

"Damn, what was that all about?" Dave questioned before jumping back in the bed with his wife. Dave knew exactly what it was about, though. It was just too bad that his wife's assumptions weren't exactly accurate.

"What choo mean what was that all about? She needs to put some clothes on. That's what that's all about." Nikki didn't respond, but her feelings were definitely hurt.

Just as she was finishing her little tirade, Tracie's cell phone rang. She grabbed it off the nightstand and glanced at the number. It was Teddy. She quickly pressed the power button, trying to silence the phone. Then she placed it back on the stand. "I wonder who that was," Dave said sarcastically.

"That's fucked up. My wife can't even answer the phone around me!"

Tracie was silent. She knew that she was in the wrong, and anything she said would be used against her. Pissed to the core, Dave could do nothing but think about all the wrongs he'd done. From Nina and the bastard child all the way to the harmless kiss between him and Nikki, Dave had a long list of wrongs. But those thoughts didn't stop Dave's jealousy from rearing. *She better be lucky I didn't fuck her little cousin like I started to,* he mumbled.

CHAPTER SIXTEEN

It had been almost a week to the day when Nina met Tony Wright, the real estate agent, on her way to work. For one, a week might not seem like such a long time, but to Nina, it felt like an eternity especially since Nina had been expecting to hear from Tony ever since the day she had given Tony her home and cell phone number to ensure a phone call. Surely, she was supposed to hear from Tony by now. At least, that's what Nina was thinking anyways. But then again, what had Tony been contemplating? Maybe Tony felt like, since he gave Nina his number first, she should get in contact with him—first! Maybe he felt like he was the catch. You know, with him being a "real estate agent" and all.

But every man in America knows that the regimen was the dog chases the cat. So why wasn't Tony in compliance with the law? Who knows? Not Nina. And she wasn't about to waste any time trying to figure it out either. Nina strolled through the vestibule of her apartment from work at about five o'clock. She tossed the mail that she got from the mailbox onto her glass table. Then, she threw her mustard suit jacket on the black leather sofa.

No sooner had she grabbed the remote control off the couch to turn on the television than the phone rang. Anticipating Tony's call, Nina hurried toward the base of the cordless phone, grabbed the receiver, and with urgency said hello.

"Wuz up, Nina?"

The voice on the other end caught Nina by surprise. She hadn't heard this voice in weeks. And frankly, she was beginning to get used to it.

"Hello, Dave. How are you?" Nina asked as she waited for Dave's all-too-familiar response.

"I'm good. How about yourself?"

"I'm doing quite all right. Thanks for asking."

What was Dave's reason for calling? *I hope he is not calling about that check,* Nina said to herself quietly, *'cause I been spent that money.*

"You must've been waiting on a phone call or something?" Dave asked.

"Naw. Why you say that?" Nina retorted.

"'Cause you answered the phone with enthusiasm, like you were waiting for somebody special to call."

Nina didn't say a word. She wanted so badly to blurt out Tony's name, number, occupation, and anything else she knew about him; but she didn't.

Instead, she just gave Dave's statement the silent treatment.

Dave immediately caught the hint. So to end the slight intermission, he changed the subject.

"So I see you went ahead and cashed that check, huh?"

"Yeah, I did. Was I not supposed to?" Nina's tone of voice was so unpleasant. And although she faked the hatred well, deep down inside, she had about as much love for this man as she had for her own mother.

"Naw, it's cool. That's what I gave it to you for." Dave sighed heavily then continued,

"You know what, Nina, let me get straight to the point since you're not in the mood to communicate with me. Listen, in the next day or so, you should be receiving another check. It should be for about $500 if I'm not mistaken. You don't have to take it, but I would appreciate if you did, okay?"

Nina was so busy rushing toward the mail on the glass table that she unknowingly just agreed with Dave. "Okay," she replied. And before Dave could hang up the phone, Nina said, "Oh, and, David, thank you."

Nina wanted so badly to say I love you to Dave before he hung up.

She couldn't give in, though. Not now. At least, not right this minute anyways.

Nina rambled through the mail for a second and finally came across an envelope addressed from David Smith to Shanina Tucker. Gazing at the envelope intently, she commenced to opening it. Sure enough, it was a $500 check inside. "Thank you, Jesus!" was all Nina could squeeze out of her trap.

Moments after Dave and Nina's phone disconnection, the sun's light began shining brilliantly through Nina's living room window. The radiance instantly permeated the entire room. Its existence was a reflection of Nina's spirits: the way she shined inside, the way her heart felt after her and Dave's conversation. It finally felt like things were starting to go her way from the baby to the new job, to the new car, down to the charity she was receiving from her soon-to-be baby's daddy. Nina felt better than she had in a long time even though the man she loved was loving somebody else.

Just as Nina was heading toward her bedroom to bask in her inexplicable joy, her phone rang again. This time, it was Tony. Already feeling exuberant, Nina committed to the two of them having a dinner date on Saturday evening. What else could go right? If she blinked a few more times, Nina just might be able to conquer the world!

Nina arrived at the restaurant that the two of them had agreed upon, called Luna's Krusty Krab, on Northfield Road at exactly nine o'clock. The night's sky was midnight blue with a few scattered clouds that looked like soft cotton floating in midair. The moon was full. It stood all alone, trying its best to illuminate the sky with what little light it could generate. Daylight saving had this beautiful September evening in northeastern Ohio, a little peachier than it would've been a few weeks prior, but the darkness fit the season. The soothing brisk wind was much calmer than the day's earlier stages. But it still packed enough punch to whisk Nina's long flowing brown-and-cream skirt back and forth continuously, if so desired.

Coasting around the semi-replete parking lot, Nina found a parking space right next to a black Chevy similar to the one she'd seen Tony in. She took a harmless glance in the Chevy's passenger-side window and observed Tony's familiar profile. From the looks of it, he was conversing on his hands-free cell phone. Or at least he had better been, Nina thought to herself because there wasn't another soul inside of his car.

Tony noticed Nina's car when it pulled up beside him. He turned to face her, then flashed his pointer finger, as if to say, "Wait a minute."

Damn he looks so good behind the wheel of that car, Nina said to herself lustfully. Nina watched Tony get out of his car and mosey his way around to her driver-side door; then, he opened up her car door. She stepped out looking like the black queen she had blossomed to be. Her jet-black hair hung loosely in a ringlet style, the cream-hooped earrings that dangled from her earlobes matching the cream pattern on her skirt; her caramel skin highlighted the deep-brown-colored body shirt that hugged her voluptuous breasts ever so snug. Her cream-and-brown Fendi bag suspended from her shoulders accentuated her brown eyes. Stepping away from the car door gave Nina enough space to get a good glance at Tony. What she saw through her peripheral vision was quite impressive. Tony was decked out from head to toe. Not too formal or too informally dressed was he. He was gracefully sporting a solid-blue long-sleeved button-down shirt that he had tucked inside a pair of navy-blue khakis. The boot-cut heel of the khakis set perfectly over the back of his cream-colored Polo boots as if they were tailored. His jet-black hair was neatly cut and shining from the grease he'd packed on earlier. His facial hairs, the little that he did possess, were trimmed to perfection. Plus, the gold watch dwelling upon his wrist had somehow snuck its face from underneath his long-sleeved shirt, causing it to shine ostentatiously.

In her mind, Nina had already given Tony a stamp of approval.

Despite his own dapper appearance, Tony was also taken by Nina's elegance: the way her skin shone in the light of darkness, how her clothes accentuated her pure essence, the way her jet-black hair hung so carefree, symbolizing what Tony thought to be her carefree spirit. "Well, well, well, I must say, you look mighty good. Fine! Better yet, Baby, you look stunning," Tony tried to express, fumbling over complimentary words.

Nina's caramel-colored face instantly lit up, like a tree of Christmas lights. Those compliments that Tony imparted did wonders to Nina's self-esteem much more so than Tony could've ever imagined. See, on the outside, what Tony saw was a beautifully dressed, perfectly toned, gorgeous-looking black woman while Nina, on the other hand, saw herself as just another pregnant black woman and a soon-to-be single parent.

"Why, thank you, Tony. You look very handsome yourself," Nina retorted, grinning from ear to ear.

Tony gently shut Nina's car door, then stepped to Nina, and hugged her tightly, took her hand, and led her into Krusty Krab.

Once inside, Nina meticulously surveyed the atmosphere. With their table positioned directly across from the smoking sections, she looked on at the smokers in total disgrace. Thick dirty-white smoke floated apathetically through the air toward their table. The smokers just continued puffing on their little white cigarettes, with the brown filters, and carrying on.

Nina, being pregnant and all, had zero tolerance for it. "Hey, Tony, do you mind if we move closer to the wall by the smoke-free section?" she asked sarcastically while smirking at the perpetrators.

Satisfied with their new table, Nina and Tony simultaneously grabbed their menus. Tony studied his closely. Nina tried to do the same, but her conscience began bothering her. Using the menu to shield her probing eyes, Nina stared at Tony uncontrollably. His face was so easy on her eyes. His teeth were so white and pretty. *Damn, you had to get pregnant, didn't choo? How in the hell are you going to tell this man you're carrying another man's baby?* was all she could say to herself.

Tony caught a glimpse of Nina's probing eye and the way she shielded her face off with the menu. "Nina, may I ask, why you're covering that gorgeous face of yours? Everything's okay, isn't it?"

Hell no, everything isn't okay, Nina thought. Here she was, out on a date with a man, and she's two months pregnant. To make matters worse, the man didn't even know. She had to tell him, though—that is, if she wanted to have any chance with him in the future. But boy, how far would he run when he finally found out?

"Yeah, everything's fine, Tony," Nina answered, thinking the total opposite. Just then, a plus-sized light-skinned waitress—wearing microbraids pinned up, who had some extremely huge breasts—came over and took their menus off the table after first taking both of their orders.

"Yes, I would like to have the blackened catfish dinner, with two sides of garlic-cheese mashed potatoes," Nina said after observing the run-down pair of white Reeboks that the waitress sported with little shame.

"What would you like to drink with that, ma'am?" the waitress asked Nina nonchalantly. Her bucked eyes were staring Nina down.

"Ah, I'll have lemonade with that. Thank you."

Tony ordered a walleye fillet, fried with extra fries on a hoagie bun. "And what would you like to drink with your meal, sir?"

"Ah, you can give me the same. Thank you."

The waitress returned with both plates approximately ten minutes later. Everything was hot and steaming. Nina's catfish was of a nice-sized portion. The aroma from the seasoned fish mesmerically tickled at her nose. Tony's walleye was very fresh looking. It overlapped the bulky-looking hoagie bun so scrumptiously. His fries looked hot and edible. When he added ketchup to them, their appearance became savory and much more than just a scrawny-looking side dish.

Nina and Tony literally demolished each and every thing on their plates. During which time, they had gotten to know each other a little better. Nina found out that Tony was the middle of three children. He had an older sister and a younger brother. His parents, who were still together, had been married over thirty years. Twenty-eight of those years, which were all spent in Cleveland, had been dedicated to his birth and raising. Tony had never been married or had he had any stray kids. He lived in an apartment building called The Americana on Lakeshore Boulevard.

Nina's background, although she wasn't shameful of it, was not as flattering as Tony's. She explained to Tony how she had grown up in a somewhat single-parent household and how her father had run away with another woman, who coincidentally just so happened to be married, when she was around ten. Nina revealed being her mother's only child. Also, how much she loved her mom and her daddy despite their separation.

"Were you born in Cleveland too?" Tony probed, now intrigued by Nina's conversation. His eyes were glued to hers.

What Tony hadn't a clue of was that Nina's conversation was leading somewhere. And although explaining to him her pregnancy was probably going to be one of the hardest things she had to do since telling her parents, she deemed it necessary.

"Naw, I was born in East Cleveland," Nina answered. Then she paused.

Tony, being somewhat of an intellectual, caught on to her silence. He knew that something wasn't right. But being that she had just poured out her whole life story, he figured that she just had some issues with her past.

"You all right?" he asked, showing his concern.

Something was telling Nina not to tell Tony. Something inside of her was screaming, "Just wait till the next date." But something else said, "If you don't tell him now, the next date might be too late."

Tony's question was interrupted by the pudgy waitress. "Did you enjoy everything?" the waitress asked as she quickly began grabbing plates off Nina and Tony's table and stacking them onto a large tray.

"Yes, everything was nice," Tony spoke up quickly. "You may bring us the check too."

The waitress slid her hand into the pocket of her apron and placed the check on the table.

"Thank you, ma'am," he retorted.

"Oh, Tony, I need to tell you something," Nina said apprehensively after the waitress's departure. Somehow, she had mustered up the courage to tell him. Where it came from only God knew.

"Please don't hate me for what I'm about to say."

I knew it was too good to be true, Tony thought to himself as his mind began gyrating around every negative thought possible. Nina was just too gorgeous. Her mind was just too sound. Everything about her was just too perfect. That's why Tony knew something had to be wrong. "Go ahead, sweetheart," he said, retaining his negative thoughts. "I'm all ears."

Nina didn't hesitate another second. She jumped out in blind faith and replied, "Tony, I'm pregnant."

Nina's confession hit Tony kind of hard. And although his blank facial expression didn't reveal much, he was actually stunned a bit. *How do I respond without offending her?* he thought before saying, "Oh, really, well, congratulations, sweetie. I'm sure some man is a proud soon-to-be father," he said, hoping not to show any rejective body language. "If you don't mind my asking, though, how's the relationship between you and him? He's not outside vandalizing my Chevy, is he?' Cause, if so, tell him his work is in vain 'cause that car is already on its last leg."

The two of them burst out at Tony's attempted joke. Then Nina took it upon herself to clear the air. "Naw, naw, it ain't like that at all. Actually, we're separated. I just thought that it would only be proper for me to inform you about it."

"Well, I'm sure glad you did 'cause I was just about to order us a couple of drinks." Tony let out another giggle. "Naw, really, though, I truly appreciate your honesty. Most women wouldn't have told me that. Oh, and, by the way, your pregnancy is perfectly fine with me. In fact, how about you go with me next Sunday to the Mike Epps and Sommore comedy show? I've got two tickets."

Nina's face lit up like the sun. She blushed uncontrollably. "Of course, I'll go with you, Tony."

"Then it's a date," Tony confirmed before drawing his wallet to pay for their meals. Nina and Tony exited Krusty Krab together, looking and feeling like a happy couple. And after stealing each other's passion with a small kiss, Nina went on her way, and Tony went on his.

CHAPTER SEVENTEEN

Carrying Jay's seed for the last few months, for Candace, had probably been one of the most exciting times in her young life. Just the mere thought of a human being growing inside of her uterus was so intriguing to her. In fact, ever since Candace first found out, she'd be eating for two; she couldn't stop talking about it. She told her family, all her friends and co-workers, and everybody else that she came in contact with long enough to strike up a conversation.

Candace's mother, on the other hand, was not too fond of Candace's pregnancy.

She thought that her daughter had rushed into it especially since Candace and Jay had no intentions on getting hitched or even engaged for that matter.

When Candace first informed her mother about her pregnancy, her mother's nonreaction was all it took to know that mom did not approve.

There was no congratulations. There wasn't a "Baby, I'm proud of you." There wasn't even a negative reaction out of her mom. She simply just gave her the silent treatment then rashly changed the subject. That hurt Candace's feelings. She felt low. Candace looked up to her mother, so her mom's approval absolutely meant so much to her. For some reason, though, it always seemed as if Candace had to work extra hard to receive that approval.

Growing up was much harder for Candace than it was for most of the other kids she grew up around in the suburban city of Euclid, Ohio. Euclid, which is a suburb of Cleveland, was similar to a melting pot with blacks and whites being the majority. Most families, with the exception of a few, were middle-income families, with a common family structure—that being, father, mother, and children. So that meant that nearly every kid she knew of stayed with both of their parents.

With her, though, things were different. Candace lost her father when she was just a little girl. He battled cancer before finally passing away. Candace's mom took it hard. She wept and mourned for many years after his death. And as much as she tried to conceal the hurt, her actions just wouldn't let her hide it. Many days of the week she took her anger and hurt out on her only child. Candace, not knowing the full extent of where everything was coming from, just took it all in stride. She just figured, being a young girl and all, that that was just the way mothers were supposed to act.

As Candace grew older, though, curiosity about her missing father slowly began to rise. She started to ask questions like "Mommy, why come I only have one parent?" Or "Mommy, where's my daddy?" Candace's mother wanted so badly to ease her child's burden and tell her all about her father, his death, and everything else that her child had no clue of. But she didn't—at least not until Candace came home with the answers to all the questions.

"Mommy, Tray Tray told me that my father died of something called cancer" was what she would come home and say to her mother after spending the weekend over to her cousin Tray Tray's house.

By age fourteen, Candace was a blossoming teenager coming into her own. She was only a freshman in high school; but her knowledge, wisdom, and understanding far exceeded her grade. Candace kept a report card full of straight As. She participated in almost every extracurricular activity. She got along great with almost every teacher that walked the halls of Euclid High School. Eventually, before the end of her ninth-grade year, she became vice president of the Student Council. With all these attributes, you'd think Candace's mother would be one of the proudest parents in the entire city. Not hardly. Actually, Candace's mother had become more bitter than she was in years prior. She would say things to her daughter like "Why were you tardy to school three times?" after reading a report card full of straight As and exceptionally great comments. Candace—now being able to understand, to some degree, the source of her mother's pain—just gave her mother the benefit of the doubt.

During her junior year of high school, Candace, now fully focused and ready to explore life, stumbled across this brown-eyed handsome guy at one of her high school's basketball games.

His name was Jayson. His friends called him Jay for short. The two of them met at the concession stand. Candace was about to pay for the hot dog and Coca-Cola she had just ordered when this guy Jay stepped up and slapped a crispy $10 onto the counter. The gesture immediately caught Candace's attention.

Before the game was over, Candace and Jay had exchanged numbers and were running off at the mouth like long-lost friends. Not too long after, Candace and Jay were going to malls together, going out to eat, and talking on the phone all times of the night.

Candace had really begun to like this guy Jay. There styles were totally opposite, but that's what attracted her to him so much. Candace was book smart and Jay was street-smart. Candace was soft and fragile; Jay was rough and rugged. Candace was a suburban girl; Jay was from the mean streets of Cleveland.

The one thing that the two of them did have in common, though, was they were both filled with love. And as time grew, they began to love each other strongly with that love. Candace and Jay literally became inseparable. But for some reason, Candace never told her mom about Jay.

One day, during her senior year of high school, Candace decided she'd bring Jay home to meet her mother. She figured that hiding their relationship had gone on long enough. It was time to introduce the two people that she loved the most to each other. The idea unfortunately wound up being a huge mistake. Candace's mom had shown immediate disdain toward Jay all this time despite Jay's exceptionally polite behavior toward Candace's mom the whole time.

Candace was absolutely disgusted with her mom after her lackluster behavior. "Mommy, I can't believe you embarrassed me like that in front of Jay," she would say. But unfortunately for Candace, about a month later, all her standing up for Jay would come to a screeching halt. She found out that Jay had been cheating on her with another girl from her school. Jay's infidelity threw Candace in a state of depression; this lasted through her senior year. She skipped prom, moped through graduation, and wept through her first semester of college at the University of Akron.

One day, out of the clear blue sky, she received a call from the one-time love of her life Jay. At first, Candace was a bit afraid to hold a civil conversation with him, fearing that her feelings would only get hurt again. She wound up hanging up the phone on him all the time. For some strange reason, though, this one particular time, Jay called Candace, and she felt inclined to talk to him. That one conversation sparked all kinds of old feelings that had been lying dormant since high school. Jay confessed his wrongs, begged for Candace's forgiveness, and did all the things necessary for her to try trusting him again. Not long after, she decided to take him back. Her newfound joy prompted her to call her mom and tell her about the breakup-to-makeup love story. Her mom didn't take the news as well as she thought. In fact, she quickly showed her disdain.

"Candace, that boy cheated on you! Now I know I didn't raise you to be stupid!"

Candace's mom's comments were like battery acid to the brain: they burned.

But what could she do? Candace was in love, and her love was blind. She'd finally reclaimed euphoria. Was it her fault that it just so happened to be with a man that cheated on her years prior? Still, feeling a slight bit of insecurity, Candace made Jay agree not to ever lie, cheat, or hold back anything that she felt she was entitled to know. Being the man that he was, Jay gladly agreed to all the terms.

After Candace's graduation from Akron U, she moved back in with her mom and got a job in Olive Garden as an assistant manager. It wasn't long before Candace moved out of her mom's and in with Jay's in the house in Richmond Heights. The rest is history.

CHAPTER EIGHTEEN

The West Bank in the Flats of Downtown Cleveland was backed up for what seemed to be a mile. There were cars lined up from the Powerhouse parking lot all the way to West Fourth Street just to witness Mike Epps and Sommore turn the Improv Comedy Club upside down.

The Improv was located downtown in an old brown warehouse-type building. From the outside, one would believe that the place was shabby; on the inside, it was just the opposite. The inside, which was on the second floor above other venues, was built like a theater, with chairs strategically positioned next to each other, all the while facing the lofty stage. The Improv was very regal.

Cars and trucks were literally bumper to bumper. One could just about feel the anticipation leaking feverishly as horns beeped in continuous rage. "Move the fuck up!" a guy screamed out of a classic red '69 Camaro to a group of females in a burgundy-colored Sebring.

The evening sky was completely clear, except for the full moon that lit up the sky. The wind blew comfortably, causing most everyone to keep their windows rolled up at least midway. The temperature was somewhere in the high forties; it was down almost thirty degrees from its earlier seventy-eight degrees. Everything about this gorgeous Sunday read perfect for a night filled with laughter and endless comedy.

After paying the parking attendant, Dave drove his sparkling baby-blue Navigator, sitting on all-chrome twenty-six-inch wheels, over the speed bump. Then, he made a right into the spacious parking lot. The lot was just about filled to capacity. Dave made his way through hesitantly until he spotted a parking space near the entrance of the Powerhouse, right next to a cocaine-colored old-school Cadillac.

"Damn, this place gotta be packed. All these cars and stuff out here don't make no sense," Tracie commented as Dave shut off the engine.

Dave and Tracie walked together boldly into what looked to be a full house. The lights were dimming above the audience, and it seemed as though the 9:00 p.m. show was about to start. The two of them surveyed the audience in search of not only their seats near the stage but also their companions Sleeze and his nameless date.

When Dave and Tracie entered the venue, all heads turned, and all eyes zoomed in. They were both as clean as the presidents' criminal record. Dave looked like a million dollars sporting a long-sleeved off-white-and-turquoise silk Armani shirt, with a pair of white silk pants to match. Its off-white-colored derby with the turquoise band was bent ever so slightly on the top of his head. The darkened atmosphere inside the venue couldn't withstand the radiance of his turquoise alligator dress shoes. And with the big-faced Jacob watch he had on, along with a set of cufflinks gleaming, Dave caught just about every woman's eye inside the place.

"Damn, Tracie, you sho'll got these niggas eyeing like a hawk in this joint." Dave leaned over and said as they both continued gazing into the audience. From head to toe, Tracie looked as if she could be an A-list movie star: her jet black with long free-flowing hair hanging low and loose set atop her semi-naked shoulders. She graced the floor in a designer blue-green draped satin dress. Her neckline hung loosely over her braless breasts. The gorgeous dress ended somewhere near Tracie's midthigh, showing off her luscious thigh and calf muscle tone. Tracie's legs looked so erotic, setting on top of the blue-greenish pumps she wore.

Her heels added a serious arch to her already-very-well-round backside. The men inside the place couldn't remove their eyes from God's fine work of art. With her off-white Donna Karan bag wedged up under her armpits, Tracie looked on in excitement.

"I dunno what choo talkin' 'bout. These hoes in here sweatin' yo' ass hard!"

Dave and Tracie matched from head to toe, with their wedding rings being as visible as could be. Together, they looked like the perfect couple.

The master of ceremonies stepped onto the stage, receiving a lengthy ovation. "What's up, Cleveland? Ya'll ready for some COMIDEEEE!"

Just then, Tracie caught a glimpse into the crowd of what looked to be someone waving at her and her husband.

"Hey, David, ain't that yo' friend over there?" Tracie said, pointing her finger near the front of the stage.

Dave and Tracie made their way through the chair-filled aisles to go to two empty chairs near Sleeze and some woman wearing a scarlet-red dress.

Dave, tugging on Tracie's hand, led the way.

Sleeze and his date stood up to greet Dave and Tracie upon making it to the table. "David, my man, what's happenin'?"

Sleeze said softly in consideration for the quieted crowd who looked hypnotized by the utter loquaciousness of the master of ceremonies. "And dis mus be your lovely wife."

Sleeze looked toward the woman who stood up with him and said, "I'd like ya ta meet ma lady fren, Tosha."

After greeting one another with hugs and handshakes, the four of them sat down to enjoy the show. "Come on now, I need ya'll to help me bring to the stage," the MC said to a festive crowd, "the one and only. Give it up for her, Cleveland, S-O-M-M-O-R-E!"

When Nina looked over her right shoulder and witnessed Dave standing with what looked to be his wife and two other anonymous people at the start of the show, it had definitely struck a nerve. She knew that the chances of seeing Dave tonight would be great, but what she hadn't prepared her feeble heart for was seeing Dave with his wife. So what if Nina looked absolutely stunning in an all-white, Baby Phat shirt and pant outfit? So what if she trimmed her hair down to a bob in hopes of a boost of self-esteem and confidence? So what if she just looked drop-dead gorgeous—period? And so what if Nina's date, Tony, who was oblivious to everything, complimented her in every way? That wasn't the point. The point was Dave wasn't supposed to be here with his wife. At least that's how Nina felt anyways. Especially since he hadn't even mentioned it to her during the few conversations that the two of them had had.

Instead of throwing herself a pity party, Nina made it her business to show her date some much-needed attention. She grabbed Tony by the hand, pulled him close, then whispered in his ear, "Baby, I really wanna thank you for taking me out and showing me such a good time."

Tony tried to respond, but Nina's luscious lips took control of the conversation, swallowing his upper lip, then taking hold of his tongue till she sucked it dry. "No, seriously, Tony, thank you," Nina somehow managed to say after releasing Tony's helpless tongue and planting a small kiss upon his lips.

"You see these big-ass titties?" Sommore said as the crowd burst out into laughter. "These titties ain't this big fa nuthin. Oh, trust me when I say they ain't this big fa nuthin. These titties are multipurpose." The crowd laughed uncontrollably. "Seriously, ya'll, these puppies is multipurpose. I use um fa milkin', suckin', and some occasional dick fuckin'."

While everyone in the audience, including those at her table, viewed Sommore in amazement, Tracie, as usual, had her sights set on something else. The man sitting directly across from her, who once introduced himself to her as

Cedric, had somehow gained Tracie's full and undivided attention. Tracie couldn't refrain from her covetousness. She gawked at Sleeze with her ever-seductive ebony eyes. Dave, as well as Sleeze's date, initially had no clue of this. The two of them were so engrossed in the show at hand they weren't even paying any attention to what was going on around them. Sleeze was, though. He was paying very close attention, as a matter of fact; he saw the way Tracie sneakily cut her eyes toward him. He saw how Tracie faked her laughter when Sommore made a joke just so her husband wouldn't become suspicious. He saw everything. He even saw the way Tracie traced her lips with her thick tongue.

"Man, Sommore is silly as hell, ain't she, baby?" Dave leaned over and said to Tracie while still giggling from the jokes prior.

Tracie looked at her husband long enough for him to revert his attention back to the show. Then, she went back to gazing. Only this time a set of eyes were gazing back at hers.

Sleeze's eye contact was penetrating, touching Tracie in the worst way. His piercing looks forced her to slip her left hand between the seams of her glistening thighs to calm her purring kitten.

Watching Tracie's subtle actions only seemed to evoke Sleeze's sinful desires. His eyes began probing Tracie's chest area. Her nipples were rock-hard. Seeing that compelled him to surreptitiously flicker his tongue for her to see. "Whew shit," Tracie sighed underneath her breath, losing all composure during their flirtatious chain of events. Tracie was so gone that she hadn't even noticed her husband checking her out.

"What's wrong, boo? Is everything aight?"

Sommore's successful comedic stint came to an end after thirty short minutes. Pleased with her performance, the satisfied audience applauded gracefully.

"Ya'll give it up again for S-O-M-M-O-R-E," the MC loudly demanded after rushing his way back to the stage. "And now it's that time. Time for you to get up, use the restroom, get choo sumthin' to eat, sumthin' to drink, use the phone, do whatever it is you need to do. It's intermission time, ya'll."

Chairs immediately began screeching, and feet began patting. Not one person in the audience gave the MC enough time to finish his statement. "Be back here in fifteen minutes. The show will resume in fifteen minutes."

The lobby outside the theater was packed from this side to that. Groups of people were bunched together, leaning against the walls, in large packs. The restaurant was filled to capacity. Even the restrooms, which were now spilling over to the outside area, were overcrowded with stragglers impatiently waiting for open stalls.

Dave, Tracie, Sleeze, and Sleeze's lovely date all walked side by side, together, down the crowded hallways. Passing by occasional clouds of cigarette smoke and loads of idle chatter, the group heard, "Sleeze, Dave, wuz happenin', fellas?" from another group of guys. Both men were getting acknowledged quite frequently and frankly were beginning to get used to it.

As the four of them continued walking, Dave caught a glimpse of a woman, very familiar looking, through his peripheral vision. At first glance, it looked like his ex-Nina, hanging on to the arm of some light-skinned brother.

Dave just wasn't certain if that was her, though. Slowing up a bit, just to get a closer look, Dave cut his deep-brown eyes toward the woman and noticed that she was coming toward him. It was Nina! Feelings of regret, guilt, mistrust, etc., all rushed Dave at once. *Damn, that's her,* he thought to himself as he looked directly at his soon-to-be baby mother.

"Hi, David, how you doing?" Shanina said, walking right past him toward the restroom. Shanina looked stunning. It wasn't just her assets either; her face displayed a look of complete satisfaction. Her skin had an illuminating glow. Dave couldn't take his eyes off her or her new hairstyle. "Hey, Shanina," Dave said before turning toward his wife and saying to her, "Baby, this is one of my workers at the club. You don't mind if I have a word with her really quick, do you?"

After staring awfully hard at what looked to be her equal in many ways, Tracic then cut her eyes, scrunched up her face, and set her arms akimbo. Looking her husband directly in his eyes, she said, "Can you what? You know what, Dave, yeah, you can go over there but make it quick. And I mean really quick." Wasting no time, Dave power walked over to Nina and stopped her in her tracks before she could go into the restroom.

CHAPTER NINETEEN

Sunday night was finally consummating. Both Jay and Candace lay together in the pitch dark, inside their bedroom, whispering sweet nothings back and forth for what seemed like forever. Jay then finally dozed off into what would become a slobbery, sedative sleep but not before coming to the stern conclusion that staying at home with his woman and not going to the comedy show was one of the best decisions he's made in a long while. It was not like Jay did not have a desire to be there. In fact, the thought of recanting his earlier decision, on turning down Sleeze's offer, itched at him severely.

Lying beside the most beautiful, kind, loyal, and trustworthy woman on the planet that he knew quickly erased the thought, though.

"Jay," the shrill voice cut through the still of the night, bouncing off the bedroom walls and echoing through the empty hallways of their two-and-a-half-story home. Jay was in the midst of a horrid dream filled with sirens, cop cars, and prison bars. He tussled strenuously with the blue-eyed officer trying to cuff him and throw him inside the back of a white Crown Victoria. He could hear his name being called by someone close.

"Jay," the voice became amplified, causing Candace to toss and turn beside her slumbering boyfriend. Jay hearkened the voice in hopes of putting a face with it. As the uniformed cop pressed down on Jay's head, forcing him into the patrol car, Jay twisted his neck around, looking for someone—anyone—in the area that could've been calling him.

"Oooouch! Jay, baby, get up." Candace clutched Jay's shoulder blade along with his bare muscular arm and began jolting him back and forth.

"Jay! Get up, baby. I'm hurting! Something ain't right. Oooouch!"

After awaking, Jay, realizing the problem at hand, leaped out of bed and rushed to get dressed. "Baby, you okay?" he sputtered frantically. Candace continued to scream. Her outcry became disturbing. Jay could barely hold his composure as he rushed to Candace's closet to grab the first few articles of clothing he could find that looked presentable. "Just hold on, baby, everything gone be all right, you hear me? Just hold on okay. You know I'm not gone let anything happen to you."

CHAPTER TWENTY

The comedy show downtown concluded itself a little after 11:00 p.m. Dave and Tracie met up with Sleeze and his date outside in the parking lot. "So wut ya finna do?" Sleeze asked Dave curiously.

Sleeze had gotten wind from a few of the folks that he knew at the comedy club of the happening after-hour spots. If Dave left it up to Sleeze, this night would be far from over. "I hear da House of Blues is da spot for da night."

Dave wanted so badly to go out to the House of Blues with Sleeze and his lady friend, but the timing was way off. Not only was Dave hurt by seeing Nina with some other guy again during the comedy show, Dave had seen some stuff transpire between his wife and Sleeze that he wasn't too happy about: continuous eye contact, provocative facial expressions, stimulating body language.

About halfway into Mike Epps's stand-up act, Dave was convinced that his wife hadn't watched a bit of the show. With all the veiled thoughts running sprints through his head, Dave just figured it'd be best for him and his wife to call it a night. "Man, you know what, Sleeze, me and my wife jus gon go ahead and turn it in for da night."

Extreme sounds of overbearing car systems, revved-up motorcycles, car and truck engines, combined with gobs of rowdy and restless folks, anxious to terrorize the streets, all amplified the parking lot. So much so that Dave and Sleeze had nearly began yelling back and forth just to make sure they heard each other clearly. "Ya goin' home dis early?" Sleeze questioned Dave while wringing his hands together with the intent of keeping warm. Sleeze's Coca-Cola–colored mink coat, with the equal Kangol, was no match for the monstrous winds that had suddenly materialized in the last two hours or so. The frigid Cleveland wind had settled its way into the fabric of Sleeze's coffee-brown-colored slacks, chilling the skin on his legs.

Tracie listened in on the whole conversation in total disbelief. She couldn't remember the last time Dave walked inside the doors of their home this early on a Sunday night. Why now? Why did he have to wait until she was having fun to want to go home? "Come on, Dave, let's go out," Tracie pleaded with her arms wrapped tightly around her husband's waist.

"Naw, baby, I'm ready to go home and relax. Maybe next time, though, Sleeze."

"Are ya sure? 'Cause we ain't gotta go out. We can go to me restaurant and have a few drinks, ya know. As a matter of fact, I tink dats wut Imma do."

"Yeah, I'm sure. Imma gon an' turn it in. But thanks again for the tickets, man." Dave said as he and his wife headed for the truck. The second Dave and Tracie drove out the parking lot, tempers began to flare.

"Come on, Dave, baby, let's go out with Sleeze and his girlfriend," Tracie blurted out, unaware of the consequences.

"Didn't I say no already, Tracie?"

"Yeah, but—"

"Then what the fuck you keep asking me for?" Dave blurted with fury. The two of them argued back and forth continuously from the time they left the Power House until Dave yanked his truck into their driveway.

"Maybe it's just me, but what I can't understand is why the hell you so scared of going out somewhere with me. Oh, what, you think you gone run into that little bitch you seen earlier?" Tracie screamed as they walked through the threshold of the front entrance of their home.

"You know what, Dave, fuck you. Fuck you and her," Tracie yelled loud enough to wake Nikki out of her coma.

Dave did his best job of ignoring his wife. Her screaming antics had become quite outrageous to say the least. Attempting to escape the mayhem, Dave tossed his keys onto the kitchen table, then thrust himself into the bathroom. Tracie's ranting and raving continued for a time. Then suddenly everything went quiet—extremely quiet. *What is this crazy woman up to now?* Dave thought as he stood up from the toilet and headed toward the door. Easing his way out of the bathroom, he expected to see, or hear, Tracie's loud mouth. But after checking his bedroom and nearly every other room inside of the house, Dave came to the realization that Tracie wasn't around. Feeling confused about his wife's whereabouts, Dave had no choice but to confront the only person that could've heard anything.

"Nikki, I hate to wake you up like this, but I need to ask you a question," Dave said after bursting his way through her bedroom door.

Even half-sleep Nikki looked stunningly gorgeous with the lavender comforter only covering part of her body. She rolled onto her back, overtly displaying her goods. "Don't worry about it," she responded as the bright glare from the television shined on her and the dried-up saliva occupying the side of her face.

"I wasn't asleep anyways. Tracie killed all that. Go ahead, though. What were you about to ask me?"

Dave's mind was preoccupied with his wife's disappearing act, but that didn't stop him from glancing lustful at Nikki, with her legs wide open. The sky-blue panty and bra set she wore accentuated her extremely fat camel toe and her firm breasts. His mind was drifting. "Uuuh . . ." he dragged before snapping out of it. "Have you seen that crazy broad around here?"

"No, but I do think I heard the door shut and a car engine rev up."

Immediately, Dave raced to the back of the house, where he noticed the back door was cracked open. He slid his feet into a pair of old white Nike's lying atop the basement stairs, crushing the back of them with his heel. *What is this woman's problem?* he asked himself aloud while walking toward the side of his home. After looking up and down the driveway, Dave concluded that his wife had left. He was puzzled. *Where could this woman have gone?* he thought while gently rubbing his head. With his face scrunched up and his forehead wrinkled, he asked himself a question audibly, *How did she move my truck, pull her car out, drive my truck back in, then put my keys back on the table without me even noticing?* With his hand cupping his chin and his mind racing a mile a minute, something clicked. He hurried back into the house to check the kitchen table. No keys! He probed the kitchen meticulously. Still no keys! Finally, he searched the attire he wore earlier at the club.

No keys! Dave was convinced. *This bitch done took my keys too!*

Tracie parked her Lexus right in front of an occupant's home just around the corner from Carolina's. The streetlight hanging directly above her car shined brilliantly, displaying not only the swirls in her pearly-white paint job but every nook and cranny that had normally gone hidden.

Sleeze and Tracie sat together—alone—inside the office of his restaurant. Sleeze, sipping on the beginnings of a freshly opened Heineken bottle surveyed Tracie closely. He watched her fully-glossed-up lips wrap themselves around the edge of a martini glass. "So where's your girlfriend, Sleeze? Did you take her home?" Tracie asked after setting her glass on the edge of Sleeze's office desk.

"Dat wasn't me gurlfren, but yes, I took'er home."

The two of them tossed back drinks for what seemed like an eternity, conversing and laughing the night away. Before they knew it, three o'clock had eased upon them like a thief in the night. Tracie noticed the time and insisted, "Sleeze, it's about time for me to get—" but before she could finish, Sleeze leaned in and stole a kiss from her luscious lips. Tracie was taken aback. Sleeze then stood up and furthered his sexual advances. Tracie's body was quivering. Her mouth was extremely moist, and her panties were soaked. She knew what she had come here for. She just didn't think that it would happen. Trying to stop him from seducing her any further, she put up a haphazard fight. Unfortunately, though, his charm was too strong for her body to resist. Tracie had succumbed.

CHAPTER TWENTY-ONE

While the doctor ran a series of tests on Candace, Jay sat anxiously in the waiting room of the Hillcrest Hospital branch of Cleveland Clinic. To the right of him was a stack of *Time* magazines, the one atop bearing the face of President George W. Bush. To the left of him, a Chinese family waited patiently on the return of their doctor. Directly in front of him was an unoccupied row of chairs connected by the arms.

The waiting room was filled with awkward silence. There wasn't a sound for what seemed to be miles. Not even an occasional voice of a doctor, nurse, or family patiently waiting. Jay's patience was beginning to run thinner than his father's hair. Sitting and waiting was not one of his best attributes. He jumped up, grabbed his cell phone, and called his homie. "Wuz happenin', man?" he asked to an alert Dave, who answered the phone on the first ring.

Dave had been hoping to receive a call from his wife who had, not even twenty minutes prior, eased off with the keys. With his spare keys attached to his wife's keychain, Dave was temporarily without a means of transportation. "Wuz up, Jay? Man, I thought choo were my wife callin'. That bitch is craaa-zee!" Dave went hush but for what only seemed to be a millisecond. "Wuz up, though? Shouldn't you be somewhere sleepin' right now?"

"Man, I'm at Hillcrest with Candace," Jay said in a mellow tone, trying his best not to irritate the Chinese family. "She was having some serious stomach pains."

"Everything's aight, ain't it?"

"I think so. The doctor already came back and told me that the baby was all right. I'm just waiting on him to finish up a few more tests. Hopefully, within the next few minutes or so, she should be getting released."

"That's good," Dave replied while peeping through the blinds in search of Tracie. The headlights of a car skimmed his window, giving Dave false hope of his wife's return.

"I wish I could come up there with you, man, but my simple-ass wife stole my keys. I don't know what the fuck her problem is."

"Awh, don't worry about it, family. I know ya heart. I ain't trippin'. I just thought I'd call and let choo know the deal, just in case. Plus, all this waitin' shit's making me tired."

"So you really using me to stay woke, huh?"

"I guess you can say that," Jay replied, giggling sensibly, trying his best to show the Chinese family respect.

Just then, Candace and the doctor emerged from the short hallway, coming from his office.

From what Jay could see, Candace's smile was stretching from one ear to another. The doctor looked as if he was trying to explain something to her. Her full attention was on Jay, though.

"Dave, man, I'ma have ta ring you right back. Here comes Candace with the doctor."

Candace eagerly made her way toward her man and nearly squeezed the life out of him.

"Hey, baa-be," she said affectionately while the doctor stood there patiently.

"Now, you make sure you eat properly, get a sufficient amount of rest, and do not forget to take your prenatal vitamins, okay? And make sure not to lift anything heavy."

After those oh-so-redundant words, the doctor disappeared, leaving Candace and Jay by themselves.

"You ready to get outta here, baby?" Jay asked, kissing his soon-to-be softly on her forehead. Relief was present upon his face.

"I thought you'd never ask."

PART 3

CHAPTER TWENTY-TWO

As the chills from the blistering winter weather whisked itself through the construction-filled avenues of Cleveland, whistling heavily and fogging up nearly every window it blew past, Dave stood upright, directly in front of the screen door, staring down each and every snowflake that fell from the sky. Each one was another contributor to the already-compacted four inches sitting atop not only Dave's street but nearly every street in the city. He could hear the salt from the salt truck right outside of his home, tapping against the sides of cars, parked next to the curb.

Directly across from him, his neighbor was putting the finishing touches on the driveway he'd been plowing for at least an hour.

Change, for the Smith family, was all but evident. In addition to the New Year sneaking its way in a few days ago and the fluffy white snow finally accumulating after Christmas, things around the house were in total transition too. Tracie's little cousin Nikki had just gotten an apartment on West Twenty-Fifth near downtown Cleveland. Unbeknownst to Tracie, with Dave's help, Nikki finally scraped up enough finances to move out on her own, plus buy herself a decent-looking used car. That left Dave and Tracie by themselves once again. With their relationship already on the ice, Nikki's disappearing act left them on the brink of a cliff.

Dave's dilemma at home, although a bit unsettling, to say the least, was no match for the one he had to face outside of his domain. Nina, who was now seven months pregnant, had put on about fifty pounds, seemingly all in her stomach area. The thought of her having this bastard of a child had Dave thinning at the corner edges of his well-groomed head of hair. It wasn't the actual birth of the child that had him frightened, though. It was the possibility of Tracie finding out. Dave knew that if she detected anything suspicious, be it monetary support, phone call, or anything remotely close to any signs of infidelity, Tracie would eventually put two and two together. Then who knows what she would do?

With nothing but danger lurking on either side of her name, one would think that Dave had better sense than to still want Nina. Oddly enough, though, he didn't. In fact, the more time passed, the stronger his feelings for her became. Nina was everything that he wanted in a woman. She was fine as hell, down to earth, free-spirited and, as far as he was concerned, the perfect woman to have a baby with—all this despite their past misunderstandings.

Tracie, on the other hand, had become nothing more than a selfish, inconsiderate, freeloading housewife, who just so happened to be carrying his last name. Her apparent apathy for Dave and their relationship was starting to get to him more than ever before. He yearned for the void in his heart because of a lack of love to be filled, but Tracie didn't care. She was too busy doing her. That attitude only made him despise her even more. It had gotten to the point where him just seeing his now-estranged wife's face caused the resentment he harbored to decay his spirit like a rotten tooth.

He still loved her, but he just couldn't stand her. That once-sexy and sensual voice she had, had now become squeaky and irritating. All the things that she used to do, unconsciously, to turn him on now turned him off. Dave was fed up.

After a little over fifteen minutes of staring down snowflakes and watching the neighbor plow his driveway, Dave began feeling a bit weary. Figuring that since his wife was gone, this would be the perfect time to get in a little early-morning siesta, then wake up refreshed. Before he even got the chance to shut the door, what he saw out of his peripheral was discouraging.

Tracie's Lexus quietly eased its way through their slushy snow-filled driveway. Dave glanced through the crack of the door in pure disgust. *Well, I guess I'll go get me a drink or two* was all that he could say to himself.

When Tracie finally arrived at home from her overnight hiatus that began somewhere close to sevenish the evening before, it was nearing nine the next morning. All night, she'd been out partying carelessly with her new confidant Sleeze and his coterie. The two of them, plus the rest of the clan barhopped and tore clubs up deep into the wee hours. Tracie's concern toward being seen in public with one of her husband's good friends was little, if any, so it seemed. She carelessly took control of every dance floor she stepped upon, raunchily shaking her rotund derriere like a salt shaker. When she wasn't shaking what her mother gave her, she was thirstily sucking down shots of top-shelf liquor like the professional drinker she'd become while hanging out with Teddy.

Eventually, this night too would end like most every other night since that unforgettable time after the comedy club did, with Tracie's legs spread eagle and Sleeze driving his manhood deep within the walls of paradise.

Tracie should've been working for Barnum & Bailey for the past few months the way she acrobatically juggled the three relationships she coexisted in. With Sleeze now at the helm of receiving nearly all the loving she had to offer, Tracie found herself fighting tooth and nail trying to give Dave and Teddy some attention too.

Unlike her husband, Teddy began paying very close attention to Tracie's sudden schedule changes. He immediately noticed things like how her weekends were somehow becoming booked up "all of a sudden." He also noticed the drastic reduction of sex the two were having and their long phone conversations, and they'd too been reduced to curtandry chats.

After two or three call me backs and a few I'll call you laters, Teddy would finally say, "Hell naw, I'm not calling you back, TRACIE! So tell whoeva the fuck you talkin' to, to call you back later. I don't give a fuck who it is."

What had become most trivial to Tracie was her husband's apathy toward everything. To her, it seemed as though the more suspicious Teddy became, the less concerned her husband was. Dave never once called and asked where she was or with whom she was with. He never fussed about the two of them barely having sex. It was like he was in another world or something. Not that his attitude made a difference or would change anything. It just stirred up Tracie's curiosity a bit.

"What the fuck you standin' there lookin like dat fo?" she asked impolitely while stumping her feet on the ceramic tile that sat underneath the sway of the front door, trying to rid the sole of her boots of the slushy snow. She then shut the door behind her.

Lately, Dave and his empire had been experiencing some troubles. The club just wasn't generating the money it once was. His marijuana operation had taken a huge hit ever since his wife and Sleeze had been creeping around. And unfortunately, for Dave, these were the only two sources of income that he had. The depletion of funds, in his mind, had to be the reason his wife was acting like such a bitch. "What choo say?" he asked her, shocked at her tone of voice.

"You heard me. I said what you standin' there lookin' like that fo?"

"Here it is. My wife is out all times of night and walkin' in my house all times of the morning, and she has the nerve to ask me a stupid-ass question like that."

"What?" Tracie said with conviction like she truly hadn't done anything wrong.

"What! What the fuck you mean what? Tracie, you must be a man 'cause you got some big balls. You walk in MY HOUSE AFTER SUNRISE DUN STAYED OUT ALL NIGHT. My silly ass don't even say shit, and you still got nerve enough to ask me some shit like 'What the fuck you standin' there lookin like dat fo?' Girl, you got some HUGE BALLS. H-U-G-E!"

Dave's voice vibrated through the decorated drywall of their ranch house like a tremor. At first glance, Tracie thought she saw her elegant crystal and china glasses shaking inside the curio cabinet.

Yeah, he's pissed now, but I bet he'd really be hot if I told him where I was and with whom I was wit last night, Tracie thought to herself while wrestling with her boots, trying to pull them off her feet. She threw them right next to the front door and then nonchalantly eased her way through the living room, right past her husband, on her way to the bedroom.

"Since you want to be so tough, why don't you take yo tough ass outside and move your car?" he demanded to his wife as she rounded the corner, strutting pompously, like the hallway had become her own personal catwalk. The tan-colored stretch pants that were pasted to her skin shook vigorously with each and every step she made. Her calves, her thighs, her ass—all moved vibrantly as she carefully put one foot in front of the other.

"Dave, you know where the spare key is, and you know how to drive. Move it ya self," she replied sarcastically without even looking back. Knowing his response, or the lack thereof, to her next statement, Tracie curtly said, "Oh, and leave me some money on the table." Before she could count to ten, Dave was gone, and he hadn't left as much as a quarter behind.

CHAPTER TWENTY-THREE

Gazing intensely through a small opening in her venetian blinds that she created with her index finger, Nina watched her new man ease his car away from the curb, next to her apartment building, then drive off into the night traffic. *Damn, that's a helluva man,* she said while quickly plopping her pregnant self down onto the sofa to catch the back end of her favorite primetime sitcom *Girlfriends.* Five or so months of dating, and somehow, Tony still made her heart race faster than a NASCAR.

After softly getting her feet upon the glass coffee table, Nina slumped back into the couch and took a deep breath. Her night out on the town with Tony was frolic and all, but hauling these fifty extra pounds around everywhere they went had definitely begun taken its toll on her. She pressed power on the remote control, and her eyes quickly widened when she saw what was in front of her. Maya seemed to be tearing her favorite character Joan, a new asshole. *What's next?* Nina thought to herself as she looked on in disgust. *First they let go of Toni, and now this. Hell, they might as well do away with the whole damn show!* she spoke to the television set, loud and clear, as if she were looking to receive a response. *They ain't doing nothing but tryna take off all the black sitcoms and replace um with them white ones. Don't nobody wanna watch no* Fashion House?

Nina's uncontested ranting was then interrupted by the tolling cordless phone. *Ring-ring-ring. Ring-ring-ring-ring-ring-ring.* The receiver sat facedown upon the kitchen counter. *Ring-ring-ring.* Wobbling all the way over, she tried her best to get to it and answer it before the caller hung up but to no avail.

Damn, whoeva it is knows I'm pregnant, she exclaimed after pressing the power button, only to hear an unfortunate dial tone.

You would think they'd give me enough time to answer the damn thing.

Nina continued her raving, with the telephone gripped in the palm of her right hand, on her way back to the sofa. The phone rang again. "H-E-L-L-O!"

Her unpleasant tone of voice mirrored the likes of a mad black woman.

Hearing such an irrational tone from the woman he so adored caught Tony off guard. "Hey, baby. What's wrong? Why you sound so upset?"

"Some smart-ass just called here and hung up the phone before giving me a chance to answer it. I mean, damn, whoeva it is gotta know I'm pregnant."

"Baby, that was me. I hung up to give you enough time to get to the phone before I called back," Tony said as he rested his car at the stop light.

"Well, you was 'bout ta get cussed out. You know better than to mess with a pregnant woman while she's tryna watch her favorite program."

The two of them conversed up until close to midnight. During the conversation, Nina was experiencing a few sharp pains here and there and decided that it would be best if they just continued their chat in the morning. Tony agreed.

After a nice long hot shower, Nina scrubbed her pearly whites, wrapped her hair, slathered her caramel-colored skin with aloe vera, slipped into her undies, and headed for bed. Once in bed, she reached over toward the nightstand to make sure her alarm was set, then turned off the lamp light. As she got ready to dig her knees inside of her mattress to pray, another sharp and intense pain shot through her entire body.

"Ouch," she said tenderly before clutching that rock-hard stomach of hers.

She waited a few seconds, hoping the pains would subside, and they did. So she proceeded, "Now I lay me down to sleep, I pray the Lord my soul to keep. If I should die before I awake, I pray to the Lord my soul to take. Our Father who art in heaven, hallowed be thy name. Thy kingdom come. Thy will be done on earth as it is in heaven. Give us this day our daily bread and forgive us our trespasses as we forgive those who trespass against us. Lead us not into temptation but deliver us from evil, for thine is the kingdom, the power, and the glory in the name of Jesus Christ I pray. Amen." Nina recited her prayer slowly and carefully with her eyes shut and her head bowed. Immediately following, she slid between the sheets and the mattress and fell straight to sleep.

Nina wobbled her way through the doors of the *Plain Dealer* the next morning just before seven. The bags she carried with her that sat beneath her eyes were showing signs of a lack of a good night's sleep. Last night had been nothing but a struggle for her. Plagued with what seemed to be endless amounts of sharp intense pains, she tossed and turned uncomfortably nearly all night and all morning. After experiencing a few others while getting herself ready for work, she had almost made a decision to call in sick but then decided against the thought and continued getting dressed.

"Good morning, Nina," one of her female co-workers blurted out as the two of them crossed each other's path going in opposite directions. Nina wasn't in the best of moods, and it was quite obvious in her response. And although she didn't speak nastily, her uninviting tone, which was normally more receptive, spoke volumes.

"Hey, Sherrie," Nina replied curtly as if it were hard for her to speak. As she slowly made her way down the aisle toward the work area she'd been assigned to, she couldn't help but to wonder about the pains she'd been having.

What if they come back? she thought to herself as she set her dark-brown handbag that matched the dark-brown outfit she was wearing next to her computer. *Maybe I shoulda just called off.* Nina managed to ease her oversized fundament into the chair lodged beneath her desk. *I hope them damn pains ain't startin' up again.* Fortunately for her, Nina's time at work went a lot smoother than anticipated.

Before long, she was speeding up the on ramp of I-90 on her way home.

The freeway was packed with rush-hour traffic. Vehicles were literally bumper to bumper, accelerating at an intolerable five miles per hour. The patient drivers sat and waited while traffic continued its snail-like pace. Others illegally rode the shoulder lane until the next exit arose. Nina, who just so happened to be in the midst of some horrifically false labor pains, sat impatiently behind the trailer of a semi-truck.

"Damn, what the hell is going on up there?" she shouted over the soothing voice of American Idol winner Ruben Studdard, seeping its way through the speakers of the car stereo system.

Ten long minutes filled with pure congestion and revving up the engine only to slam on the brakes finally ended when the fast lane began to move. "It's 'bout damn time," Nina said, cautiously weaving through heavy traffic in pursuit of the fast lane.

Nina entered through the back door of her apartment building just after three thirty. Two guys, who were parked a few cars down from her, whistled and tooted at her on her way inside as they sat in a green older-model Chevy Monte Carlo, smoking what looked and smelled—and seemed to her—to be a blunt filled with weed.

"You gone let me stepdaddy sumthin" unfortunately, for her, was the only jargon she could interpret as the two guys continued yelling disrespectful comments.

Nina trudged her way to the front of the building to retrieve her mail, which was shuffled inside her mailbox. Sauntering back toward her door, Nina searched through the mail out of curiosity. Her penetrating eyes lit up immediately when she saw David D. Smith addressed on one of the envelopes. She couldn't stick her key in the door fast enough. Flinging all her things to the couch, Nina tore open the envelope. *Three hundred dollars,* she said disappointingly.

She had become so accustomed to the larger numbers she was starting to get ungrateful. *I guess I can't complain though. Three hundred sho'll beats not getting nothin'.*

Nina scanned around her apartment with the mail still tightly gripped inside of her mitt in total disbelief. Her apartment was filthy. The carpet was filled with what looked to be old potato chip crumbs, blended with dirt. A small pile of dishes from the night before were left stacked inside the sink. Mail from Lord knows how long, along with other miscellaneous paperwork she'd been too lazy to put up or throw away, covered part of the glass coffee table. The more she observed, the worse it began to look. *I'm not finna clean this shit up,* she said, tossing the mail onto the dust-filled coffee table with the rest of it.

Talking to herself was something Nina had adopted during the beginning stages of her pregnancy. Seven months in, she'd become a professional.

Let me go in this kitchen and fix me sumthin' ta eat. On her way toward the kitchen, the phone rang. *This could only be one person,* she said on her way to the phone's base. With her eyes rolled toward the back of her head, she took a deep breath and said, "Not now, Tony. I just got off work, baby. You're starting to become a pest."

Nina grabbed the receiver and gently pressed the power button. "Hello."

"Hey, baby," the caller on the other line said freely. Puzzled at whose voice she was hearing, Nina responded, "Who is this?"

"Dave!"

CHAPTER TWENTY-FOUR

Jay awoke Sunday morning to the legendary sound of the late Luther Vandross singing "Dance with my father again . . ." Luther's voice was lowly and distant as if it were coming from the downstairs stereo. Even from afar, that melodic piano, mixed with the late great sound of Luther's ever-exhilarating voice, soothed Jay's aroused ears. As he listened in on the emotional lyrics to the song, he couldn't help reminiscing about his past, which caused him to have mixed emotions.

The more Jay thought about his past, recollecting how he was raised, the more he thought about his father and their uncanny resemblance. His facial structure, his complexion, his grade of hair, and his stature—all matched those of his old man. *Damn, I look just like that man,* he said as he peeked at himself in the mirror.

His father passing down his genes to him was not one of the reasons Jay was upset with him; he was mad about his father's attitude toward life and the way he treated people. Jay's father had this I-don't-care-about-anybody attitude; and unfortunately, that attitude affected everybody around him, especially the people that loved him. He abused Jay's mom and got her hooked on damn near every drug manufactured. He had Jay and lived up to his fatherly duties for all of a day. He stole, cheated, and lied to everyone else, not caring what bridges he burned or whom he crossed. At first, Jay would always say to himself and his Big Ma, "I'm never going to be like that"; but as time went on, he was starting to pick up minute characteristics. The most notable one was they both sold marijuana and at a very young age. Jay hadn't thought about it before, but while reminiscing, it struck him that that was something that he and the old man had in common. Then, there was the child and the girlfriend. Just like his pops, he too was about to have a child with a beautiful young woman who loved him to no end. Jay, though, afraid that he might end up like him, vowed not to become the person his father was. He loved his woman dearly and couldn't imagine hurting her. And his unborn child, his connection with it, was untraceable. Hurting these two people, like his father once did, was something he just couldn't envision. He also couldn't see becoming the renowned "marijuana dealer" that his old man had become, but he had. Something had to give. Something had to change—and fast—before his life spiraled out of control, and he wound up being the exact same scumbag that donated sperm for him.

"Jay," Candace hollered. Then she hollered it again, nearly to the top of her lungs this time. Jay sat at the foot of the bed with his head hunched over. He was so engrossed in his thoughts that he didn't even notice Candace walking through the threshold of the bedroom. "You okay, baby?" she asked with concern while watching Jay slowly lift his head up to look her dead between her eyes. Jay had quickly switched his focus and was now daydreaming about the time he'd slapped that crispy $10 bill on top of that counter. It had seemed like just yesterday to him. Now with that same woman, he had conceived a child.

"Yeah, I'm okay. Why you ask me that?" he asked, scared that she could see through his soul and spot all the mixed emotions he struggled with.

"'Cause I've been calling your name ever since I started up the stairs. I was trying to tell you that I made you some breakfast. It's downstairs on the kitchen table."

"Thanks, baby," Jay expressed before palming the back of his head. With the same hand, he gently traced down the back of his neck, then inhaled and exhaled deeply.

Jay's body language was still insinuating to Candace that something was wrong. So she stood in front of him, watching intensely, and inquired, "Baby, you sure you're okay? 'Cause it seems to me like something's truly bothering you."

Jay took hold of Candace's hands and pulled her close. Still sitting on the edge of the bed, he wrapped his arms around her waist, kissed her stomach, and then squeezed her tightly. "Baby, you know I love you, right?"

"Of course, silly, why would you ask me something foolish like that?" Candace's arms were around Jay's head. Her now enlarged breasts were smashed up against his forehead.

"Because I dunno. I was just thinking about my father, me becoming a father, and a husband and all that."

"Relax, baby. You're going to be a great father and a great husband too. Trust me."

"If it's up to me, I'ma be there every step of the way 'cause I do not want my child to have to go through what I went through with my parents. I mean, who knows where I woulda been without Big Ma?"

"Gone downstairs and eat cha food," Candace insisted just before planting a soft kiss on Jay's lips. "And you make sure you leave all that worrying to me."

CHAPTER TWENTY-FIVE

The late-afternoon sky was clear and still as blue as the ocean's seashore. Not a ray of sunlight could be spotted for miles. Surprisingly, the bleached-white snow upon the sidewalks had been a helping culprit in keeping the streets lit.

Side streets were filled with kids playing blissfully. The day just seemed so pure and innocent. The breeze from the wind was even light and easy enough to handle. Despite all the dirty snow, flinging filthily from beneath the treading of car tires, most every vehicle on the road somehow managed to remain clean.

"Damn, man, ya'll picked a helluva time to wanna quit on me," Dave said as he pressed upon the gas pedal, coasting through the light, as it changed from red to green.

The New Year hadn't started off so great for Dave. The government had just passed a new law in November that took effect in January, banning public facility smoking in Ohio. This hurt many of the local bars and clubs, Dave's being one. This public statue, along with a few changes as far as female dancers went, had his club faltering heavily in service revenues.

Now with this new problem arising, Dave's patience was beginning to wear thin.

"Well, can't we just restructure the contract?" His eyes, along with his mind, were on everything but the road as he drove a hasty forty-five miles per hour down Harvard Avenue on his way to the club. One minute he's playing with the radio trying to shift CDs in the changer; and the next he was leaning over the passenger side, rummaging through the glove compartment for his Cleveland Brown's lighter.

"So I guess there isn't too much I can say to convince ya'll to stay then, huh?"

He lit the perfectly rolled cigarillo, sitting inside of his ashtray, with the lighter. After rolling back the sunroof, he took a long drag from the blunt. "Okay then," Dave said to the manager of the BDS, a.k.a. Big Dick Slangers, after realizing their leaving was nonnegotiable, "if you ever have a change of heart, though, just know that my door is always open."

Losing his Wednesday-night male act was definitely going to be a huge blow especially since business as of late had already become somewhat stagnant. Not only had the club's income slowed down a bit, Sleeze had been unable to come through for them on their usual packages.

Sleeze had been telling the two of them for the past few weeks that he was out. Dave didn't believe him, but there was little he could do about it since Sleeze was the only person he and Jay ever dealt with.

"Sleeze, wuz up?" Dave said after dialing him up on his phone.

"You ain't heard nuthin' new yet, huh?"

"Nah, man. Ain't nuttin' changed. Believe me, when it does, you'd be da first tah know. Yuh'ear me?"

Yeah right, Dave thought to himself as he drove into the gated parking lot of his club. Sleeze hadn't even attempted to call Dave ever since a few days after the comedy show. The only time he'd heard from Sleeze was when he called Sleeze. Even then, Sleeze made Dave feel like those calls were pestering.

After parking the truck, Dave shut off the engine then just sat. His intentions were to go inside and help his crew open up the club, but life's trials, along with the weed, had become so overwhelmingly depressing he couldn't find the strength to rise up from the leather chair. He threw his head back against the headrest and shut his reddened eyes as small clouds of marijuana smoke began seeping its way through the opening of the sunroof.

Wuz up, family? Dave expressed in a loud tone as he tried his best to speak over the stentorian sound of the speakers just above his head. After musing for nearly an hour inside his truck, he finally made his way inside the club to help his employees open up. Fifteen minutes in, somehow, Dave still had earlier problems on his mind.

"You talk to Sleeze lately?" he asked, eager to hear Jay's response.

"Speak up. I can't hear you."

"HAVE YOU SPOKEN TO SLEEZE LATELY?"

"Naw, I ain't talked to that cat in about two weeks. But listen," Jay insisted, chiming in hesitantly as the bass in his normally deep voice suddenly began airing out like a deflating balloon. When Jay first called Dave, Sleeze was the last thing on Jay's mind. The things he had on his heart to tell Dave far outweighed Sleeze, money, weed, or anything else for that matter—or so he thought. His voice cracking with every word proceeding from his mouth, Jay struggled to tell his best friend the disturbing news he had been informed of. "Man, I don't even know how to tell you this."

"TELL ME WHAT! NIGGA JUST SAY IT," Dave shouted, eager to hear what the only person that really ever cared about him, besides his parents and his pregnant mistress, had to say.

"Man, I was down at Monroe's last night, right? This same crazy shit 'cause you know I'm normally sleep round this time, right? But N-E-ways, I'm down there having a few drinks with them you niggas off the top, and one of um got to talking about Tracie. So I'm like 'Tracie who?' but in an inviting tone, so he wouldn't recognize my true motives. And dude was like the one with the white Lexus."

"Oh yeeeah! What he say about her?" Dave's eager voice was completely smothered in nervousness. He tried his best to disguise it, but it was just too obvious.

"Some shit about that's his bitch and how he heard she was fuckin' some nigga wit a Benz. He got ta talkin' 'bout how he wanna fuck her up."

"How you know if he was talkin' about her, though?" Dave interrupted.

"'Cause the nigga was even talkin' about you! I'm guessin' he didn't know who I was 'cause he was just spillin' shit out. He was holl'n, talkin' 'bout she got a husband, the nigga owns a club, and he be fuckin her while her husband be at his club. Man, dude was talkin' real crazy."

"So tell me this, though. How could the dude know me but not know you? Man, now you know that's some bullshit." In a sigh of relief, Dave began giggling.

His weakened voice still seemed extremely frail and mellow. Jay-Z's song "Dig a Hole" was nearly drowning him out completely.

Dave contemplated heavily on the things Jay said as he sat silently on the other end of the phone line, waiting on Jay's response to his question.

His festering anger was evident to the concerned employees. They watched him pace back and forth unconsciously behind the bar for most of the conversation. After realizing Jay was not going to respond, out of anger and pure disgust, Dave berated his best friend with a series of questions, "And, man, why you wait so late to tell me anyways? You coulda told me dis shit when you first got up. Damn, man, I thought we was supposed to be niggas? I mean don't choo think it woulda been a lot smarter to tell me in the morning while it was still fresh on your mind and I'm at home with this bitch?"

"Wait, wait, wait, hol' up, bruh!" Jay demanded, aggressively halting the tirade.

"You actin' like I did something wrong here. You need to be checking your wife, bruh, not me!"

Silence crept its way through the phone line. Dave didn't speak another word for over thirty seconds; Jay didn't either. The music in the background even faded slowly.

Dave was oblivious to everything, except for the horrid thoughts now lurking through his mind. How the possibility of some young punk having his wife bent up in every direction was more of a reality now than ever before and not just one punk but apparently two. Dave's life flashed before his eyes. All the years he and Tracie spent together—both as friends and lovers, husband and wife—were up for question now. Dave could think of nothing else to say now to his friend but "Man, my fault. I'm trippin'. I guess . . . I guess, I am taking it out on the wrong person, huh?"

"Man, don't worry about it. I know that's a hard pill to swallow."

"Hell yeah, it is. But hey, I'ma get back wit you after I call this woman, aight? Oh, by the way, what was dude's name again?" Dave immediately dialed Tracie's cell phone.

His index finger shook nervously as he cautiously pressed each number. It took about four complete rings; then Tracie finally answered.

"H e y,   b a b y ."
Young Jeezy's raspy "Yeeeeah" adlib clouded Dave's end of the line. She could hardly hear his response.

"Baby, I can't hear you. What did you say?"

"I said I'm on my way home. Be there when I get there."

"For what?"

"'Cause I said so."

PART 4

CHAPTER TWENTY-SIX

Jayson Hill Jr. was born at 5:00 a.m., March 12, 2007, at Hillcrest Medical Center to the proud parents of Jayson Hill Sr. and Candace Michele Jones.

Just like his daddy, Big Jay, little Jay was born with a full head of extremely good hair. His eyes were a pretty light brown. His complexion, tan, just like his mother's.

Big Jay never left the room one time while his son was being born. He watched Candace intensely as she strained, screamed, pushed, and called on Jesus on a number of occasions during labor. Until he saw the miracle of his son's head easing its way out of Candace's vaginal passage, though, Jay assumed labor to be nothing more than a complete overburden.

The doctors let Jay cut his son's umbilical cord. Tears streaked down the sides of his face as he snipped nervously at his newborn's flesh.

"Baby, you a Soulja," he yelled out to Candace as the doctor wiped the baby clean of the blood, cleaned his nose and mouth, then wrapped him inside of some pure white blankets. They handed little Jay over to Big Jay. Jay's excitement was very visible. He looked on in pure amazement as his son screamed as loud as his underdeveloped lungs would let him.

"Let me see um, Jay," Candace asked anxiously.

As the mild celebration continued, Jay's Big Ma, whose ailing body somehow still managed to get around quite well, had come to enjoy every single minute of it. Watching her grandchild and his girlfriend bask in their creation was somewhat surreal to her. It was something she hadn't gotten the chance to experience with her own children. After surveying the hospital room with aging eyesight, Big

Ma removed her pop-bottle-sized glasses, lowered her gray-haired head, shut her eyelids, and prayed a blessing over the proud new parents and their precious child.

Candace's mom, however unfortunate, looked on in pure resentment. For some reason, she just couldn't find it in her hardened heart to like or accept Jay as a part of her daughter's life. She just didn't believe Jay to be worthy of her daughter. "Ma, do you wanna hold the baby?" Candace asked her mother.

"Naw, that's okay, baby," her mother shunned as her countenance slipped and fell from the sudden invitation from her daughter to hold her first grandchild. Her mother then looked over at Jay in disgust and grunted as Jay stood over Candace and the baby, showering the both of them with endless kisses. Jay was proud to be a father, and there wasn't a thing she could do about it.

CHAPTER TWENTY-SEVEN

Almost two weeks had come and gone since Candace and Jay had their son Lil Jay. In which time, Dave hadn't seen or heard from his best friend, except for when he stopped up for a visit at the hospital and when Jay made that ecstatic phone call informing of Lil Jay's birth. Dave understood his friend's avoidance, though. In fact, he was careful himself not to even call unless under extreme circumstances to give him and his family some much-needed time alone.

Coincidentally, for the past two weeks or so, Dave had been waiting eagerly for a similar phone call concerning his own child. Nina, whose due date was over four days old, was expecting to have her child any minute now. She had been calling Dave periodically ever since the date lapsed. With every phone call she made to him, both their conversations reeked of anxiousness.

"You ready to be a father?" she would ask him. She'd then express her nervousness by saying, "David, I'm scared." This affection, however minute, was rare and hadn't been practiced by the two of them since back when they were together. Dave was definitely enjoying every second of it, and strangely enough, boyfriend and all, so was Nina.

Fresh from the Marriott Hotel that he'd been shacking at off and on for some two months now, Dave drove his truck into his driveway and parked directly behind his now-estranged wife Tracie's Lexus. He was shocked to see that she was even at home. Ever since the fight the two of them had gotten into after Dave allegedly found out about her promiscuity, she too had been in and out of their home like a robbery.

Dave entered his home and walked right past Tracie like she didn't even exist—no hi, how are you doing, or anything. The two didn't speak one word to each other. Well, at least not until Tracie's pitchy morning voice yelled belligerently, "Damn, nigga, you could've at least spoke, wit ch'yo ignorant ass!"

Dave just ignored her harsh remarks and made his way toward their bedroom. He was on a mission to get a few articles of clothing from his closet to hold him over at the hotel. Tracie, following as closely behind as possible, just continued her rage of bickering and carrying on. Fed up with her berating, Dave turned toward his wife and yelled, "Tracie, shut the fu—just shut up."

"You SHUT THE HELL UP!" she screamed back as she grabbed hold of the front of her lavender gown, trying to cover up her visible and obviously large breasts. "So what, every time you hear a rumor or some bullshit concerning me, you gon just up and leave, huh? That's some shit a woman would do!"

Everything that Tracie was saying was spot-on, and Dave knew it.

Running away from the situation was not going to make it any better.

In fact, it was only going to do for their relationship what they so dreaded just a few years ago: tear it apart. "So what we gon do David, huh?" Tracie asked submissively, following him down the basement steps and over toward the washer and dryer.

"Are you gon' come home or what, baby? 'Cause I miss you."

Her soothing words penetrated Dave's soul but not like they once would've. Her voice was so soft and childish, almost like when they were teenage friends. He could feel the heat from her body inching up from behind him as he checked the dryer for the whites he'd put inside there a few days prior.

"Boo, you know I put them whites inside your drawer already," Tracie conveyed, seductively as she bent over and wrapped her arms around Dave's torso. Her voluptuous breasts rested comfortably on the small of his back. With her hands searching the crotch of his pants, Tracie desperately tried to wake the savage beast.

"Tracie, c'mon now! What choo doin'?" Dave fought his best fight trying to ward off Tracie's sexual advances, but watching that lavender gown fall gracefully from her otherwise naked body was just too much for him to bear. He quickly slipped out of his blue jeans and button-down polo shirt and then stood anxiously in front of his wife wearing a bright-white T-shirt and likewise boxer shorts. Almost immediately, his rock-hard johnson forced itself from behind the slit in his underwear. Tracie licked her succulent lips thirstily as she prepared her throat to take in all nine inches of him.

Dave leaned as far back on the dryer as possible as his wife dropped to her knees in hot pursuit. "Damn, Tracie," he moaned as she began licking the tip of him like a lollipop. The tingling sensation that his body felt was uncanny. *Why now?* he thought to himself. *Why would she wait all this time to become spontaneous?* Tracie's gorgeous skin tone began glowing from the exuding perspiration seeping from her pores. She tried gripping Dave's thighs, but her tips were just slippery. So instead, she took hold of his dick and swallowed it, sucking back and forth sloppily.

"Wait a minute, baby, "Dave managed to say with what little breath he could muster. Using both hands, he aggressively grabbed her beneath her underarms and pulled her to her feet. Then he shoved his tongue inside of her mouth.

"How you want it, daddy?" she asked sensually after somehow managing to break their passionate lip-lock.

Dave threw Tracie's healthy body against the dryer, made his way inside her slippery cave, and began stroking unconsciously. Melodramatic moans forced their way out of lips as she struggled to hold herself up by the edges. Her breast bounced up and down rhythmically. Her hair flung around wildly. The excess flesh upon her thighs jiggled loosely.

With his arms clenching her sweaty thighs, Dave flexed his toned-up muscles and continued digging into his estranged wife. His climax became more visible with each and every stroke.

"David . . . put a baby in me," Tracie pleaded in the heat of passion after falling forward and wrapping her arms around him. She dug her nails deep inside the skin of his back as the strokes became more and more intense. Finally, Dave culminated, shooting everything he had, built up within his loins, into Tracie.

"So did you think about what I said earlier?" Tracie inquired while lying in the bed, underneath the blanket with Dave right next to her; he had dozed off over twenty minutes ago while Tracie just lay there in deep thought. Reflections of their marriage, her infidelity, and all their disagreements clouded her mind for what seemed like forever. Part of her wanted Dave to come back home where he belonged, but then there was another part of her that had fallen too far for Sleeze.

She knew that messing around with someone so close to home, like Sleeze, was like playing Russian roulette with her life, but it was just too late. She had gone way too far to turn back now. "David!" she shouted with aggression after he unintentionally ignored her to continue counting sheep. "I know you heard me!"

"What, Tracie? DAG!"

"I asked you a question. Now, answer it."

"I must've been asleep when you asked, so that would mean I didn't hear you. Now what choo want?"

Tracie turned her body toward his, then tucked the blanket underneath her armpit. "I said what did you think about what I said earlier?"

"What did you say earlier? I can't remember."

"David, come on now. You know what I said about you moving back in and us starting over. What did you think about it?"

After a long pause, he said, "I don't know if that would be a good idea, Tracie. Maybe we both should just take things slow, you know. I feel as though there's a lot of things we still have to discuss, and until we can sit down and do that—you know, face the truth—we'd both be doing ourselves a grave big injustice."

The look on Tracie's face was one of pure perplexity. She was hurt. She couldn't believe that her husband had the audacity to say such a thing after what they had just finished doing. She sucked his dick sloppier, nastier, and better than she had ever done before. She totally submitted herself to him sexually, and this was the result. Bullshit! "So what then? What's next?" Tracie curtly asked before being rudely interrupted by the ringing of Dave's cell phone on the dresser.

"Hello?" Dave said, ignoring Tracie's question.

"Okay. I'm on my way." And without so much as an explanation, Dave threw on some clothes and shoes and told Tracie, "Baby, I'll see you later. I gotta take care of some business." He stormed out of the door.

CHAPTER TWENTY-EIGHT

After hastily making his way into University Hospital's parking lot, Dave flew dangerously through the narrow lanes and crookedly parked his truck next to an older-model two-toned Lexus and a gray Honda Civic.

He then jumped out and ran recklessly toward the hospital, weaving in and out of parked cars, grazing bumpers along the way. All that he could think about was Nina's panicking voice, screaming, "Dave, my water just broke. We're about to have the baby." Even him having passionate sex with his estranged wife and discussing a possible return to his domain couldn't overpower the connection he felt to Nina and their life that she hoarded in her stomach.

Dave broke the threshold of both automatic sliding doors and then power walked over to the information desk. "Can you tell me what room Shanina Tucker is in? She's having my baby," he said, gasping and panting while nervously conveying everything to a high-yellow assistant, whose focus was more on the painting of her fingernails than assisting anyone.

"The delivery room is about halfway down that hall and to your right, sir." Before the indifferent assistant could verify his name, Dave was down the hallway and gone. With anxiety exuding his person, he rushed down the inner hallway, hoping to see a sign or a trace of anything resembling a delivery room.

Damn, I think that was it there, he said after he unknowingly walked right by it. While he turned back toward the delivery room to enter, something came over Dave. Butterflies consumed his stomach. His salivating mouth began to dry up. Things quickly became blurry.

"Sir, are you looking for someone?" the nurse asked while exiting the same doors that Dave's now-feeble body was so scared to enter.

"Yeah, I'm looking for Sha . . . Shanina Tucker's room. She's having my baby."

"Well, sir, you're in luck' cause she's in this room right here." Dave began making his way into the delivery room, but before he could completely cross the threshold, he noticed out of his peripheral the familiar face of a guy that he once saw.

I know that guy from somewhere, he said to himself, then entered the room.

When Dave entered the delivery room, it's nearly filled to capacity. Both doctors and nurses were strategically positioned around Nina. Her mother stood just behind the commotion, looking on equivocally. Equipment scattered about the room, making it hard for a layperson to come any closer from where they stood. Nina, whose sweaty face brightened ever so slightly when she noticed Dave's entrance, lay painfully amid the tumult while doctors and nurses uttered in unison, "Push, Nina! Push! That's good."

With her legs bent at the knees and spread apart, Nina grabbed hold of the side of the bed, took a deep breath, and then pushed. Her screams and moans could be heard from outside the room. She pushed and pushed for nearly five minutes until the most beautiful and precious life-form squirmed out of her stretched vaginal passage.

Dave looked at Nina in total amazement. She gazed back at him in full relief. Their baby boy had finally been born.

"Where's my son at, Nina?" Dave curtly inquired while sitting atop the catholically stiff mattress that the Marriott Hotel provided. Ever since Lil Kevin Smith was born a little over two weeks ago, Dave couldn't stop thinking about him. He could still hear his son's feeble cry from the last visit out to Nina's.

Lately, for Dave, all the things that had once been so constant, so sure, and so reliable now seemed to be in total disarray. His marriage was all but over. His disconcerted living quarters, although his name was still on the lease of his and his wife's house, were now the inside of a mediocre hotel room. His club was suffering tremendously, and his illicit drug activity had all but been put to a halt. The only thing that was constant—and that he was sure of—was that he now had an innocent child who would depend on his love, support, nourishment, and affection for the rest of his natural life.

This fact alone was what kept him emotionally stable.

"Where do you think he's at, David? He's in his crib." Nina knew Dave's true intention behind asking about his son. Yes, a part of it was genuinely wanting to know about the well-being of his child, but another part of him was curious as to who was around him too.

"Now, is that the real reason you called?"

"Yeah, that and I wanna know what nigga you got over there with my lil man. Oh, Nina, let me ask you this question too," he said while rising up off the bed to walk toward the window. "Why did you have that dude at the hospital with you while you were having my son?"

The sudden but potent question startled Nina to the point where she nearly burned herself of the bottle that she had been heating up for Lil Kevin. After gaining her composure, she answered with a question, "Dave, come on now, you on that? I told you that he was already over my house. Shit, at least, he was nice enough to take me to the hospital. I mean, he didn't have to, considering that that wasn't his child that I was carrying. Since we're on asking questions this morning, I got one for you," she shot back quickly.

"What?"

"Did you tell Tracie that you had Lil Kev yet?" Nina knew that asking that question plus personalizing it by saying their son's name would only intensify the guilt that Dave would have had he not told Tracie.

"Come on now, Nina, you know I ain't told Tracie about Lil Kev." Guilt rushed toward him immediately just as Nina had anticipated. Even with Tracie's cheating and him moving out of the house, telling Tracie about some baby he's had with another woman was a no-no, at least for right now anyways. Dave knew, though, that he couldn't hide it forever. Eventually, the light would shine upon his dark deeds. He just hoped that he'd be ready to answer and explain himself when time came.

After his and Nina's long conversation, that spanned from their child to the remote possibility of them getting back together, Dave then threw on a brown-and-blue short-sleeved Polo shirt, some blue khakis, and a pair of suede loafers and headed out to his Navigator.

Upon keying the ignition and pulling out of the hotel parking lot, he immediately fired up the blunt of hydro that he'd copped last night from one of the young hustlers off Brightwood. He'd only smoked part of the blunt the night before, and he was so high that he had to put it out and head to bed.

Dave, taking two hard pulls of the blunt, let the smoke roll from his mouth to his nostrils, exhaled slowly, then put it back into the ashtray. He then grabbed the remote control to his car stereo and then turned the volume up nearly to its zenith.

He bobbed his head slightly as Jay-Z uttered the words "Thirty's the new twenty. Nigga, I'm so hot still . . ."

After driving for a ways, Dave began to contemplate heavily about his current position in life. The state of his marriage, his club, him living out of a hotel room, even his finances, as well as the condition of his truck for some reason were starting to annoy him. As for the truck, it wasn't like the Navi had lost its luster or anything.

His problem with the truck was that it was nearly four years old.

He'd already seen countless versions of the newer addition too. Dave reminisced back to when he and Jay first bought the Navi and the Escalade and how they had the whole city in AW, especially when they painted them and put sounds, rims, and TVs in them too.

That's what it is, Dave said to himself, having an epiphany while pulling up to the light at Hayden and St. Clair.

I need to step my game back up. Just then, a black-on-black with black 22-inch rims Bentley GT pulled up beside him. Dave took a deep breath and then reluctantly nodded his head. *Yup, that's what it is. I've got to step my game back up.*

CHAPTER TWENTY-NINE

"Jay," Candace yelled halfheartedly to her boyfriend who was getting dressed for work.

"Baby, I need you to grab me a Pampers out the back room closet before you come up, okay?"

Damn! Wuz wrong wit him? Jay asked as he walked up on his child screaming obnoxiously.

"He dun boo-booed on himself." Jay then handed the Pampers to Candace. While wiping between her son's legs and coating him with baby powder, Candace managed to convey to Big Jay that she was planning on going to work soon and that the two of them would probably need to find a babysitter.

"Why can't choo ask you mom if she'll babysit him?"

"Jay, come on now, you know how my mother is. Shoot, the last thing I need right now is for her to say something nasty toward my chile. You already know I'll disown 'er," she said, chuckling.

"Come on, baby, you ain't giving your momma enough credit," Jay retorted, looking anxious to exit.

"Girl, dunno black woman in the world dislike their grandchild. I don't care if she like the father or not."

As Jay reached for the doorknob in anticipation of leaving, Candace said, "What about your grandmother?"

"I dunno about Big Ma. She getting up there." After pausing, Jay said with authority, "Candace, call yo' momma and ask her. If she says no, we'll figure sumthin' out. Plus, I need to talk to her anyways."

"You want me to call her now?"

"I don't care when you call her. Just make sure it's sumtime today. Don't forget to tell her I need to talk to her too."

"Okay, baby," she replied, reluctantly while watching her man walk out of the front door. Candace hesitantly grabbed the phone, then began calling her mother. *I dunno why this boy insists on letting my momma watch our baby,* Candace thought to herself while dialing her mom's number.

And what does he want to talk to my momma fo? she spoke softly before being interrupted by the sound of her mother's voice.

"Hello, Momma."

"Yeees," her mother curtly responded.

After a moment of awkward silence, Candace said, "Momma, I have to ask you something." Her mother didn't respond. Candace just continued, "Well, Momma, I'm planning on going back to work soon, and you know that Jay works from seven in the morning till six or seven at night—"

"So what are you trying to say, Candace?" her mother said unemotionally. Candace's mother knew exactly what Candace was trying to say. In fact, her mother was surprised that it had taken Candace this long to ask. She had been expecting this call for the last several weeks.

"Well, Momma, I was just wondering if you had time to babysit my son. I'll pay you." As Candace's mom began to answer, Candace hastily interrupted her, saying, "Momma I can understand if you say no. I just didn't want to take my son to any ole body."

"Well," her mother said, with a huge smirk upon her face, "I guess I can watch him for a few days." Candace's mother had been waiting on this invitation for quite some time unbeknownst to Candace. In fact, she was taken that her answer would surprise her daughter, but what she didn't know was what Candace was about to say next.

"Thank you, Momma. I'll call you back later to let choo know when. Oh, and Jay told me to tell you that he has to talk to you." Candace was so excited that she accidentally hung up the phone on her mother.

Jay wants to talk to me. What the hell he wanna talk to me fo? her mother said loudly as she stood stiff-looking puzzled with the receiver still pressed up against her hear.

Jay and his crew finished painting and putting the shingles on the roof of the house that they were rehabbing at around six o'clock in the evening. Candace had called Jay not even thirty minutes earlier to relay the good news about her mother wanting to watch the baby. "Did you tell her that I wanted to talk to her?" he had asked her.

"Yes, baby," Candace replied.

While sitting at the drive-thru window, waiting on the six-pack of Heineken he had just ordered, Jay called Candace's mom. "Hello, Ms. Jones," he said in a timorous tone of voice.

"Yeees," she replied back. Before long, the two of them were engaged in a very cordial conversation. And to Jay's surprise, Candace's mom was much nicer and a lot more receptive than he could've ever imagined.

"Thank you, Ms. Jones. You really made this a lot easier than I expected," Jay said. Then, the two of them hung up the phone.

CHAPTER THIRTY

"Cedric," Tracie screeched in a slightly frantic tone of voice, "quit playing so much now. Slow this thing down." Sleeze had just purchased a new candy-apple-red Aston Martin nearly a week ago, and he was anxious to see what it possessed under its hood. What better way to do that, he thought, than with a beautiful woman like Tracie, riding shotgun? Sleeze whisked his car methodically through the highway traffic, on 271, doing well over one hundred miles per hour. Tracie, gripping the armrest firmly, gazed out of the window in amazement.

"Do you see the look on these people's faces when you pass them by?"

The two of them rode for a while, then headed back to Sleeze's restaurant.

"Baby, can you have someone bring me out a catfish dinner? I'm kinda hungry."

About ten minutes later, one of the waitresses set Tracie's fish dinner and soft drink on the table. Sleeze, unconsciously following closely behind the waitress, sat down at the table opposite Tracie.

"Why don't cha eat in da back?" Sleeze asked Tracie before leaning in and stealing a kiss from her.

"I dunno. I guess I just feel like eating out here. Is that okay wit choo?"

"It's okay wit me, baby girl," Sleeze said, tittering at Tracie's innocuous remark. After briefly looking out of the window at the setting of the sun, Sleeze then got up and went back into his office, leaving Tracie all alone.

* * *

"Damn, this baby's kinda fillin' up quick, ain't it?" Dave asked his bartenders as he helped them do the usual rotating of the liquor and things.

"Yea. It hasn't filled up this early in a long time," one responded back.

Seeing the Reason this packed during happy hour was a beautiful sight to Dave especially since his regulars weren't due to come in till the strippers began to dance at 9:00 p.m.

"Can you handle the rest of this?" Dave then asked his bartender in hopes that she'd say yes. Dave was feeling really good, and for some reason, he just wanted to jump into his truck and ride.

"Yes. I think I can handle it, Dave," the bartender reluctantly responded, hoping that Dave could hear her disinclined spirit. Unfortunately for her, he took her for her word.

"Okay then. I'm finna make a run. I'll be right back, all right?"

Dave jumped into his Navigator and headed up to Harvard. With no particular destination in mind, he just rode.

With the music blaring and his mind preoccupied with all the events that had transpired earlier that day, Dave was fortunate to see his phone, which sat in between his cup holder, flashing the words *Jay*.

"What up, homie?" Dave said after pressing the Alt button on his remote control to semi-silence the humming coming from the back of his truck.

"Shit, my nigga. I'm just callin' to check up on you. Make sure Lil Kev ain't runnin' you ragged," Jay responded.

"Hell, I need to be the one checkin' up on you for that one. You must've forgotten my son doesn't live with me," Dave said, chuckling.

After jesting back and forth with Dave for a few minutes, Jay finally got to the significance of his call. He told Dave about how he and Candace's mother had finally resolved their differences and how eager Candace's mom was to watch the baby. Jay also told Dave about the surprise party that he and Candace's mom had planned for Candace at the Civic Center.

After receiving his verbal invitation with gratitude, Dave unconsciously changed the subject. "Man, Jay, I think I'm 'bout to switch da game up on deez niggas."

"Switch the game up? How? Nigga, what da fuck is you talkin' 'bout?"

"Nigga, come on now, read between the lines," Dave said and then huffed.

"Man, 'bout a week ago, I'm at the light on Hayden in the Clair, and I run into this nigga in a Bentley on twenty-twos, black on black with black rims. The bitch was niiice, right?"

"Right, right."

"So anyways, I nod. Then he nods. I go my way, and he goes his. Well, coincidentally, I run in to the same guy again today at the car wash on MLK off Corlett."

"Oh yeah!"

"Yeah," Dave retorted as he pulled up to the light on Lee and Harvard.

"Only this time, we exchange names and numbers, and somehow or another, we get ta talkin' business. I get ta tellin' him about Sleeze and how shit ain't the same, and he tells me how he can make it better."

"You didn't say dude's name, did you?" Jay said with discontent, fearing Dave may have told him Sleeze's handle.

"Come on, man, you know me better than that. But listen, though, dude was talkin' really sweet, and I wanted to know before I do my thang if you wanted in or not."

"Man, Dave, I'm gone sit this one out, my nigga. I think it's 'bout time for me to take it somewhere else."

With a tone of disbelief, Dave retorted, "Take it somewhere else? What choo on, Jay? I know you ain't squarin' up on me."

"Yea, if that's what you wanna call it. Dave, ya nigga is getting tired. I gotta focus on Lil Jay now."

"Focus on Lil Jay? Nigga, you actin' like I ain't gotta lil one to focus on. Man, I'm 'bout to go hard," Dave said just before riding past Carolina's.

As Dave glanced to the right of him, he could see the extremely bright-red paint job on what looked to him like a new Aston Martin.

Seeing that flawless Aston parked out front of Sleeze's restaurant instantly made Dave a bit envious. All that Dave could think about was the possibility of that being Sleeze's new car. If it was, that was all the more reason for Dave to step his car game all the way up.

While making a right onto the street immediately after Carolina's to park and confabulate with Sleeze, Dave unintentionally screamed into the phone, "I know this nigga Sleeze ain't bought no Aston Martin!"

"What choo say, wit ch'yo loud ass? I can't hear shit choo sayin'. Your phone is breakin' up."

"Naw, I was saying that I think this nigga Sleeze dun copped an Aston Martin on the candy-apple-red side. Jay, let me ring you back after I finish hollerin' at this nigga."

After parking his car beside the building, Dave rushed anxiously over to the car then meticulously scanned it. "This muthafucca is COLD! And he got twenty-twos on 'em. Man, he killin' um," Dave shouted aloud with intensity as if talking directly to someone.

Dave then left the car to enter Carolina's. With his mind preoccupied with talking to Sleeze, he walked straight over to the takeout register and asked one of the servers, "Can you tell Cedric to come out here please?"

The server then walked back to the kitchen to get Sleeze, but before Sleeze could make his way to the dining room, Dave turned around and spotted his wife, Tracie, stuffing her face with a healthy piece of fish. She had been so engrossed in her meal that she didn't even notice Dave mosey his way up to the register.

"Tracie," Dave shouted with a perplexing look upon his face. "WHAT DA FUCK YOU DOIN' UP HERE?" he said in a low tone. Just as he was starting to approach her table, Sleeze appeared from out of the back, unaware that Dave had just called Tracie's name.

Dave's primary reason for entering "Carolina's" was to congratulate Sleeze on his new ride, but that had all been a distant memory. All he could imagine now was horrific thoughts, like the possibility of Sleeze and his wife creeping around. What if he's fucking her? What if she sucked his dick? *You trippin', Dave. She's just eating here.* Dave's mind wondered back and forth about all the potentials, and then he just flipped.

All the customers eating and drinking inside the restaurant looked on apprehensively as a now-heated Dave tramped aggressively toward Tracie. They could recognize the furious look upon his scrunched-up face as he stared through Tracie's soul. They could feel the anger exuding his person as his skin began brightening and his eyes began watering. With his fist balled, and his upper lip and nostril turned upward, Dave, who stood over Tracie, confused and vexed, asked, "What the fuck you doin' up here? And don't say no bullshit either 'cause I'm not in the mood."

Jumping to conclusions was the exact thing that Dave didn't want to do, but his emotions couldn't be contained.

Trembling at her heels, Tracie chewed her food nervously while thinking of a plausible excuse. The only one she could manage to come up with, though, was "What choo mean what am I doin' here? I'm eating. What it look like I'm doin?"

"Since when you start eating up here?" With the tension escalating rapidly, Sleeze looked on with trepidation, wondering whether or not he should intervene or let Dave and Tracie handle it responsibly. After realizing that the two of them weren't going to be able to resolve things by themselves, Sleeze began making his way over to the table.

"I ain't gotta take this shit. I'm gone," Tracie screamed, thrusting herself from the chair.

"Gone where, Tracie? Yo' car ain't out there," Dave said after realizing that he had never seen her car.

"What the fuck! You think I'm stupid? Ain't no Lexus out there."

"Nigga, you don't know what the fu—"

"Hey, hey, hey," Sleeze interjected in what seemed to be in the nick of time.

"What's da problem, Dave?" he then asked with that distinctive Jamaican accent.

"What's the problem? What the fuck you think the problem is? You know what, Sleeze, let me get outta here, fo I have to fuck sumthin' up!" Dave then busted through the glass doors, looked to his right, and spotted Tracie about to turn the corner on foot.

"Tracie." His resounding voice could be heard for blocks. "I know you hear me," he said while jogging to catch up with her.

Turning the corner, he noticed Tracie's Lexus parked midway down the street.

"What choo park all the way down there fo?" Dave shouted as Tracie hustled to get down the street to her car.

"'Cause I knew if you saw me, you'd do some stupid shit like this." After fiddling with her keys inside the driver-side car door, Tracie finally managed to get inside and slam the door before Dave could get to her. She then hurried to key the ignition.

"Naw, bitch, you did it 'cause you knew you was fuckin' that punk-ass nigga, and if I saw yo' car, I was gone find out." Dave's voice could barely be heard by Tracie because of her completely sealed windows, running engine, and midlevel music playing; but she could still hear him, though.

"It's cool, though, 'cause I'm fuckin wit somebody else anyways." Dave's voice was getting much closer. "And I got a baby by her." Tracie heard the words *and I got a baby by her* loud and clear, and it stung her to the core. When she heard it, she wanted to jump out of the car and kick Dave's ass, but now wasn't the time. She was in the wrong right now, and she felt that her best bet was to go home and regroup.

With the window cracked a bit now and the music on low, Tracie put her car in drive, exited the parking space, and listened intently for ammunition as Dave continued to rant.

"Yeah, bitch, and you gone get out my house too. Matter fact, you ain't gotta leave 'cause I'm leaving. Keep that punk-ass house!"

After nearly two hours of struggling with Lil Kev, trying to rock him back to sleep so she could manage to get a bit of shut-eye too, Nina finally completed her task. Lil Kev was now out cold with his thumb lodged into his mouth. Nina slowly eased him off her knees and then set him onto the couch.

"Fat boy, you's a handful," she whispered while running her hand gently across the little bit of new growth that Lil Kev was starting to get.

It was approaching 11:45 p.m. With intentions on going back to work in the next couple of weeks, Nina was trying to set a schedule so that she and her son could be in bed at a certain time. Once she completed that, she would then be able to get up, get him to a babysitter, then get to work promptly. Because of this new schedule she was trying, she'd previously tried to inform everyone, including her boyfriend, Tony, not to call after 9:00 p.m. so she could be in bed by ten o'clock. The only problem with that, though, was she had forgotten to inform her baby's father about the new scheduling. *Who the fuck is this calling this time of night?* Nina said to herself while rushing over to the phone as it seemed to ring endlessly.

"Who is this?" she then asked.

"Who it sound like, Nina?"

"I thought I told you not to call her after nine o'clock, Dave," she questioned, forgetting that she hadn't told him anything of that sort.

"You ain't neva told me no shit like that, and if you would've, I would'na listened anyways. I hope you didn't forget I got a child over there."

"Boy, what do you want?" Nina asked, realizing Dave had a valid point. Despite the true joy Nina felt when she heard Dave's voice on the other line, she tried to play tough.

"Nina, I need to talk to you." Her face immediately began glowing.

"Well, talk. I'm listening."

"I'm not talkin' about on the phone. I need to see you. Can I come over?"

"Dave, I just put Lil Kev to sleep. I'm tired now. Come on." Nina's resistance was futile. She wanted to see Dave just as much as he needed to see her, but putting her guards up had become all but instinctive to her.

"So what if you just put him to sleep? If he wakes up, then I'll put him back to sleep. He's my son, remember?" Nina didn't even put up a fight.

"Boy, come on. And you better be quiet."

It took him nearly twenty minutes to get there; and when Dave finally arrived, he noticed that, again, Nina had left the front door ajar. He then strolled directly into the hallway and tiptoed quietly into the dark apartment. Nina, wearing nothing but a white tank top and pink translucent panties, sat next to Lil Kev on the couch. "Be quiet," she whispered. "You see, he's sleeping."

Dave wound up telling her every single detail from the time he left the club until the time he chased Tracie down the street. Nina, intrigued by the juicy details, listened on intently.

"So you think she heard you when you told her about Lil Kev?" she asked, elated that Dave finally had the courage to tell Tracie about their son even if it was at such an inopportune time.

"Hell yeah, she heard me," he exclaimed while giggling quietly. "Shit, the way I shouted that, I wouldn't be surprised if the whole street heard me."

The two of them talked for another few minutes before talking slowly became touching. Touching then quickly became rubbing. Rubbing became kissing, and before the two of them even realized it, they were on the floor next to the couch their son was lying on, having uninhibited *raw sex.*

Early the next morning, the two of them were awakened by Nina's ever-ringing telephone. Still groggy from the night prior, Dave reached unconsciously to retrieve it.

"Hello," he answered, not caring who it was.

The sound of a man's voice answering Nina's phone startled Tony.

"Who is this?" Tony asked inquisitively.

"This Dave. Who is dis?" The two of them hadn't had any contact with each other other than a brief encounter at the hospital, and they certainly hadn't spoken a word to each other, so they were both in a state of shock at their encounter.

"Uh, this is Tony. I was calling to speak to Nina," Tony conveyed respectfully, now realizing that the man on the other line was Nina's baby's father. Tony, for obvious reasons, wasn't particularly fond of Dave answering Nina's phone, especially at this time of morning. His mind ran rampant about all the potential things Nina and Dave could've been doing together so early. Initially, he'd give thought to Dave strictly visiting their son but quickly dismissed that, figuring Dave must've spent the night when he recognized the sluggish tone of his voice.

"Hold on a min, fam." Dave shoved Nina a few times as she lay nearly lifeless next to him on the floor. Dave had put it on Nina last night, leaving her body and mind totally exhausted.

"Nina," he said with vigor a couple of times before finally getting a response out of her.

"Tony's on the phone."

"H-E-L-L-O." Nina's apathy was apparent. She didn't want to talk, explain herself, or any of that. All she wanted to do was go back to sleep.

"You sound like you're asleep, Nina. If you need me to, I'll call you back."

"Okay. Bye." Just like that, Tony and Nina's conversation began and ended. The resignation in her voice said everything.

PART 5

CHAPTER THIRTY-ONE

The date was the Fourth of July. The time was approaching 7:00 p.m. To no one's surprise, Northeastern Ohio had been completely bombarded with impromptu fireworks displays, the remnants of which could be witnessed about the overspread streets. Side streets were filled with the parked cars of owners who were attending a planned event of some sort. Normally, around this time, Jay and Candace too would be preparing to attend someone else's get-together, or they'd be on their way to watch the fireworks at Euclid High, Candace's former school.

Today, though, Jay had a little something of his own planned for him and Candace.

"Come on, baby, now messin' wit choo. We gon' be late," Jay complained while slipping his feet into a cream-colored pair of Maury's.

Jay's ensemble looked fitting for just about any occasion. To go along with his cream gator shoes, he wore a cream-and-brown long-sleeved Sean John shirt with a pair of brown slacks. Covering his eyes were a pair of brown Valentino shades trimmed with gold. His gold-faced Movado watch with a black band set just outside his right sleeve with cufflinks.

Candace complemented her man well, wearing a strapless cream-colored dress made by Roberto Cavalli that hugged her curves to death. Her matching high heels accentuated her assets beautifully.

"Okay, baby. I'm coming," Candace assured him as she ran her French-manicured fingernails through her jet-black hair while admiring herself in the bathroom mirror.

The two of them hopped into Candace's Explorer and headed to their destination.

"Baby, I'ma call my momma and make sure everything's all right with Lil Jay," Candace said while reaching for her cell phone.

"Come on now, baby. Lil Jay's all right. Sit back and enjoy the ride," Jay retorted.

After they made a left onto Euclid Avenue from Richmond Road, then making a right on Babbitt Road, it didn't take long for Candace to notice that they were headed the same route that they'd normally take to get to her old high school. She kept quiet, though, thinking Jay might be getting on the freeway a different way. But when he turned onto Tracy Avenue, Candace immediately said, "Jay, I know you ain't got me all dressed up to go to no Euclid High School again. I dun got my hair and nails done, plus a new dress, and you got me goin' to the same place we damn near go to every year," Candace nagged on, but Jay just kept silent.

The parking lot of the high school was jam-packed with parked cars and others waiting in an extensive line to get a parking space when Jay and Candace got there. Numerous kids ran recklessly in between the parked cars, chasing one another with lit sparklers, clutched between the palms of their hands.

Directly ahead, the two of them could see the amateur fireworks show that was apparently supposed to keep the seemingly restless crowd occupied until the official show was to start.

After moseying through the parking lot for nearly five minutes, they finally found themselves a parking space. Jay put the truck in park, shut it off, and they got out. Candace, looking like a supermodel, walked over toward the throng of people but quickly stopped and turned around when she noticed that Jay wasn't beside her.

"Jay, what choo waitin' on?"

"For somebody who didn't even want to come up here, you sure sound eager as hell to get over to them fireworks," Jay said sarcastically while walking over to her.

"I know one thing," Candace said as the two of them made their way toward the multitude. "You sho'll better have one helluva night in store for me after dragging me up here again!"

"Oh shoot, Candace! I almost forgot. I got something to show you. Follow me over here, okay?" Jay asked her eagerly as they made a sharp left turn, avoiding the baseball diamond where the fireworks and the crowd were, and began heading toward the school.

"What now, Jayson? You know what, boy, you're really starting to work my last nerve. And where are we going anyways?"

The two of them entered the gymnasium door attached to the school. At once, Candace could hear chatter coming from around the corner, which was odd because school was out for summer vacation, which meant no one should've been in the building at the time.

Knowing that, Candace instantly began to ponder on why Jay would want to go inside her old school.

"Jay, why are we inside of my old high school?" Once making a left down the hallway, Candace began to notice that the chatter that she'd heard earlier was coming from some very familiar people. As they walked closer, she could see that some of the people were her family members, friends, friends of Jayson's, and some of his family members too.

"Okay, Jay," Candace said with a look of ambiguity upon her face, "what the hell is going on?"

The two of them continued walking down the narrow hallway. Candace, looking more timorous by the second, could barely think straight. She wanted badly to run and ask one of her family members, who were a little farther down the hall, what the hell was going on.

"Baby, do me a favor," Jay said while holding his woman's hand. The two of them were now standing directly across from the basketball gymnasium on one side and the concession stand on the other. Out of her peripheral, Candace could see Jay's best friend Dave positioned behind the counter of the stand.

"What, Jay?" Candace managed to sputter, shaking from nervousness. Candace's and Jay's friends and family weren't making it any better because they just stood there staring at Candace and Jay like they were both butt naked in a room full of nuns.

"I want you to go over to that concession stand and order you a hot dog and a Pepsi."

"Do what, Jay?" Candace's heart was beating so hard and fast that she thought everyone else could hear it too.

"Just go do what I said, baby." Moving as slowly as she possibly could, she did as her man instructed her. The hallway instantly got quiet when she finally approached the stand.

After looking back at Jay, Candace finally mustered up enough courage to say, "Dave, can I please have a hot dog and a Pepsi?"

With a devilish grin, Dave said, "Coming right up, Candace." Dave quickly made her a Pepsi, dressed up her naked hot dog, and then set it on the counter. But before she could grab it and begin to turn around, Jay came from behind and slapped a crispy $10 bill onto the counter.

"Do you remember this, baby? Do you remember that day at the basketball game when I saw the most beautiful girl in the world about to buy that hot dog and Pepsi? It was at that time that I knew I wanted to marry you, but all I could afford to do at the time was buy you that meal."

"J-A-Y—" Candace tried to interject but couldn't manage to find the words to say. She shook nervously in anticipation of what was to come, after which a few tears fell from her moistened eyes.

"Come on now, baby, let me finish. Now I know we've had our ups and downs, and I haven't been the best man in the world, but I'm trying my best, though. And I promise you this, Candace," Jay said as he kneeled onto one knee.

"If you give me the chance to be your husband, you will not regret it. Candace, will you please marry me?"

The crowd had now closed in on the two of them. Nearly everyone was in tears. Candace's face was now completely covered. She had been crying from the time she realized what was about to happen till then.

"Yes, baby, yes. I'll marry you," she conveyed with excitement as Jay began sliding this gorgeous four-carat ring on her finger. Everyone applauded as the two of them hugged and kissed for what seemed like an eternity.

After a brief celebration amid the corridor, the newly engaged couple and their semi-vas entourage all dispersed from the area in pursuit of the much-anticipated engagement party at the Civic Center on Mayfield Road.

Upon exiting the school building, everybody was befittingly entertained by the gorgeous display of multifaceted fireworks.

"That's perfect timing," Jay said to Candace while wiping away one of the many tears that still lay atop her glowing face, then planting a wet kiss upon her lips. "Baby, you sho'll did it this time. I didn't see this one coming at all."

Once observing the vast and extremely beautiful grand finale from the parking lot, everyone in Jay and Candace's entourage, including themselves, began walking toward their vehicles. Jay, showing vintage signs of chivalry, escorted his fiancée over to the passenger-side door of her truck and then politely opened it. She kindly thanked him, then hopped up in the truck. With her eyes affixed on her man and his every move, she watched as he and Dave began walking over to this pretty powder-white car with likewise rims that she couldn't quite figure out the make of. Candace, after watching the two of them slap hands and embrace in excitement, impatiently opened up her door, then hollered, "Dave, whose pretty car is that? Is that yours?"

Dave and Jay made haste toward Candace's side of the truck. "You like that car, Candace?" Dave asked with an enormously big grin upon his face.

"Yeah, I like. It's pretty. What kind is it, though, a Porsche?"

"Yeah, it's the new 911 seven-speed automatic. I just got it yesterday."

"That's a nice car, Dave, I must say. Did those rims come with it too?"

"Naw. Those are twenty-one-inch Dub X-16s. I got'um shipped in."

The three of them talked a brief while longer till Jay finally announced to the group that it was time to head out to the engagement party.

The engagement party was a huge success just as Jay had planned it to be. Everyone who attended the party enjoyed themselves. They ate good, they drank good, and they danced until their hearts were content. Both Jay and Candace just looked on in pure satisfaction. Even Candace's mom, whom Jay had gotten approval from to marry Candace and throw the party, was in good spirits.

She sat in a corner all by herself, looking on at her daughter and future son-in-law dancing while listening to Al Green sing "Let's get married t-o-d-a-y. Let's get married."

With the two of them both tipsy and having the time of their lives, Jay and Candace kissed, hugged, and looked at each other as if they didn't want to leave this very moment.

"Baby, I love you with all my heart," Candace confessed to her husband-to-be.

"I know you do. And that's why I married you. I love you with all my heart too, and don't choo forget it." With that, the two of them entertained their guests until the blissful party came to an end. Then, they safely made it to the embassy suite that Jay had reserved especially for this night.

The suite had a beautiful trail of rose petals leading from the door to the bed. Upon the bed, there was another array of various flower petals adorning it. Buckets of champagne were being chilled inside the bathtub. Jay grabbed one, popped the cork, and poured himself and his fiancée some.

"This is to us, baby," he said, holding up his glass.

"To us," she happily repeated as a tear slid down her gorgeous face.

They then toasted and took sips from the expensive champagne. Shortly after, they danced a bit, then stripped each other naked, and made passionate love until the sun came up.

CHAPTER THIRTY-TWO

It had been about a month since Dave's best friend Jay's unprecedented proposal and engagement party, and somehow, Dave was still in the same blissful mood that he was in on that very day. Watching Jay propose to such a deserving woman as Candace was one of the happiest moments of Dave's life. The two of them were meant to be, and he knew it.

That's why his participation in the event was a must.

Despite his previous marital problems, Dave felt like he was in the best position in life that he'd been in, in quite some time. He and Nina, his new baby's mother, had gotten back together. He had a little boy who could've been mistaken for his identical twin at his age that was totally and completely dependent upon his love and nurture. He gave up the house to Tracie and was living in Nina's small apartment. But the two of them had already begun the construction of a new home they'd decided to build in Aurora, Ohio.

The drug game, despite its risks, were paying off heavily too for Dave. He bought the new Porsche, which he was obsessed with without even having to trade in his truck. And his pockets were now as thick as the glasses on his second-grade teacher. Everything was going well.

The one regret Dave did have was the fact that he took Nina from such a good man. Nina had explained to Dave that Tony was such a nice, respectful guy and didn't deserve to be treated the way she'd treated him. Just hearing that from his girl made Dave a bit regretful, but he had to have Nina even if it was at the expense of a good guy.

With the power hole rolled back and haze smoke billowing out the roof, Dave did a modest fifty-five miles per hour in a thirty-five-mile-per-hour zone, down MLK Boulevard, listening to Rick Ross rap "Everyday I'm Hustlin'." After stopping at a red light, he got a phone call.

"Who the fuck you think you are sendin' me some divorce papers?" Tracie shouted angrily.

"You call yo'self a man, tryin' to sneak and do some shit like that? Fuck you, nigga!"

Instead of reacting negatively and saying something he might regret, like he'd normally do, Dave just chuckled apathetically and then replied, "Tracie, you have a good day too!" With the most pleasant of look upon his face, he softly hung up the phone. Dave was already aware of the type of response that those divorce papers would provoke from Tracie. That's the reason he elected to keep them hidden.

Once the light changed, Dave stepped on the pedal, again, en route to his destination. No sooner had he reached the next light than his phone began ringing again.

"Tracie, come on," he said, thinking that it was her pestering him about those papers.

"Tracie? Nigga dis ain't no Tracie," his new friend Joe with the Bentley said.

"Dis Joe!"

"Oh, what up, Joe? My fault. I thought choo were Tracie again, callin' me about them damn divorce papers. What up, my nigga?"

"Shit. I just wanted to see if we were flyin' high today," Joe said while slightly giggling. *Flyin' high* was the phrase they used to represent Dave buying a package from Joe.

"Hell yeah, we flyin' high as soon as I handle this extra point," which meant Dave only had one kilo left to sell. "What is it, two o'clock right now? Let's try to hook around four. That should give me enough time to take care of some business, aight?"

"I'm on yo time, my nigga."

"Aight, I'ma get wit choo then."

"Aight."

After his phone call with Joe, nervousness immediately consumed Dave's mortal body. His arms shook feverishly as he made a right turn into the Reason. For some reason, every time Dave spoke about drugs with Joe or anyone he sold them to, he'd be overtaken by this scary feeling.

Dave knew the amount of time that cocaine and crack carried compared to weed, which was his drug of choice; and every time he thought about the possibility of him getting caught, it haunted him.

With his mind stuck on his last kilo and the person with whom he was to sell it to, Dave unconsciously unloaded the few supplies that he had in the trunk of his car into his deserted club. Then, apprehensively, he ran and retrieved the dope from the new trap house he had acquired just across the street. After contemplating as to whether or not he should even sell the drugs, Dave then said audibly, *Man, this shit ain't nuthin'.* Then he headed back toward his car.

The meeting place was the Plaza on 105 and St. Clair. Dave had been parked in the huge lot in between a chameleon-painted '85 Cutlass on twenty-sixes and a black Pontiac Sunfire for nearly ten minutes, and he was getting very restless.

"Man, what the fuck is takin' Rocco so long?" he hollered aggressively, then picked up the phone to dial his number.

"Rocco, man, what the fuck is takin' you so long? I'm 'bout to pull," Dave yelled.

"Hol-up, hol-up, Dave! I'm at the light on Lakeview. I'll be there in a second."

"Man, if you ain't here in the next two minutes, I'm gone."

Nearly two minutes after, Dave saw Rocco's black Cadillac DTS pulling up in front of him. Rocco parked his car directly in front of Dave's but in the next row.

Then, he shut off his engine, exited his car, and walked over to Dave.

"Wuz up, homie?" he said after plopping down on Dave's soft black leather interior, then gently shut his door.

"Shit, man, let's handle this business," Dave replied while reaching underneath the driver's seat to retrieve the work. He then handed it to Rocco, and in return, Rocco handed him a nice-sized brown paper bag. "I hope it's all here 'cause I ain't got time to count it," Dave said while looking in the bag at the huge bundles of dead presidents that occupied it.

"Come on now, Dave, you know I ain't cut like that."

Dave threw the bag in the back of his car, then said to Rocco, "Aight, my nigga, I'ma holla at cha."

Rocco reciprocated. Then Dave keyed the ignition and quickly vacated the premises. A sigh of relief then came over Dave as he began cruising down 105. He successfully pulled off another score! There's twenty-five grand in the bag! As he cranked up "Pushin' It" off the same old Rick Ross CD, all sorts of emotions began running through him.

His desultory thoughts leaped from hooking up with Joe at four to him nearly acquiring enough money to finish the construction of his new home. Unfortunately, though, all those joyful thoughts were suspended when he rode past B&Ms and a black Dodge Charger. A blue unmarked police cruiser turned off the side street, onto 105st, and immediately jumped behind him. Dave's heart instantly dropped to the floor of his Porsche in terror.

With the Charger on his left and the unmarked cruiser on his right, Dave, scared to death, wisely dismissed the thoughts of a high-speed chase and just began hoping that they were looking for someone else. Then the covert lights of both police cars began flickering, and Dave's suspicious were confirmed.

CHAPTER THIRTY-THREE

"Nell, man, you see the news last night?" Tay yelled emphatically through his cell phone to Nell, who was half asleep at the time.

"Naw, why? Wuz up?"

Tay took a hard pull on his Maverick cigarette, then replied, "Swear, this nigga Dave got caught with the brick and twenty-five stacks!" To the two of them, this was an awful lot of money.

"What! You talkin' 'bout Jay's homie Dave?" Nell inquired as his half-shut, crust-filled eyes began to enlarge. His enthusiasm became so apparent that his baby momma, who was in the other room, hustled her way into the bedroom and asked, "What's wrong?"

His baby momma was really nosy. Hearing Jay's and Dave's names only piqued her interest, compelling her to fish for more info.

"Nuttin', baby," he replied as he began to wave her out of the bedroom.

For the next ten minutes, Tay ran down the whole scenario to Nell almost exactly as how nine action news reported it; he did manage to fabricate and exaggerate a bit of it to make it more dramatic.

"So you mean to tell me them niggas doin' it like that?" Nell asked in a dragging voice as his diabolical mind began contemplating.

"Hell yeah, they doin' it like that," Tay retorted.

"You thinkin' what I'm thinkin, Tay?"

"You know it!"

"Aight then, my nigga. Meet me over here in fifteen."

"I'm gone." Tay couldn't believe that Nell was so game. Tay had been plotting for hours on how he would manage to coax his friend Nell into doing the unthinkable, and here it was. Nell brought it to him.

"You have a collect call from Dave," the automated phone service stated, "who is an inmate at the Cuyahoga County Jail. To accept this call press 0. To deny, press 5."

Nina quickly pressed 9, then waited anxiously for the sound of Dave's voice.

"Hello," Dave said indifferently.

"Hey, baby! How are you? Is everything all right? What took you sooo long to call, David?" Nina rambled on, concerned.

"I was worried sick about you!"

Bombarded with a multitude of questions, Dave didn't know which one to answer first. What he did know, though, was he was glad that his woman, from the sound of concern in her tone, was going to ride with him win, lose, or draw.

"Hey, baby! I'm aight," he responded, trying not to sound defeated. What Dave really wanted to express to Nina was that he was sick to the core about getting caught with that $25,000 and the brick of cocaine, but his pride wouldn't let him.

He knew that in order for the two of them to make it through such a difficult situation together, he had to stay strong for the both of them.

With Lil Kev in one arm and the phone occupying the other, Nina sat on the couch, feeling totally confused.

Ever since she'd first found out about Dave's arrest, she couldn't dismiss the thoughts of her making a huge mistake in leaving Tony. Why didn't she just keep her and Dave's relationship the way it was? Was she being punished? What if she just broke it off with Dave right now and tried to get back with Tony? Would Tony take her back? All these different thoughts and questions continued to permeate her mind even during her conversation with Dave.

"So what am I supposed to do now, Dave? I mean your son and I—we're out here by ourselves." Nina's voice was now one of anger and discontentment. "And what the hell you doing getting caught with a kilo of cocaine? Cocaine, David?"

"It ain't even like that, Nina," he tried to convince her as he shifted his weight over to the right side of his body because of the pain that began setting in from him standing. Dave then explained the situation to Nina as best he could but with as little detail as possible for fear of incriminating himself. Then, the two of them were abruptly interrupted by the automated system, which stated, "You have sixty seconds left for this call."

"Nina, listen. I'ma need you to get in touch with Jaye Schlachet, spelled *S-C-H-L-A-C-H-E-T*. He's my lawyer. See what his retainer's fee is. Then, pay it for me. Don't worry about what it cost. Whatever it is, I'll replace it. Tell him to come and see me as soon as he can, okay? Also, I'ma need you to go check on the club, okay? I'ma try ta call you back later on tonight, aight? If I don't, though, be expecting a call in the morning."

"All right."

"Nina," Dave said just before the automated service informed them that they only had ten seconds left.

"Yes, Dave?"

"I love you," he spoke with sincerity, "and I need you to hold me down."

"I love you too, and I got choo" was all Nina said and all the phone company would've let her say because the phone shut off immediately afterward.

It took Nina a while to finally get in contact with Dave's lawyer, this after having to locate his information. Nina made sure that she explained the situation to the lawyer just as Dave told her to. She was exact in nearly every detail, fearing that the lawyer might misunderstand something and possibly hinder her man's release. Nina's body cringed a bit when the lawyer informed her that his retainer's fee would be $2,500. Then, she thought about Dave's assurance that she'd get her money back, and she breathed a sigh of relief.

"May I bring the money to you today?" she asked him.

"You may, but I doubt that he'll get out today," Mr. Schlachet said.

"Why not?"

"Because he doesn't have a bond yet, ma'am."

"Okay, so what's a good time to meet with you, sir?"

"I'll be in my office at around 4:15 p.m."

"I'll be there."

"All right. See you then."

Rush-hour traffic was pretty mild in Downtown Cleveland. Normally, around four o'clock, RTA buses would be at the head of a host of other vehicles clustering the downtown main streets. Contrarily, today one could count the number of vehicles occupying Ninth Street on two hands. Despite this, buses still wrapped themselves around Public Square's turnaround, anticipating a huge crowd to come storming out of Tower City and fill up those completely vacant seats.

Nina parallel parked her Cavalier alongside a parking meter across from Johnny Q's Steakhouse. Johnny Q's—an elegant meeting and eating place for most lawyers, judges, and other prominent individuals—was directly neighboring the building that Nina had been driving around downtown for the last ten minutes. *There it is,* she spoke in relief after leaning her body over into the passenger seat to gaze out of the window at the address on the building. Finally, she'd found this lawyer's office. Now, all she had to do was grab Lil Kev from his car seat, then rush, and pay the man before she began contemplating emptying most of her savings and had a change of heart.

As soon as they approached the building, Nina could tell that it wasn't an ordinary downtown building. This completely glass, with smoke-black-tinted windows, building's architecture exuded one of prestige. The landscaping just in front the entrance was meticulously trimmed and had a short protective black gate around its edges. Just off to the side of the building was a large white fence with white chairs and tables that accommodated the remnants of Johnny Q's customers, who preferred the outdoor scenery.

Upon entering the building, Nina and Lil Kev crossed paths with four middle-aged white males and a younger balding black male, who, by their attire and ever-obvious confidence, appeared to be prominent attorneys.

Despite their cocky arrogance, every one of them nearly broke their necks trying to watch Nina, with Lil Kev tucked underneath her arm, as she made her way over to the security desk. Her skin-tight Rocawear jogging outfit left nearly nothing to the imagination. With her breasts bouncing rhythmically to the sound of her high heels, and her ass jiggling loosely, Nina commanded attention.

"Excuse me," she spoke in her most seductive tone.

"Can you pleeease tell me where Mr. Schlachet's office is?" Oddly enough, the fat, pale, and out-of-shape security guard, completely unfazed by her sexual innuendos, didn't even look up at her. He just nonchalantly responded, "All attorney's office numbers are on the bulletin board to your right."

Disgusted with his response, Nina could do no more than roll her eyes at him and mumble under her breath, "You fat ugly muthfucka," then walked herself and her baby over to the board.

Later on that night, after finishing all her errands, Nina decided she'd obey her man's commands and stop to check on the club. Just thinking about the Reason evoked so many emotions for Nina that it was ridiculous. Like the night she and Dave had first met. Or all the money she'd brought in from all the "ballers" that used to trick with her.

Even the night that she had had sex with the guy in the Dodge Magnum just to get back at Dave. All these different thoughts began to spring up with each light she passed. Then, finally, Nina arrived at the front of the club. To her surprise, the Reason was boarded up at both the windows and doors. Sadly, it now looked more like an eyesore than a prominent club that had just been closed for investigation. Part of Nina really wanted to stop, look, and reminisce on all the club memories; but instead, she just shed a tear and continued rolling past.

CHAPTER THIRTY-FOUR

"**M**an, Tay, my muthafuckin' legs crampin' up on me, man," Nell whispered submissively from a kneeling position.

"Man, we been here foreva. Why 'on't we just come back tomorrow night?"

"Man, hell naw, we ain't comin' back no tomorrow night," Tay argued in a resonant voice. After realizing how amplified he sounded, Tay looked around, then began whispering, "Nell, man, I knew you was gone do this shit. It's too late to be tryna back out now. Now, we've been watching this nigga for the past three nights, and he's been coming home at eleven every night. So what the fuck! So what if it's eleven fifteen? The nigga gone be home soon. And as soon as he gets here, we gone do what the fuck we gotta do."

Tay and Nell was kneeled down between a row of bushes, alongside Jay's neighbor's house, waiting anxiously on Jay's return. Ever since the news broke that Dave had gotten arrested with all that money and drugs, the two of them had begun plotting to rob Jay. They figured that if Dave had gotten caught with all that stuff and Jay was still out there, apparently, Jay still had something. Plus, ever since that basketball game at the creek, when the two of them got into it, Tay had developed a strong hatred for Jay.

"Man, you hear that?" Tay said in a susurrus tone.

"Naw, man, what choo talkin' 'bout?" Nell retorted.

"Shhh, listen!" Tay could hear the roaring engine of what appeared to be a large vehicle approaching.

"That sound like a truck coming to me," Tay said while gripping his 9mm Glock firmly. Nell then reached between the bushes to grab his chrome .38 special too. The two of them began scooting through the connecting bushes and rustling through the dirt, loose leaves, and debris toward the front of the neighbor's house in hopes of getting a good look at the approaching vehicle.

Then, suddenly, the bright headlights of what looked to be a Cadillac Escalade began shining brightly on the very bushes that the two of them were in. It slowly turned into the driveway. Then, it inched its way up on the Explorer just in front of it, shifted into park, then shut off. Tay and Nell, with guns in hand, waited thirstily for the driver to exit the vehicle.

"You ready, Nell?" Tay asked.

"Hell yeah," he responded. Then the door opened. The driver hopped out of the truck, slammed the door . . .

"Aey, nigga, don't make anotha move," Tay demanded lowly but aggressively as the two of them jumped out of the bushes. He quickly pressed the cold tip of the 9mm Glock to the back of Jay's head.

"Yeah, nigga, don't move," Nell repeated as he stuck the .38 special into Jay's side.

"Listen, nigga, don't say nuthin'. Just lead us in the house to the money."

With the gun still smashed up against Jay's head, Tay began gazing inside the truck in hopes of spotting a few bricks.

"Man, WHAT MONEY?" Jay responded nervously, hoping his frantic words wouldn't get him killed.

With what little courage Nell managed to muster, he said, "Nigga, you know what money. Quit playing 'fore we pop you."

"Man, all I got is two hun'd and fifty dollaz to my name. Ya'll can have that."

"Nigga, we 'on't want no two-hunid fifty dollaz," Tay said angrily as he nudged Jay's head forward with the gun. Then, through his peripheral, Tay noticed what appeared to be an attic light from the neighbor's house whose bushes they'd been hiding in turn on.

"Listen, if you don't open that door and lead us to this money, one of us gone die tonight. And trust me, it ain't gone be me or my homie."

When Jay heard the word *die* released from Tay's mouth, his life instantly flashed before him. *How could this be happening?* he thought to himself. He'd just had a new baby boy. Not long after, he'd proposed to Candace, the love of his life. To top that, he didn't even sell drugs anymore!

Why him? Then, out of nowhere, it hit him; the voices behind those black face masks weren't any ordinary voices. If he wasn't mistaken, those were the voices of his archenemy, Tay, and Nell.

But why them and why him? he thought. *The most we ever had was a little scuffle.* Then, without thinking of the consequences, Jay blurted out, "Come on, Tay, man, why you doin' dist a me?"

"Nigga, my name ain't no Tay," Tay shouted, then unconsciously pulled the trigger. *Pow-pow* was all you heard. One of the two bullets instantly ripped through the back of Jay's head while the other one grazed it.

Blood simultaneously splattered upon Tay's faded black hoodie as Jay's helpless body fell forward.

Nell couldn't believe his eyes. Everything was now moving in slow motion. He watched as Jay's face smacked the driveway pavement. Nell then looked over at Tay in utter disbelief. Why did he shoot him in the head?

Was it that serious? Who the fuck is this guy I'm with? All these questions filled Nell's mind before he told Tay, "Man, let's get da fuck outta here." With that, the two of them raced through Jay's backyard, hopped his fence, then rushed to the getaway car parked just on the other street.

When Candace heard those gunshots so close to her home, she immediately jumped and looked through the bedroom window to see if Jay's truck was in the driveway. It was. "Jay," she then yelled as she began walking through the upstairs hallway in search of him. "Jay," she yelled again, but he wasn't responding. *Where is this boy at?* she asked herself in fear of the possibility that those gunshots were for him.

Holding the edges of her house coat together, Candace hustled downstairs and decided she'd check the outer perimeters of her home. "Boy, quit playin' so much," she said as she opened the side door and stepped down the stairs. What she saw next nearly stole the life out of her body: her beloved, fiancé facedown, sprawled out on the concrete. "Jay, baby, get up," she said as she rushed over and tried to pick his lifeless body up out of the pool of blood he lay in. Tears instantly covered her entire face as she said his name again. From the looks of it, Jay was long gone. Realizing that she was now covered in nearly all the blood that Jay's body contained, Candace looked at her hands, arms, and chest and then uninhibitedly yelled, "NOOOOO!"

CHAPTER THIRTY-FIVE

It took nearly two weeks, three separate seventy-two-hour investigations, and a host of phone calls from his lawyer and Nina before Dave finally received a $25,000 bond. He was charged with drug trafficking, a felony of the third degree, which carried a sentence of anywhere of one to five years.

Normally, this wouldn't seem like a lot of time, especially for someone who'd been bagged with a kilo of cocaine and $25,000. But for someone like Dave, who just recently had a baby and had never so much as seen the insides of a penitentiary except on TV, it was an awfully long time.

During the two-week period, they seized his Porsche, his Navigator, and blue CTS that he'd just purchased from the auction. They boarded up his home on the Westside that Tracie unfortunately was still staying in and his trap house and shut down his infamous club the Reason. Losing his possessions only added to the stress of being locked up. So to him, it was an utter relief when the CO screamed, "Smith, pack it up." Dave quickly packed up what little he had, then sat patiently by the door for the CO.

Fifteen minutes later, the tall overweight CO came and unlocked Dave's door, then took him down to the bullpen.

The bullpen was nothing more than an undersized holding cell used to hold inmates who were either just admitted, waiting to be released on bond, or waiting to be scanned as part of a nationwide warrant search.

Inside the bullpen, inmates had the luxury of clustering together onto two adjacent six-feet-long-two-feet-wide hardwood benches, using the restroom on one stainless steel toilet, and washing their hands in one stainless steel sink. They also sometimes had to fight over the use of one highly coveted payphone that hardly ever worked, and when it did, it was subject to take their money.

There were over fifteen inmates packed inside this congested twelve-by-eight-feet space.

The benches were filled. There were inmates holding up the walls and some stretched out upon the floor. Dave stood at the front of the cell by himself with his back toward the door.

"Man, this some bullshit," he mumbled furiously while surveying the different inmates. To him, they all looked like dopeheads and alcoholics. So to keep them at a distance, he made sure he stood as far away as possible.

Without any warning, one of the guards yelled, "Step back!" Then he said, "I need inmate Smith to step out." Shocked to hear his name called so quickly, Dave took a gander at the room to see if there were other Smiths inside. Before he could turn toward the door, the officer shouted, "Smith, let's go! Don't let me call you again!"

After running Dave's name through the nationwide warrant check, the CO then took him over to retrieve all his personal property. Next, he had Dave sign some papers, pointed toward the door, and then told him, "You're a free man. Be safe."

"Thanks, man," Dave retorted with relief as he shoved the door in great anticipation. Nina, who had been waiting patiently just outside the door, immediately held her arms open wide when she saw Dave come through the doors.

"Hey, babe," Nina said ardently as she ran up to him and squeezed the life out of him. The two of them French kissed passionately like nobody else was around. Then, Nina, whose eyes were bloodshot red from the stream of tears that flowed down her face, remembered the news about Jay and lay her head on Dave's solid chest. "Baby, I've got some bad news to tell you," she mumbled.

Instantly, Dave's mind began racing rampant. *What could she possibly be talking about?* he thought. He knew about Jay getting shot in the head because that was practically the talk of the county. Everything else, though, he was unaware of. Jay being shot in the head was terrible news to him, but last he heard, Jay was in critical condition, which is why he hastily yelled, "Ain't nuthin' wrong wit my son, is it?" Nina impotently shook her head no.

"Then what's wrong?" Curiosity quickly ate at the core of his being. He wanted to know, and he wanted to know now.

Before he could say another word, Nina somehow managed to say, "It's Jay."

The second that he heard Jay's name, Dave breathed a sigh of relief.

Thank goodness, he had already heard from Candace that Jay was in critical condition, or he would've been a complete wreck.

"Baby, I already know. Somebody shot him. He's in critical condition, right?"

Nina's crying quickly transformed into loud wailing. Then, before collapsing into Dave's strong, protective arms, she screamed hysterically, "David, he's dead."

Dave clutched Nina's biceps, leaned back, and hollered, "He's dead!"

"That's impossible. He can't be dead, Nina, 'cause I just talked to Candace the other night, and she said that he was still in critical."

Reluctant to continue, Nina struggled to say, "Baby, he died last night." Not knowing what to do or where to go, Dave just wrapped his arms around his woman and continued shaking his head. "What da fuck! What da fuck! What da fuck" was all he kept saying.

CHAPTER THIRTY-SIX

Jay's funeral service, which was held at Gaines Funeral Home off Ninety-Third and Union, was packed beyond belief. If it hadn't been so far in the inner city, one might've mistaken it for the president's home going. Cars were lined up for miles down the normally traffic-friendly street. Bentleys, Benzes, Maseratis, and Caddys all sat out front of the undersized funeral home.

Just these cars alone drew tons of onlookers, and nosy individuals just curious to see who everyone was. Not every vehicle in the myriad of cars was luxury, though. There were some family members and friends who came to pay their respects in more conservative cars such as Hondas, Fords, and Chevys. Because of the lack of parking space, people began irrespectively parking in some of the neighboring homes' driveways and front lawns.

Dave, Candace, and Jay's grandmother had rented a black stretched Cadillac Escalade for their transportation. The chauffeur had it parked in front of the Cadillac hearse while its trunk was setting directly parallel to the funeral home's forest-green canopy.

Candace, her mother, Jay's grandmother, Dave, and Nina all sat together in the front row; nobody else was able to sit with them.

Every single seat, besides theirs, inside the funeral home was filled, though. There were loads of people holding up the walls and lined up out in the hallways.

The place was so packed that if the fire marshal would have come to inspect, Gaines Funeral Home would've gotten a hefty fine.

As far as the attire went, everyone was properly dressed for the occasion.

The front-row seaters, though, were clad impeccably. Dave had on a navy-blue Ralph Lauren purple-label tailed suit, with cream-and-blue matching gators. Usually, his attire would be flashy and ostentatious but not this time. From the Stella McCartney shades down to the Ralph Lauren socks, Dave was very neat and moderately dressed. Everything fit on him just perfectly. Likewise, with the women. They too were dressed very conservatively. All the ladies intentionally wore figure-friendly black strapless dresses down to their knees, along with matching high heels.

Jay's ensemble stole the show. His embalmed flesh was covered by an extremely expensive three-piece pearl-white, Armani suit. His feet were being smothered by the best pearl-white gator and sock that Maury had to offer.

Because of the damage to his head from the shooting, Candace elected to style it with a custom-fitted Polo hat made exclusively for him; there was also a veil covering his face that if the viewer chose, he could lift up to glance at Jay. For the many people that decided to attend the event, it was definitely one home going to remember.

With the line to view Jay's body still well out to the sidewalk and the service running extremely late, the director approached the reverend, requesting to shut the casket, so that the services could proceed. The reverend approved, but when the director began shutting the casket, all hell literally broke loose in the place. "No, no, no, stop, man, stop. Don't close that muthfuckin' casket on my nigga" was just one of the emotional outbursts screamed before a crowd of people rushed to Jay's lifeless body. Feeling helpless, sympathetic, and somewhat scared, the director decided to leave it open for the eulogy.

"Jayson was a good man," the rev preached to the sobbing crowd. "He was a well-behaved grandson, a faithful future husband and son-in-law, and an honest and trustworthy friend."

The words cut through the front row like a knife. Dave tried to stay strong for the women, but just the thought of never seeing his best friend again forced him to hunch over, almost wedging his head between his legs. Nina, who wasn't as close to Dave as anyone else, including Candace's mom, still showed her empathy by rubbing Dave's back invariably.

Anyone with two eyes could see that the women in the front row were taking Jay's death extremely heard, but no one was taking things as hard as Dave. Not only was Jay and Dave best friends, he was like a brother to Dave. They had known each other practically all their lives. They spent weeks at a time with each other. They traveled together. They hustled together. They pretty much did everything together. Unfortunately, the one thing they didn't do together was quit selling drugs; and from the rumors swirling, this could've possibly been the motive for his best friend's murder.

Dave would've loved to question the validity of those rumors, but every time he'd even attempt to, his conscience would take him back to the day of his arrest and just days after—when Jay was killed. Something in Dave's heart was telling him that when Jay said he was done with hustling, if he had said the same, they probably wouldn't be having this funeral. Sadly, it was all speculation now.

Despite all the grief of having to bury his best friend, there was something that gave Dave a bit of comfort. Hearing the reverend say that Jay had been baptized and was now going home to be with the Lord touched Dave.

He never knew that Jay had been baptized. The two of them had never really talked about God much. So hearing that Jay had done such a courageous act in giving himself to the Lord, for Dave, was sweet relief.

Maybe I need to think about being baptized too, Dave thought. That thought was quickly dismissed, though.

The funeral service finally ended nearly an hour after its scheduled time.

All the guests were then instructed to exit the funeral home for precautionary measures before the casket was to be closed.

The pallbearers then transported Jay's body out to the Cadillac hearse. Dave, still grieving heavily over the loss of his best friend, stood in awe, watching the whole process. The tears flowed uncontrollably as he witnessed the pallbearers slide Jay's body into the hearse and shut the door.

Damn" was all he could conjure, still in a trance.

After coming to, he then noticed the enormous crowds of people on hand. Initially, he wanted to just walk right past everyone and hop straight into the limo, but he didn't. He knew that doing that would've been rude and selfish, considering the majority of the people were here for his moral support. So with reluctance, he took it upon himself to go and speak with some of the folks.

Ironically, the same communication suddenly began to lift his spirits.

"So, ya'll going over to the burial, right?" he asked almost jovially to a group of mutual friends of Jay and his.

"It's at Riverside over on West Twenty-Fifth," he informed them, then paused to hear their response.

"All right then, I'll see ya'll there." On his way to the limo, Dave spotted his girlfriend, Nina, in what looked to be a white hard to Sebring, sitting alongside the limo. Without hesitation, he darted over to her driver-side door and said with a playful grin on his face, "Whose car is this, Nina? It bet not be a nigga's car."

"Boy, shut up. I rented this." She laughed, then patiently waited on her man's next words.

"Look, are you going over to the burial, Nina?"

"No. That's what I was just tellin' the girls. I'm not going to be able to make it 'cause I told my mom I'd pick up your son right after the funeral." Just then, Dave was nearly swiped by a truck trying to squeeze between him and an idle car on the side of him.

"Damn, she came mighty close," Nina said.

"Anyways, Candace's mom was just telling me that she'd watch the kids for the night, so we can go over Candace's if that all right with you?"

"That's cool."

"Okay, baby. I'll see you later. Love you," Nina said affectionately before leaning outside the car window to kiss her man.

"I love you too, baby. Now get that ass home," Jay said with laughter.

As soon as Nina drove off, Dave could hear his name being called from the other side of the street. He glanced toward where the voice had come from but didn't see anyone, so he headed toward the limo door.

"Dave, boy, I know you hear me callin' you," the woman said again as Dave was opening up the limo door. Emerging from a new Lexus RX 300 was his ex-wife's cousin, Nikki. She stood tall between her car and the opened door, so he could see her.

"N-I-K-K-I," Dave said after turning and squinting to get a clear visual of the beautiful specimen standing before him.

"Is that you?" Nikki wore a black business suit and some black heels that stressed her sensuality and sex appeal to a T. The black suit pants hugged her thick but firm thighs to the point of suffocation. Her rotund rear could nearly be seen from the front as she stood waiting for Dave to make his way over to her. Immediately, they hugged, holding each other for what seemed like an eternity.

"Damn, Nikki, how have you been?" Dave asked, grabbing a firm hold to her triceps, then leaning back to survey the young woman that he was once extremely infatuated with.

"I should be asking you that. How are you holding up, Dave?"

"I guess I'm all right," he answered while unconsciously glancing down at Nikki's newfound cleavage, which happened to be effortlessly protruding out of her blazer. Nikki saw him but didn't comment.

"I heard you and my cousin were no longer an item. Is that true?"

"Yeah, that's true, Nikki!" Dave's countenance dropped a little.

"Well, how about you and I go out and grab a bite to eat and maybe a drink or two? On me," Nikki offered persuasively.

"And we can go in my new truck, which I've noticed that you haven't said anything about."

"I was just about to ask you who did you stick up to get that pretty thing?"

"Boy—gone," Nikki said, then hit him on his shoulder softly.

"Naw, but seriously, Nikki, I wish I could, but I got a new lil boy and a baby mother that loves me to death. Plus, she'd kill me if she knew that I went out with another woman, especially one as gorgeous as you.

"Boy, stop! Anyways, congratulations, Daddy!"

"Thanks."

After seconds of awkward silence, Nikki persisted, "All right, but it's just some food and a drink, Dave. And if it makes you feel any better, you know I'm not the one to tell anything."

Nikki's offer was extremely enticing, especially since Dave knew that if there was anyone that he could trust to keep their mouth shut, it'd be Nikki.

Going with his better judgment for once, Dave said, "I know, Nikki, but I can't. Not this time. A man got to stand up for sumthin' in his life, or he'll continue to fall for anything."

"Well, at least take my number then," Nikki insisted.

"Naw, not this time, Nikki, but we'll see each other around."

"All rightee then, Mr. David Smith. I'm proud of you."

"Likewise, baby," Dave said as he turned his head toward the limo.

Turning back, he yelled, "Nikki, you goin' to the burial site?"

She just smiled, then nodded her head yes.

"Okay, I'll see you there." Dave then jumped in the limo.

"Who was that, Dave?" Candace asked curiously.

"Ashes to ashes and dust to dust," the reverend recited while standing amid the large cemetery crowd.

Dave was literally a wreck after witnessing his best friend get lowered into the ground. Hanging on to every word the reverend spoke, he tried keeping his composure but just couldn't hold back his tears. He couldn't stop contemplating on past memories while simultaneously thinking about the fact that he'll never get to see his friend above ground again. Still, in all his hurt, Dave amazingly found enough strength to reach his arms around Candace, who stood beside him, and whisper in her ear, "Listen, I know that this is hard, Candace, but stay strong." Candace's somber face looked as if somebody had just thrown a glass of water on it.

"Whateva you need, Candy, if I can do it, consider it done. You my family and always will be. I don't care who I'm with or where I'm at, you and Lil Jay are foreva gone be a part of my life."

Before he could say, "Always remember that," Candace grabbed hold of him and practically bear hugged him to death.

"Thank you, Dave. I really needed to hear that."

Soon after the reverend finished his brief sermon, a large red dump truck filled with dirt, drove over toward

Jay's burial site. The driver then backed the rear end up to the hole where Jay was placed. The driver was in the process of dumping the dirt onto Jay's tomb until the family, with the cemetery's consent, instructed him to pour it beside the hole; they wanted to shovel the dirt manually. The driver complied, and soon the family, along with friends, began shoveling the dirt and throwing flowers into the six-foot hole that would now be Jay's permanent address.

Once complete, everybody said their good-byes and made plans for later before retreating to their cars. Dave, again, wound up being one of the last ones to the vehicle.

On the way over to the limo, Dave happened to notice that one of the cars leaving had stopped alongside the limo he came in. They must be talking to Candace, he figured, not recognizing the Monte Carlo. At first, he was a bit curious as to who it was but then blew it off as just another concerned person. But as he got closer to the limo, he couldn't help noticing the facial structure of the woman in the passenger seat. It was Tracie. *Who the hell is the dud with her?* he asked himself, not knowing Teddy's Monte Carlo.

"Don't act like you don't see me, Dave," Tracie said sassily, with her done-up head sticking outside of the window.

"How you doin', Tracie?" Dave replied apathetically.

Dissatisfied with his curt response, Tracie, drunk and slurring, said, "Oh, so you can't come over here and speak, huh? I guess you dun had a baby wit ch'yo lil stripper baby momma, and think you da shit, huh?"

Trying to be the bigger man, Dave just responded, "Tracie, now is not the time. People are grieving right now."

"Yeah, whateva, nigga!" she yelled. Just as Dave was shutting the limo door, Teddy, being the inconsiderate person that he was, sped past the limo, then erratically cut in front of it.

"I'm kinda glad you left her alone," Candace said.

"Nina's a waaay better match for you. Plus, I like her." The two of them just looked at each other, then laughed.

The get-together at Jay and Candace's home was set for 6:00 p.m.

Candace, who had been at home by herself ever since the burial ended, tried her best to make her abode as comfortable and inviting for the guests as she possibly could. She cleaned her house from top to bottom, doing everything from dusting to wiping nearly every dirty crevice that she could find. She fluffed couch pillows, cleaned streaky glass windows, and threw away every idle book, magazine, and piece of paper that looked out of place. Contrarily, if any miscellaneous stuff happened to be Jay's, not only would Candace keep it, she'd dust if off like an old-cherished trophy, then neatly stack it inside Jay's closet.

It was long before the entire house was spotless.

After cleaning, Candace decided she'd put some nice appetizers together to keep her company occupied and their stomachs satisfied. She made a tray filled with nothing but cracker-based appetizers: crackers with cheese, crackers with tuna, and crackers with different meats. She fried bags of wingdings, tossing some in barbeque sauce and others in her special homemade buffalo sauce. She also fried up gangs of mozzarella sticks, adding sides of marinara to each serving. By the time Candace finished, she had one huge smorgasbord of appetizers, just waiting to be devoured.

As Candace was placing one of the trays of food onto the dining room table, her phone began ringing.

"Candace, is it cool for us to drink over there tonight?" Dave asked eagerly, then proceeded without giving her a chance to answer, "'Cause, if so, I'm at the State Store now. So let me know."

"Who is this? Dave?" she inquired, not sure if it was who it sounded to be.

"Yeah, Candace, it's me." The interference in the phone plus the few people talking in the background made it hard for Candace to hear.

She was now convinced that it was him.

"Yeah, I guess it's cool. Just make sure you have someone to drive you home. We don't need any more accidents."

Dave didn't respond to Candace's comment. As far as he was concerned, this murder was far from an accident, but now was not the time to address that. Plus, Candace's concerns were genuine, and her pain was sincere, so he had no reason to get upset with her.

After the pause, Dave said, "All right then. I'll be over in a minute. Do you want anything?"

"Yeah, I do, Dave. Buy some pops and different juices and stuff. I forgot to pick some up from the store."

"All right. Is that it?"

"Get some of that Patrón too. I like that stuff."

"Oh, so you drinkin' now, huh?"

"Boy, just get the drink." Candace laughed mischievously. Then in a serious tone, she said, "Oh, and, Dave, thanks for everything."

"Candace, you don't gotta thank me. You're like a sister to me."

"I love you, Dave."

"I love you too, Candace, but we gone stop dis mushy stuff," Dave said while giggling.

"I'll be there in a minute."

CHAPTER THIRTY-SEVEN

The atmosphere of Jay's home-going celebration was just as Candace had hoped it would be. Although there were quite a bit more people than she had first anticipated, everything worked out just fine. Dave and the rest of the men had the basement occupied; they drank and played cards and C-LO all night, occasionally coming upstairs to check on Candace and the women. The women were upstairs, sipping casually and getting acquainted with one another. This went on till about 11:00 p.m.

Then, suddenly, an almost-unwanted guest happened touring the doorbell.

"Tracie," Candace said with a dumbfounded look upon her face. The utter shock of the guest standing before her was evident.

"And if you don't mind my asking, who is your friend behind you?" Candace had never met Sleeze before.

Sleeze stood behind Tracie like a confident bodyguard. His tight-blue muscle shirt accentuated every inch of his muscular upper body. Candace, who was surprisingly impressed by Tracie's new man, was a bit confused because this wasn't the guy she'd seen Tracie with at the burial site.

"Oh, this is my good friend Cedric," Tracie replied before Sleeze could step out from behind her and offer Candace his hand.

"Well, it's . . . it's nice to meet you, Cedric," Candace stuttered as she had been taken aback by Sleeze's firm handshake.

"Nice ta meet ya too. Ya mus' be Candace," Sleeze said with that alluring Jamaican accent. "Me heard a lot of good tings about choo. Please, let me say I'm sorry about 'ur lost. Jay was a friend of mind, and a good man."

Insensitive Tracie, getting a little jealous from all the touchy-feely business, said, "Dang, Candace, you gone let us in or you gone make us stay out here all night?"

Candace's good nature and inherent hospitality wanted to just let them right in.

Intuition told her, though, that she might want to lay some ground rules first.

"Cedric, thank you for coming. You can go ahead downstairs. All the guys are down there. There's plenty of food and drinks down there too." After looking apprehensively at the two of them, Sleeze slid past them on his way to the basement.

"Tracie, you and I need to talk."

Candace then cased outside and closed the door behind her.

"Tracie, you know Dave's here with his girlfriend. Now, I don't want any shit outta ya'll. This is my man's home-going celebration, and I want it to go right. All I'm asking is that you be respectful."

Cutting Candace's lecture short, Tracie replied, "Girl, come on now, you know me betta than that."

"All right," Candace said, opening the door behind her, then, entering it.

"Come on," Tracie eagerly followed behind.

The party continued on deep into the midnight hour. Upstairs, the women were still chatting up a hurricane and laughing and giggling like everyone had known one another forever.

Occasionally, Nina would catch Tracie giving her this extremely disrespectful stare, but Nina would just look her off and continue in the festivities. Downstairs, however, was a different story. The minute Dave locked eyes with Sleeze, Dave said, "Man, what da fuck you doin' here?"

Sleeze, trying to add some humor to the tensed environment, answered, "Well, I'm happy to see you too, Dave." Then he giggled.

What Sleeze failed to realize, though, was this wasn't a giggling matter.

"Oh, so you think shit's a game, huh?" Dave said angrily before attempting to rush Sleeze.

"Hol' up, hol' up. Dave, chill, man" was what the fellas said before grabbing him and restraining him. "You cool, Dave? You cool?" they asked before turning him loose.

"Yeah, I'm cool," Dave lied. Every thought and emotion that he had the night that he saw Sleeze and Tracie at the restaurant reappeared.

All that he could think about was hurting Sleeze.

After letting the situation calm down, something hit Dave. *Damn, I wonder, is he here with Tracie?* he asked himself. Then, out of nowhere, he blurted, "Oh, you must be here with Tracie, huh? That's cute. That's real cute." Immediately, Dave, letting his emotions get the best of him, shot upstairs in search of his ex-wife.

"I knew it," he said after reaching the top of the stairs and seeing Tracie drinking at the kitchen table with another female.

"Oh, so dis how you do it, huh?" Dave asked her with complete hostility.

"You come up in here wit a nigga's friend. Bitch, choo ain't shit!" Seeing Tracie earlier with Teddy didn't affect Dave negatively as much as seeing her with Sleeze. It's just something about knowing that his old friend was with his ex that burned deeper than anything.

"Fuck you, Dave!" Tracie screamed. Immediately, the entire upstairs got quiet.

One could hear a pin drop. Nina quickly stood up from the couch after hearing her man and a fuck you in the same sentence.

"So, what choo mad cuz I moved on. Ain't nobody said nuthin' to you about choo having a baby by anotha bitch."

"Nina, LET'S GO!" Dave demanded with authority after grabbing Nina by the arm. The people downstairs were all at the top of the stairs looking on, in suspense.

"Candace, thanks for everything. We'll see you." Dave and Nina then stormed out the front door.

"But, Dave," Candace said, filled with concern and a bit of guilt for letting Tracie in; then she followed the two of them outside.

The party quickly moved its way to Candace's front lawn. Everybody looked on from either the porch or the nearest window, eager to see what would happen next. Tracie, definitely the one to make the night one to remember, then stepped off the porch and yelled, "Yeah, BITCH! You betta get in that car!"

Nina was just about to shut the car door when she heard Tracie's derogatory bark. Instantly, she leaped out of the car at Tracie. Before Tracie could react or even blink, she had a fiery-hot Nina on top of her, gripping her hair with one hand and mercilessly punching every part of her face with the other. With her arms penned down by Nina's knees, Tracie could do little more than scream and yell for someone to get Nina up off her.

Sleeze attempted to come over and help Tracie but was halted by a ferocious Dave standing over the two women.

"Sleeze, if you touch either one of these women, I'ma fuck you up!" were Dave's exact words before breaking up the catfight.

Finally, Dave and another guy managed to separate the two women. There was blood everywhere. Nina's beige top was covered in it and stretched at the neck. Tracie's top four buttons on her pink button down were gone, and her shirt was opened for the public. Her upper lip was busted, her nose was bleeding, and her left eye was already swollen shut.

"Yeah! I bet that be the last bitch you call anybody," Nina said, huffing and puffing as Dave grabbed her by the waist and forcefully pulled her toward the car.

"Shut up and get in the car," Dave told her. Nina complied. Then with a crowd of shocked witnesses including a bunch of nosy neighbors, Dave and Nina hopped back into their car and skirted off.

CHAPTER THIRTY-EIGHT

Early the next morning, which happened to be a Sunday, Dave awoke to a nasty hangover and an empty bed. Groping around Nina's side of the bed to make certain that she was absent, Dave then yelled "Nina" but got no answer. Then, almost simultaneous to his call, he heard the door open. He started to yell her name again, but the pain from the last yell was so excruciating that he decided against it. Nina entered the apartment, holding Lil Kev by the lever on his car seat. After setting her keys on the kitchen counter, she then intuitively walked straight into their bedroom.

"Look, Lil Kev, there goes Daddy! You see, Daddy?" Nina set the car seat on the edge of the bed, unfastened her son, then picked him up, and laid him upon her shoulder.

"I woulda woke you up this morning before I left, but you were sleeping so comfortably."

With Lil Kev still upon her shoulder, she went and sat on the bed opposite Dave.

"I talked to Candace this morning."

Just hearing Candace's name brought back regretful memories. All the drinking, arguing, and fighting that went on were unnecessary to him now. But what could he do? How upset and disappointed Candace must've been at him for his display. He had to somehow call and apologize, hangover and all.

"Oh yeah! What ch'all two talk about?"

"You know what we talked about. We talked about last night."

Feeling completely embarrassed, Dave asked, "Was she mad at me?"

"Mad at choo? Mad at choo fa' what? I'm the one she shoulda been mad at out there fightin' like I'm in high

— 267 —

school or something. I felt sooo . . . stupid when I woke up this morning."

Looking at Nina while she talked caused Dave to ignore her words and concentrate on the swelling underneath his woman's eye. *How bad does my ex-wife look,* he thought, *if Nina has a little swelling?*

Turning back in, he heard her say, "So I apologized for my behavior."

"You think I should call and apologize too?"

"I mean . . . it couldn't hurt nuthin'."

With that, Dave grabbed the phone and called his best friend's fiancée. The phone rang a few times before Candace in her normally jubilant voice said, "Hello!"

"Hello, Candace," Dave retorted with a bit of trepidation.

Recognizing the voice, she then said, "Good morning, Dave. I'm surprised you're even up this morning. You were a little tipsy last night. Oh, and, by the way, you know I'm a little upset with you."

Guilt immediately consumed Dave. How could he possibly have behaved himself like that, at his best friend's home-going celebration?

"Candace, you know I didn't mean for that to go down like that." It was a lame apology, but it was sincere, and it was the best he could come up with on such short notice.

"Boy, I ain't thinkin' about what happened at that party. Shoot, I don't blame Nina for whoopin' her ass. Shoot, if Tracie woulda called me a bitch, I woulda whooped her ass too."

The two of them laughed out loud until they clutched their stomachs.

"Girl, you are sil-ly."

"Shoot, I'm serious." She giggled again.

"Naw, but the reason that I'm mad at you is I told you not to drive home drunk like that. Boy, that's dangerous. You know ya'll could've stayed over here."

"Candace, you know what, I am sooo . . . sorry. I completely forgot about that. My mind was on the two of them. My intention was to either let my homie drive or stay there, but I just forgot. Hell, I even left him at ch'yo house with the rest of them."

The two of them talked for a few more minutes before Candace said, "Well, Dave, let me get off this phone and get my son ready for church."

"Church?" Dave cried in total shock.

"You gone go to church smellin' like a bottle of Patrón?"

"Boy, shut up. Shoot, I'd rather go to church smellin' like a bottle of Patrón than go to hell smellin' like perfume."

"Amen to that, sister."

In the background, Candace could hear Nina's loud voice screaming, "Candace, he needs to be trying to go to church too!"

"Okay, girl," Candace responded as if Nina were on the phone too.

"All rightee then, Candace, we'll probably stop by later. What time will you be back?"

"Probably 'round two. Bye, Dave."

Dave and Candace's conversation ended, but the one about church sure didn't.

"Dave, I'm serious. I think we should go to church too," Nina pleaded.

"Go ta church fa what, Nina?"

"What choo mean fa what? 'Cause that's what we're supposed to do, hear the Word of God."

For some reason, Dave wasn't a really big fan of church. He was always under the impression that church was for the holy ones. And with his past, not to mention the throbbing hangover he had, going to church would make him feel like nothing more than a hypocrite.

"Just think about what's been goin' on lately. Plus, Dave, we've got a son now. We need to start setting a good example for him."

"I' ont know, Nina. You know I got this hangover and all," Dave said, making up excuses.

"I can't be in church with liquor coming out my pores."

"Refusing to accept his worthless excuses," Nina said. "Get dressed, Dave. We gone ta church." Then she walked out of the bedroom.

"And I'm not taking no for an answer," she hollered.

Initially, Dave was reluctant. He looked on with apathy as he watched Nina rip and run through the narrow hallway of their small apartment, looking for her and their son something appropriate to wear for the occasion. At one point, he even got back in bed and threw the covers over his head, hoping Nina would just go without him.

Nina was adamant, though. She snatched the covers from off him, tossed them to the floor, then said, "David, GET DRESSED NOW!" Eventually, Dave got up and got dressed.

Dave, Nina, and Lil Kev arrived at Greater St. Joseph Baptist Church on Euclid Avenue at around ten o'clock. Greater St. Joseph was a small modern-looking church that neighbored an old apartment building and a car wash. Its parking lot was small but fenced in; gravel, rock, and dirt was what the surface of it was comprised of. The building, which was made of brick, was painted white and was peeling at the bottom. In the front, there was an old worn sign that read Greater St. Joseph Baptist Church in blue letters. Just above the doors stood a cross, symbolic of Jesus's death.

As soon as they entered the double doors of the small family church, Dave became a nervous wreck. Filled to capacity, the church could fit no more than two hundred people; but those two hundred looked more like two thousand to him, especially since he didn't know anybody.

"Oh, look, everyone, we have some wonderful guests," the pastor said to the three of them as Dave and Nina with her son in her arms stood like a deer in headlights.

Instantly, the place got completely silent. The air became stiff. Everyone then turned to see the new guest.

The pastor, clad in a nice blue three-piece suit, stood smiling. "Welcome. Welcome."

Dave, who wasn't too fond of the greeting, was no longer a nervous wreck; he was terrified. Nina was okay at first, but she too became nervous after the announcement.

"Baby, come on. Let's go sit back there," she said, pointing to an open area in the back of the pew. Her nervousness and anxiety compelled her to pick the first spot she saw in sight.

Dave and Nina, with the little one still firmly embraced in her arms, cautiously eased and scooted through the crowded last row in quest for the open area Nina spotted. Without any hesitation, they sat. Finally, the spotlight was off them.

The choir then sang a lengthy a cappella song. During which time, the pastor eased out of sight. Toward the song's end, the congregation applauded, and the pastor returned; he was now draped in an all-white robe, lined in red silk with red crosses on either sides of his chest.

"Let us pray," he said, cuing the multitudes to bow their heads. The place went dead silent, allowing the pastor to pray a powerful and heartfelt prayer. Dave, who wasn't even a spiritual person, could feel something moving on the inside. Nina could too just not as much as Dave.

"Today, the message that will be preached is called 'The Light that Shined upon Darkness.'" The pastor then broke out into a song, "I-I-I . . . know the Lord. He heard my cry-y-y . . ." The choir, systematically following his lead, sang, "I-I-I-I-I-I."

After the song, with no delay, the pastor jumped straight into his sermon.

"Everybody, turn your Bibles to the gospel of John. Today, I'll be preaching out of John 1:4–5." And it read, "'In Him was life, and the life was the light of men. And the light shines in the darkness, and the darkness did not comprehend it.' Folks, let me get straight to the point. It's gone be some things in your life that happens to you that you can't and won't even understand. People flippin' the script on you."

"Amen."

"Come on now, pasta."

"People hatin' on you and all kinds a stuff," he said then paused. "You know they flipped on Jesus, right?"

"All right now!"

"You know they hated on Jesus, right?" The audience began clapping and hollering.

"Hallelujah! HALLELUJAH!" one woman yelled uncontrollably as if she'd caught the Holy Ghost.

The pastor waited for the congregation to calm then continued, "Listen, ya'll, verse 5 says, 'And the light shines in the darkness, and the darkness did not comprehend it.' So tell me, what light are they talkin' about? Who is this light?"

Nearly everyone in the church screamed, "Jesus!"

"Who?" the pastor asked.

"Jesus!"

"How many of ya'll know that when Jesus shows up, all that nonsense gots to flee?" The crowd erupted again.

"Listen, ya'll, in John 8:12, Jesus said, 'I am the light of the world, and he who follows me shall not walk in darkness but shall have the light of life!' So in other words, if they gone hate on you like they hated on Jesus, give'um something to hate about. Gone and shine. You got the light of the world anyways." The pastor went on for over thirty minutes, preaching one of his most powerful and profound sermons ever. Dave, who was totally captivated by the Word of God, hung on to nearly every word that was spoken.

Then, there was an altar call. The pastor, knowing how difficult it was for some people to stand up and confess their belief in the Lord, concluded with a Holy Spirit–inspired speech that touched everyone's soul.

"Listen up, ya'll. This here is the most important part of the sermon. All the lip service I just gave ya'll don't mean a thing without this part here. It's some people in here that are hurting. It's some people in here that are going through some stuff. Death of a love one, divorce, sickness, disease—hell, even court cases. Pain don't discriminate. Hurt don't discriminate. And we all know that death don't discriminate. Let me let ya'll in on a little secret: Jesus don't discriminate either. He said in John 3:16, 'For God so loved the world, that he have his only begotten Son that whosoever . . .' You hear me? I said whoeva believes in him should not perish but have everlasting life. So listen, whoever is going through these things right now, I hear God saying to you that he loves you and wants to be your God, your father, and your friend. He says he hears your cry. And his reply is 'Come unto me all who are weary and heavy laden, and I will give you rest. Take my yoke upon you and learn from me, for I am gentle and humble in heart, and you shall find rest for your souls.'"

On cue but without instruction, the choir stood up and began humming the tune "Come to Jesus." Dave, feeling the spirit of the Lord tugging at the core of his soul, fought hard to stay in his seat like the rest of the congregation. But when the pastor said, "You don't want to die in your sins. Get up to heaven and hear the Lord say, 'I never knew you. Depart from me you workers of iniquity.' Romans 10:9 says if you confess with your mouth Jesus as Lord and believe in your heart that God raised him from the dead, you shall be saved. Come on up here and confess so you can be saved from hellfire." Dave jumped up and unconsciously made his way to the altar. By the time he even realized what he'd committed himself to, half the congregation was clapping joyfully while the other half was surrounding him.

With tears of joy streaming down his face, Dave grabbed the pastor, hugged him tightly, and whispered in his ear, "Thank you. Everything you said was spot-on. It was like somebody told you about my life before I got here."

The pastor, with a huge grin upon his face, looked Dave directly into his eyes and said, "Somebody did tell me about your life."

"Who?" Dave asked curiously.

"God."

EPILOGUE

It had been over two months since Jay's vicious murder. Rumor on the street was that Tay and Nell had done it. Dave had heard the rumors swirling, but he didn't want to believe them. He knew both Tay and Nell, and he just couldn't picture the two of them wanting to murder Jay in cold blood.

They had all grown up together. Yeah, Jay and Tay had a little dispute on the basketball court, but that wasn't enough for him to want to kill Jay.

Dave's dismissal of the rumors ceased, though, when police began questioning people. Apparently, they'd tried to question the two of them, and they went on the lam. The two of them immediately went from people of interest to prime suspects. Police began raiding every place that they thought Tay and Nell could be at. Unfortunately, they were nowhere to be found. Nobody had seen or even heard from them. All that they said to Dave was "They're guilty!" Now, the question that Dave was asking himself was, what was he going to do if he happened to run into one of them?

Normally, this would've been a no-brainer: murder their asses, and that would be that. Things just weren't that simple, though. Dave was now on bond for a pending drug case, and more importantly, he had a newfound relationship with God. He couldn't just go around taking vengeance upon all his enemies and say to hell with the repercussions. So after contemplating heavily about it, Dave wisely decided to let God's justice prevail.

While sitting on the couch, watching Lil Kev entertain himself by mercilessly tearing off the head of a stuffed teddy bear inside his playpen, Dave and Nina heard the evening news anchorwoman say, "Good evening. We have breaking news." Dave and Nina immediately turned toward the TV.

"Tonight, at around nine thirty, a man and a woman were both fatally shot inside what appears to be a red Aston Martin," she said as the car appeared on the screen, riddled with bullet holes.

"This all happened on Harvard Road, just outside of a restaurant called Carolina's. The alleged suspect was said to have driven off in a newer-model Chevy Monte Carlo. The victim's names are not being released at this time. We'll have more on this breaking news at eleven."

"What the fuck," Dave yelled.

"What? Did you know them, baby?" Nina asked, concerned about her man's sudden emotional outburst.

"I think that that was Tracie and that dude Sleeze," he said in a lackluster manner. The news had deflated him. Yeah, he was at odds with Tracie and Sleeze and the whole relationship thing, but the last thing that he wanted was to hear that they had been killed.

"How you know it was them?" Nina asked.

"'Cause don't nobody else in the city got a red Aston Martin. And from what I hear, he and Tracie are inseparable now. And Carolina's is Sleeze's restaurant."

"Damn, that's messed—" Nina said before Dave interrupted.

"Shhh, shhh, shhh," Dave said after seeing Tay's and Nell's profiles appear on the screen.

"In other breaking news, apparently, the two suspects involved in the murder in Richmond Heights nearly two months ago have been captured. The two suspects, now, identified as Dionte Jackson, and Darnell Walker, were captured and taken into custody inside an Atlanta Hotel. We'll have more on this story later on as well."

With his eyes glued to the television, Nina watched as a tear slid down Dave's face. Not knowing what to do, she just grabbed hold of him and squeezed him as tight as she could.

Printed in the United States
By Bookmasters